"I'm not sure what I want, Miles," Lilia murmured.

"I only know what I don't want."

"Tell me."

"I don't want this ... this hunger building up between us again."

"Has it?"

She nodded, unable to answer aloud. "Miles, when you touch me, it sweeps me back in time. I feel like I did with you ten years ago."

"Is that wrong?"

"It must be. This isn't ten years ago. This is *now*. If something happens to us, I want it to be new, different. I don't want a repeat of my past. It hurt too much."

"I won't hurt you, Lilia. I give you my vow."

At the word of solemn promise, she slipped back in time to their wedding night. He had given her a vow then—one meant never to be broken.... Did she dare believe him again?

Dear Reader,

As always, it's difficult to know where to begin when talking about this month's Intimate Moments lineup. We've got so many wonderful books and authors that I guess the only place to start is at the beginning, with Kathleen Creighton's American Hero title, *A Wanted Man*. And I promise you'll want Mike Lanagan for yourself once you start reading this exciting story about reporter-on-the-run Mike and farmer Lucy Brown, the woman who thinks he's just a drifter but takes him in anyway. Like Lucy, you'll take him right into your heart and never let him go.

In *No Easy Way Out*, Paula Detmer Riggs gives us a hero with a dark secret and a heroine with a long memory. *Days Gone By* is the newest from Sally Tyler Hayes, a second-chance story with an irresistible six-year-old in the middle. Kim Cates makes her first appearance in the line with *Uncertain Angels*, the story of a right-side-of-the-tracks woman who finds herself challenged by a do-gooder in black leather. In *For the Love of a Child*, Catherine Palmer brings together a once-married couple and the voiceless boy whom heroine Lilia Eden hopes to adopt. When little Colin finally speaks, you'll have tears in your eyes. Finally, there's *Rancher's Choice*, by Kylie Brant, whom you met as our 1992 Premiere author. I think you'll agree that this book is a fitting follow-up to her smashing debut.

Enjoy!

Leslie Wainger
Senior Editor and Editorial Coordinator

Please address questions and book requests to:
Reader Service
U.S.: P.O. Box 1325, Buffalo, NY 14269
Canadian: P.O. Box 1050, Niagara Falls, Ont. L2E 7G7

Chapter 1

Miles Kane knew how to stalk a leopard through thick African brush. He could assist an elephant during labor and birth. He knew how to calm a wounded cheetah, how to tranquilize a sick lion, how to separate an angry black rhino from her calf.

But sitting in a hotel room in Springfield, Missouri, Miles wasn't sure he could pick up the telephone and dial seven simple digits.

Lilia Eden. Her name was printed in navy ink across the top of the portfolio. With one finger, Miles traced the swirl of the capital *L*. The business address beneath the name told him the interior design firm she owned was only two short blocks from his hotel. He could walk over there, introduce himself. Or he could phone.

Easy enough, Miles thought. Just lift the receiver and punch the numbers. Then say, "Hello, Lilia, this is Miles Kane. You might remember me. We were married once."

Sure. Sliding the file from his thigh to the bed, Miles stood and walked to the window. He held the curtain back with a finger and studied the city three stories below—a network of avenues and streets, uncountable fast-food res-

taurants, neon signs, cars gliding soundlessly past the hotel. The American Midwest.

Miles knew his thick British accent made him stick out
like a sore thumb. His Zambian passport had created a slight
hubbub in the hotel lobby that afternoon. He didn't fit. And
neither did Lilia. So what was she doing here?

Miles shut his eyes and leaned his forehead against the
cool pane of glass. His Lilia had been a child of Africa, a
beautiful, enchanting spirit who raced down the long white
beaches of Kenya's coast. Her dark brown hair flew behind
her and her laughter echoed off the tops of turquoise waves.

If he held his breath, Miles could almost see Lilia's warm
gray eyes and the smile that filled her face with sunshine.
She had always worn white clothes—loose cotton shirts and
flowing native skirts. He recalled her tiny bikini, a startling
sugar-white against her deeply tanned legs and arms, and the
perfect flatness of her stomach.

Shaking himself to dispel the memory, Miles dropped the
curtain. His hotel room seemed suddenly dark, cold. He
stared at the folder on his bed. The surprise of seeing Lilia's
name on it had begun to fade. Now that he thought about
it, the seeming coincidence made sense. In preparation for
building three wildlife adventure hotels in the U.S., the
British corporation for which he worked had taken bids
from top interior design firms in the United States. Miles
himself had written the initial contract with Creative Interiors, a New York-based company. Creative Interiors had
made a computer search of its franchise owners' special-
ties. And Lilia Eden had been selected to develop the decor
for the three resorts.

Miles strode across the room to his bed and picked up her
file. Creative Interiors had prefaced the package with a letter. He read it again:

Dear Mr. Kane,
Thank you for selecting Creative Interiors. We know
you will enjoy working with one of our top designers,
Lilia Eden. Because Lilia grew up in Kenya, she has a
deep understanding of the African ambiance you wish
to evoke with Habari Safari Hotels.

Lilia is highly trained, and she brings to her work a special flair that has earned her respect and recognition from her clients and peers. With her exotic background, Lilia will assist you well in designing rooms, lobbies, restaurants and special meeting chambers. She has agreed to cut back her local schedule in order to devote her time to the personal selection of fabrics, wall and floor coverings, architectural elements and special artifacts to enhance the beauty and appeal of your unique project....

Miles scanned the rest of the letter, then tossed it aside. Lilia did sound perfect for the job. He had spent two years working full-time on the hotel project, and he had made it clear he wanted the best designer available. If he called off the arrangement, Creative Interiors would want an explanation. Could he tell them he had once loved Lilia Eden so much that he had built his every dream on spending the rest of his life with her? Could he tell them how it had all ended and his world had come crashing down? Could he confess that just the thought of seeing her again made his heart quake?

How many years had it been since that August on the beach? Ten? Where had they gone?

Miles flipped open the portfolio and studied the photographs of the beautiful home and business interiors Lilia had created. One page featured a list of awards, but no picture of the winner. How had Lilia changed in ten years? How had he changed?

Miles dug out his passport. With a grunt, he shook his head at the signature the equatorial sun had left on the visage staring back at him. His face looked as though it had been carved from an outcrop of craggy granite, all sharp, chiseled angles, deeply embedded blue eyes, a stony mouth. Five years as an assistant game warden in the thick of the Zambian brush country, three more years carting tourists from one game park to another and then two years of desk work, travel and stress—the sum of it could make a man look like hell.

As he dropped the passport on the bed, Miles worked his fingers through his blond hair. At least he still had a thick head of hair. It wanted trimming, and the top had been bleached to a pale gold by years in the sun, but it was all there. Maybe Lilia wouldn't be too shocked.

Of course, he had put on about thirty pounds of solid muscle since he was twenty-one. He'd been a scrawny kid back then. No chest to speak of. Still didn't know what she'd seen in him. Lilia had been so beautiful—the most fascinating girl he'd ever set eyes on. He had felt like a bull elephant in musth in those days. Blazing hormones, he supposed. He'd have done anything for Lilia. And did.

But, of course, it had all come to naught. She had gone on with her life, and so had he. Maybe she'd married again. Of course, she still went by her maiden name.

Miles tapped his fingers on the desk beside the phone. Then he rubbed his damp palms on his thighs. Might as well get it over with. She'd probably decline the job after she found out they'd be working together, anyway. Or maybe she wouldn't even remember him.

Grabbing the receiver, he jammed his finger on the seven buttons in quick succession. While he listened to the rings on the other end, he tried to make himself breathe. One ring. Two. Maybe she wasn't there.

"Good afternoon, Creative Interiors. This is Lilia Eden speaking. How may I help you?"

Miles let out a breath. She sounded exactly the same. Airy. Musical. Beautiful.

"Hello?" Her voice held that familiar questioning ring to it. "Is anyone there?"

Miles rubbed his palm around the back of his neck. He cleared his throat. "Lilia," he said. "Miles Kane speaking."

"Oh, my gosh!"

He could hear her fumbling around with the phone. At least she remembered him.

"Lilia," he tried again. If only he could sound professional, instead of wobbly and uncertain. "Lilia, this is Miles Kane—"

"Where *are* you?"

"I'm right here. In Springfield."

"Oh, my stars." She was breathing hard. "Springfield, *Missouri?*"

He grinned. "I've been traveling a bit, but I think so. How've you been, Lilia?"

"Well . . . fine. You?"

"Fine, too." This wasn't going well. He picked up her portfolio. "At any rate, I've been given your name by Creative Interiors."

"Why?" It was only a moment before she was back with a torrent. "You're not with Habari Safari, are you? You *are,* aren't you? You're building the three wildlife adventure hotels. And I'm supposed to design the interiors. Did you plan this? Did you know it was me?"

"Which of those questions am I meant to answer?" Miles felt a flood of warmth pouring through him. Lilia had always talked too fast, blurting things out in a delightful tumble of words. She was exactly the same—full of energy, life, enthusiasm.

"I am with Habari Safari," he acknowledged. "Have been for five years. I proposed the wildlife hotels some time ago, and management put me in charge of the project. I've contracted builders, architects, even zoos. And I did select Creative Interiors to handle the interior design work."

"But did you know I was the designer they'd chosen?"

"I did not. Your file was waiting with your company's introductory letter when I arrived at the hotel this afternoon."

She was silent for a moment. "I never thought you'd be building luxury hotels."

"Nor did I. I didn't expect to find you an interior decorator. I thought you might be teaching. Children were always hanging around you, pulling at your skirts, begging you to play. We could hardly take a walk down the beach without two or three of them—"

"Well, you never know, do you?" she cut in. "Anyhow . . . things change."

"So what have you been doing since . . ." He raked his fingers through his hair. "Did you ever get married again?"

Now he'd done it, Miles thought. Blurted it out, just like
that. He had about as much tact and finesse as a rhino.

"No," she said after a moment. "I've never *been* married."

Miles caught his breath. So that was how she chose to remember it. He didn't suppose he could blame her. On the
other hand, they *had* been married. He clearly remembered
that night—Lilia slipping out the back door of her house,
then running down the moonlit sand to meet him. Brief
moments when they'd exchanged vows at the home of that
young Lutheran missionary. And then afterward, those
sweet hours beneath the overhanging cliffs....

"I never got married again, either," Miles stated bluntly.
"Never had the desire."

"Look, Miles, it's been so nice to hear from you—"

"When did you complete university?" He wasn't going
to let her slip away this easily.

"A long time ago, really."

"After that, you studied design, of course. Own a house
here, do you?"

"Yes."

"Whereabouts?"

"Walnut Street."

He jotted down the name of her street at the top of her
portfolio. "I've been in Africa myself. Never really wanted
to leave before now."

"So you work for Habari Safari."

She sounded distant. "I was with the game department.
Would've stayed with it, but I kept having recurrences of
malaria, you know."

Of course she knew, Miles realized. He had fallen sick
with malaria less than twenty-four hours after their secret
wedding. Fever had raged through his body. His parents had
rushed him to the Mombasa airport and put him on a flight
to Nairobi. He had stayed in the hospital there only two days
before they had evacuated him to Lusaka to undergo treat-
ment with the Zambian doctor who was a longtime family
friend. It was the malaria that had separated Miles and
Lilia. And it was the malaria that had finally torn them
apart forever.

"At any rate," he went on before she could say anything, "I went to work for Habari Safari. Tourists, you know. Started out in the bush, then moved into the offices. When I proposed building these hotels in the United States, the management jumped on the idea. They'd been looking for a way to expand. They asked me to organize the project, and then to act as chief of operations. It's been good fun."

"How nice."

Miles wrapped the telephone cord around his hand. The more he had talked, the quieter she had grown. The breathless quality had evaporated from her voice. She sounded fragile, as if she might fade away from him.

"So, when shall we start working on the design?" he asked. "Are you free this afternoon, Lilia?"

"Um, no. Not really. I promised I'd take my son to the park."

Her *son*? Miles swallowed. Lilia had a son? But she'd never been married—except to him. A rush of ice flooded his veins. Then . . . the child had to be *his* son! Before the malarial fever had seared away his chances of fatherhood, he had created a baby. That night under the cliffs, Lilia had conceived their child. His son!

"And I'm not really sure about the design project after all," she was saying. "It's very complicated. I hope you don't mind. I know Creative Interiors will locate another decorator for you, once I explain the situation. Well, good to talk to you again, Miles. Bye."

The phone went dead. Miles stared at it, listening to the dull buzz. Ten years. He'd had a wife. A son. He'd lost them both once.... Was there a chance in the world he could have them back?

Lilia replaced the receiver on the telephone and sank into her chair.

"Lilia? What is it? You're pale as death." Jenny Larsen shoved a wallpaper sample book into the tall bookcase on one wall. "Was that Miss Maddie? Is Colin all right?"

"No, it wasn't about Colin." Lilia knotted her trembling hands together. "So, did you find Jane's butterfly-green stripe?"

"Don't change the subject, Lilia." Her young assistant sat on the corner of her desk. "Who was that on the phone? You sounded like a zombie."

"I feel like one," Lilia said with a forced laugh. "Gosh, I can't stop shaking. That was Miles Kane. He's right here in Springfield."

"Who's Miles Kane? Some guy you used to know? An old flame?"

"You might say that. We were sort of married once."

"Married!" Jenny shrieked. "You never told me that! What do you mean, 'sort of married'? Either you were or you weren't."

"We were *sort of* married, just like I said." Lilia stood and pulled a length of drapery fabric from the row of bolts along the wall by her desk. She studied the pale mauve paisley print. "It happened a long time ago."

"Back when you lived in Africa?"

Lilia nodded. "I had just graduated from boarding school. I was eighteen, I guess. Doesn't seem like ten years could have passed so quickly, does it? I was spending my last summer on the beach with my folks before flying off to the States to start college. Two or three of the luxury hotels had put me to work baby-sitting. It was technically illegal, since I didn't have a work permit, but I'd done it for years. I loved kids, and parents requested me year after year when they came to the coast on holiday."

"You know, every time you start talking about Kenya, you sound so wistful."

"I wouldn't trade those days for anything in the world. But I was a wreck that August. Just thinking about leaving home was killing me. Africa was home to me, of course. It still is, in a way."

"And then along came Miles Kane, right? Handsome, debonair..."

"I wouldn't exactly have called Miles Kane debonair. More like a shaggy lion on the prowl." Lilia smiled at the memory of the tall, thin young man with his mane of thick blond hair. From the moment they had met, his pursuit of her had been bold, relentless, ardent. "Miles is a little...rough-edged, you might say."

"So you guys fell in love and got married? Just like that?"

Jenny looked so incredulous, Lilia had to laugh. "Well, not just like that. We did think it over pretty carefully. It was complicated. See, Miles had come to Kenya from Zambia. His parents had flown the whole family over for a beach vacation."

"Zambia? Were his parents missionaries, too?"

"No. Back when Zambia was a British colony, Miles's grandfather sailed down from England to start a copper-mining venture there. After Zambia's independence, Miles's father became a citizen and continued in the copper industry. The family has a home in Lusaka, and another estate out in the country. Miles was never interested in the business, though. He'd planned to study wildlife management."

"Okay, so you met on the beach while he was there for a vacation. Summer love. This sounds like *Grease*, or something. You know, John Travolta and Olivia Newton-John."

Lilia pulled out another length of fabric. It might sound like a silly case of puppy love, but what she'd felt for Miles Kane had been adult, deep, an abiding love that she had never quite been able to shed—even to this day. She ran her palm across the nubby nap of the silk fabric.

"It was a little reckless, I guess," she said softly. "We were swept away."

"So you got married, and then what happened?"

"I wondered that myself for a long time." Lilia rerolled the bolt of fabric and returned to her desk. It was time to end the conversation and get back to reality. Colin would be expecting her. She had a new life now, plans of her own. Dreams that didn't include Miles Kane.

"Miles came down with malaria," she said as she began sliding file folders into her briefcase. "Taking antimalarial pills had always been a part of my daily life. It's just something everyone does at the coast where the mosquitoes can be thick at times. But I guess the Kanes, being from Zambia, didn't know about the pills. Miles broke out in a fever the day after we married. We hadn't told our parents that we'd gotten married, and his folks just rushed him to Zambia without even letting me know what was going on."

"You tracked him down, didn't you?"

"I worked at it for almost two weeks. I was frantic. Communication in the Third World is primitive at best, and between countries like Kenya and Zambia, it was nearly nonexistent. It was practically impossible to get through. My parents were packing me up for college and all. I finally managed to get hold of Miles's father at the copper-mining headquarters in Lusaka. That's when he told me the marriage had been legally annulled."

"Annulled!"

"Like it had never happened. When I asked Mr. Kane why, he told me Miles wanted it that way. Miles considered the marriage just a 'childish whim'—I'll never forget those words—and he wanted to get on with his life. So I flew to the States, started college and got on with my own life." Picking up her briefcase, Lilia gave Jenny a brief smile. "That was that."

As she started for the door, she could hear Jenny hurrying to keep up. "But why did Miles call you today? What's he doing in Springfield, Lilia? Maybe he wants to make up or something!"

"Make up?" Lilia swung around, the buried anger and hurt rising to the surface. "You 'make up' after a spat, Jenny. You 'make up' when you've been going together. Miles Kane *married* me. He promised to love, cherish and protect me for better or for worse until death parted us. I loved that man with everything I had. He let me go, and I'll be damned if he's ever going to get me back."

Bristling, Lilia stalked across the parking lot to her car. But as she slid onto the seat, it occurred to her to wonder which hotel Miles was staying in...and whether he still had that thick mane of blond hair... and if his eyes were still as blue as the ocean.

Chapter 2

A son of his own! Miles pushed open the hotel room curtains. He felt like a caged lion, trapped in this tiny room, in this unfamiliar city, beneath this slate-gray sky. He had a son! He had to get out of the room or he'd explode.

Grabbing his passport, he stuffed it into the belt pouch that fastened around his waist. He tucked his shirt into his trousers to cover the pouch, picked up his room key and headed for the door.

A ten-year-old boy, he thought as he strode down the hall to the elevator. What had *he* been doing at age ten? Playing soccer in the dirt with his African chums, no doubt. Shooting black mamba snakes from the trees with a .22 rifle. Riding his horse to the river and watching the giraffes take a drink, their long legs spread-eagled and their necks straining down to reach the water.

Did his son know how to play soccer? Was he familiar with the rules of football? Not the slow-moving American game with helmets and padding—real English rugby in all its bloody glory. Did his son have his own cricket bat? Could he ride a horse? Did he know how to handle a gun? Could he trail a lion's spoor through the brush?

Of course not. Miles felt his stomach twist into a knot as he stalked across the marble floor of the hotel lobby and emerged onto the street. Lilia had brought up their son as an American. The boy probably played baseball. Ate hamburgers and hot dogs. Wore blue jeans instead of khakis. She probably hadn't taught him a word of Swahili, and of course he wouldn't know how to speak Bemba or Lozi.

Miles would put that right immediately. The first thing he would do was to pack up Lilia and the boy and fly them straight back to Zambia for a long holiday. Miles stopped walking and stared at his reflection in a store window. What was he thinking? Lilia had practically hung up on him that afternoon. She didn't want to see him. She'd never even told him about their son. Maybe she didn't intend for the boy to know he had a Zambian father named Miles Kane. Maybe that was why she had been so blunt, so final.

The knot in his stomach tightened. His face in the window looked pale, stony. Did his son have blond hair, too? Was it thick and unruly? Did Lilia have to wet it down every morning as Miles's own mother had done to his tangled golden mop? Were the boy's eyes blue like his—or gray like Lilia's?

Damn, why hadn't she told him? Anger bubbled through Miles. He'd lost ten years. Ten years! He'd never get them back. And, of course, he would never be a father again. The malarial fever had taken care of that. Permanently sterile, the doctors had told him. His life-giving seed was dead. Destroyed forever by the high fever that had raged in his body for almost two weeks and had nearly killed him.

Oh, he was still very much a male. His urges were as strong as any man's—stronger than most, he sometimes thought. He didn't lack anything in that department. But he'd been forced to accept that he would never be a father. Never watch his children grow. Until now.

Who would have thought that one brief night of passion on the beach could have resulted in a baby? The notion had never even entered his mind. He had been too distraught over Lilia and the loss of their love to think beyond it. Finally, he had shoved her memory deep inside, so far down he sometimes believed he had forgotten her.

But Lilia had carried his dream to America. She had silently nurtured the life he'd sown inside her, and then she had given birth to their child. His son.

Miles stuffed his hands into his pockets and started walking again. Lilia might have borne a difficult burden living as a single mother all these years, but somehow he couldn't find it in his heart to forgive her for not telling him. She had kept a secret that wasn't her right to keep! She had robbed him of his only son!

He recalled the bitter anger he had felt when his father had come into his hospital room ten years before. The fever had broken, and he was finally out of danger. All he could talk about was Lilia. He had told his parents about their marriage, and he had begged his father to try to call her.

Then, one dismal afternoon, his father had sat on the end of Miles's hospital bed and broken the news. He had reached Lilia's parents by phone. Lilia was already in America, Mr. Eden had told Miles's father. She was happily attending college, making wonderful grades. Dating. It would be much better, Lilia's father had insisted, if Miles agreed to Lilia's desire to annul the marriage so she could go her own way. She wanted to make a life for herself in America where she belonged.

Miles fumed as he bulled down the street. Of course Lilia had wanted to go her own way! She had been pregnant with his son—and she wanted the child all to herself. Well, so much for Lilia. Maybe she hadn't been as beautiful and honest as he'd thought at the time. Never mind. He could put his memories of her aside, as he'd done for the past ten years. He had lived without her, and he could easily do so again.

But he couldn't forget his only son. Never.

Miles spotted the sign just ahead. Creative Interiors. Maybe he had been unconsciously walking in this direction all along. He would go inside and confront her. He would demand to see the boy.

But how could a father fill in ten lost years? he wondered as he stood on the threshold. With love, that was how. With a slow building of trust. He could do it. Damned if he couldn't.

Miles pushed open the door and walked into the air-conditioned room. There she was, her back to him as she searched through wallpaper books. Slightly heavyset. The long brown hair cut and dyed blond. Miles grunted with satisfaction. Easier to let her go if she'd changed this much.

"Lilia," he announced. "I've come to talk."

"Oh, you caught me by surprise!" She turned. "I didn't hear you come in."

She was walking across the room, and Miles tried his best to make her fit the image of the younger girl he had loved with such passion. Her bosom was about three times as large as it had been. Her lips were painted pale pink. Her nose seemed to have taken on an upward tilt.

"Can I help you?" she asked.

"Lilia, it's Miles here. I thought we should have a chat."

"Miles!" She laughed, a sort of high giggle Miles couldn't remember at all. "Oh, I'm not Lilia. I'm Jenny Larsen, her assistant. Lilia's gone for the day. She left early so she could take her son to the park."

The mention of his son steeled Miles's determination as he adjusted to the somewhat welcome news that this wasn't Lilia. "I see," he said. "Which park would that be then?"

"I'm not sure. But you could try her at home if you want. I have her number right here."

He followed Jenny to the desk. He checked it for photographs, but there were none. The desktop was clean, neat, organized. Of course. "She's home now, is she?" he asked.

"Maybe." Jenny shrugged, staring at him. "Lilia told me you had called. She was shocked."

"I'm sure she was. It was a bit of a surprise to me, too. The hotel project, you know. I didn't realize I'd be working with her on the design."

"Oh, that's why you called! You're with Habari Safari, aren't you? Wow, this is amazing. Like a circle...the two of you brought back together after ten long years...ten thousand miles from where you met...it's so romantic."

Miles cleared his throat. "Mmmm...well, odd enough. I suppose I'll ring her up. What's the number?"

Jenny handed him the receiver and punched the buttons. "Lilia's not really mad," she confided in a whisper. "You just caught her off guard. Hang in there."

Miles watched the young woman drift to the other side of the room out of hearing range. He was thankful for that, anyway.

"Hello?" Lilia's voice again. Why did the sound of it send a weight into his stomach?

"Lilia," he said. "Miles here. We should talk."

"How did you get my number?"

"Jenny. I'm at your shop."

There was a long silence. "Miles, I really don't think we have anything to say to each other. It's been ten years—"

"Yes, it has. That's reason enough for me."

"Well, I'm not interested—"

"I am. I'm very interested." He could hear the anger in his voice, and he knew if he didn't keep it under control, she would back off completely. He couldn't lose her...couldn't lose the chance to see his son. "You signed a contract with my company, Lilia. I think we should put aside the past and get down to business. You did grow up in Africa, and you obviously have a feel for the sort of mood we want to create in our hotels. Habari Safari and Creative Interiors are expecting you to handle the project. It's the least you can do to meet with me and discuss the details."

He could hear her breathing on the other end, a shattered sound. "I want out of the contract, Miles. I'm not comfortable with this."

Of course she wasn't comfortable, he thought. She didn't want him invading her privacy. She didn't want him staking a claim to the boy.

"Perhaps you're not comfortable," he said. "I'm not exactly pleased myself at the moment. But we are professionals. We're adults, and we do have an agreement. We'll have a meeting on neutral ground to discuss a plan of action—whether that means working together or restructuring the project with a different designer."

"All right," she conceded softly. "Where?"

He searched his brain for a good place. If they met at her shop or a restaurant, she wouldn't bring his son. He had to see the boy.

"The zoo," he said. "I've been speaking with the Springfield Zoo about their cheetah breeding program. We hope to participate in that project once our hotels become operational. Set the cheetahs loose in large enclosures. Natural environment. That sort of thing."

"I've never felt very comfortable with zoos," Lilia returned. "All those cages. It depresses me to see the animals cooped up."

Damn, she was being difficult. "You'll like this zoo. It's different."

"Well..."

"We'll meet this afternoon. Four sharp, at the gates." He ran a finger around the inside of his collar. "And bring... bring the boy."

"Colin would enjoy the zoo." She still sounded tentative. "Okay. I'll meet you at four."

"Right, then. Four o'clock."

He hung up and started for the door. Colin. His son had a name. An English name. Had Lilia been thinking of the boy's father when she'd named him?

"So, is Lilia going to meet you?" Jenny asked, cutting into Miles's path.

"At the zoo."

"Oh, good." Jenny seemed to have taken a personal interest in the whole affair. "It'll be just like when you were in Africa together, won't it?"

Miles studied her. "What's the boy like? Colin."

"Oh, he's great. Cute, sweet, a real charmer. But she isn't bringing Colin, is she?"

"Yes, why not?"

Jenny colored. "Oh, nothing. It's just... well. Nothing. I hope you have a great time. Anything I can do, just let me know."

"Right." Miles shouldered past her and pushed open the door. As he stepped out onto the street, he felt the knot in his stomach twist. In less than an hour, he was going to meet his son. Colin. Colin Kane.

And Lilia. He'd be seeing her, too. He ought to get a haircut.

Miles leaned against the stone entrance wall of the Springfield Zoo and peered into each car that passed through the parking lot. He'd decided not to bother with the haircut and had driven his rental car to the zoo almost immediately. He'd been waiting more than half an hour, and his patience was thinning. He checked his watch. Two minutes until four.

A gray compact car pulled into an empty space opposite the gate. The front door opened. A long leg emerged, and a white canvas sport shoe touched the pavement. Denim jeans. A white shirt. Miles's heart slammed into his ribs. The woman leaned into the car for a long time, fiddling with something in the passenger seat. Finally, her shoulders emerged. Then her head.

She turned. Their eyes met. Her face paled, but he had no doubt. It was Lilia Eden.

"Hi," she called from across the parking lot. "Just a minute."

As he watched her walk around the back of her car, his mouth went dry. She was totally different. And exactly the same. Her hips were still small, but they were gently rounded now. The long sheet of brown hair was gone. She had cut it short, just at her jawline. His twinge of disappointment was mollified when he realized this new look suited her even better. Her hair swung and shone in a light, bouncing style that matched her easy, loping stride.

Her deep, golden tan was gone, faded almost to alabaster. Miles hadn't imagined that porcelain skin could look so ethereal, so fragile. Lilia had seemed to glow when she looked at him a few moments before.

She was as thin as ever, but her bosom had filled out. Her breasts pushed against the fabric of her white shirt, and Miles suddenly remembered the first time he had touched her. As if it had been only moments ago instead of ten years, he knew how her breasts had felt in his hands . . . against his lips.

She was reaching for the passenger door now. Miles straightened and started across the pavement. She pulled open the door. He held his breath. In a moment he would see him. Colin. His son.

Lilia reached inside and cupped her hands around something. Then she lifted, and a tiny, scrawny, fuzzy-headed child emerged into the open air. As his feet touched the ground, the boy backed up into Lilia's legs and stared straight at Miles.

Miles stopped dead-still on the pavement. This wasn't a ten-year-old boy. The kid couldn't be more than two or three. He appeared to be a mixture of races, with some undecipherable legacy that had bequeathed him a pair of bright, chocolate brown eyes, pale, golden skin and a froth of tawny, lambs-wool hair. He was a thin sparrow of a waif, all eyes and knobby knees.

Miles looked from the boy to Lilia. Where was Colin? *This* certainly wasn't his son!

"Miles," Lilia was saying as she approached, leading the child by the hand, "I'd like you to meet Colin Eden. My son. Colin, this is Miles Kane."

Miles swallowed and stared down at the little stranger. His visions of a strapping blond cricket player evaporated. His anger at Lilia's ten-year deception faded to dismay, confusion.

This boy didn't smile. Didn't say a word. But he looked up at Miles as if waiting, expecting something.

"Colin?" Miles repeated the name dumbly. He couldn't believe it. For less than an hour, he'd had a son. He'd been a father. He had built a world of hope. Now his dream had been dashed.

"Colin is my son," Lilia said for the second time.

"I see."

Lilia couldn't think of a response. Staring into Miles Kane's blue eyes had taken her back suddenly, in a rush of memory, to that blistering August afternoon on Diani Beach. They had met just this way. Walking toward each other, awkward but determined to bridge unfamiliar territory.

Lilia realized she would have recognized him anywhere. This man was Miles. Her Miles. She had known his voice the moment he spoke on the phone, and his physical presence still mesmerized her after ten years. As she remembered, he seemed to carry all of Africa with him—big, brash, bold, larger than life.

If anything, he was more handsome, more heart-stopping than before. He was just as tall but now filled-out, with the solid muscle and brawn of a full-grown man. The African sun had molded his face into deeply tanned planes and angles. His hair was thick and unruly and as golden as the long savanna grasses. His eyes shone with the blue of an equatorial morning. He was everything she remembered. He was the man she had loved with an aching passion that had swept away all reason.

Lilia felt a tiny hand tug at her finger. Pulling herself together, she managed to assemble a sentence. "Colin is two years old," she said, then added, "two and a half."

"So this is Colin." Miles couldn't seem to get past it. But his attention had shifted from his shock over the boy to a disconcerting realization that Lilia had exactly the same effect on him as ever. Her gray eyes held him, fascinated him, drew him in. Her warm smile turned his heart upside down.

To break the spell, he dropped to his haunches in front of the boy. "Pleased to meet you, Colin," he said. The brown eyes blinked. "You're a lucky little bloke, you know that? Not many boys have a mum as pretty as yours."

Colin gave the barest hint of a grin. Then he whirled around and buried his face in Lilia's knees. Miles glanced up at her. She smiled, then bent to lift the boy into her arms.

"Come on, Colin," she said softly. "Miles is our friend. Let's go see the animals, all three of us. Maybe we'll find a giraffe. Would you like that?"

As they headed into the zoo, Lilia settled Colin on one hip. He was heavy, but she knew he wouldn't be able to walk the long distance around every exhibit. Though he had lived with her for almost a year, he wasn't strong, and the effects of his birth mother's early neglect were still evident.

It hadn't taken as long as the family services agency had predicted for Lilia to earn Colin's trust. In fact, he was almost too closely bonded to her these days, in the opinion of the social worker assigned to the case. After all, Lilia had been warned, her home was still considered preadoptive. As was standard in such cases, Lilia had agreed to accept Colin as a "legal risk"—aware that his birth mother's rights had not been terminated.

Lilia had never worried too much about the situation. Although Colin's birth mother had visited him and brought gifts for a few weeks, that had quickly tapered off and the woman hadn't seen her son for eight months. When Lilia felt confident that Colin's mother had no further interest in him, she had hired a lawyer. Last month, her attorney had petitioned the court that parental rights be terminated based on abandonment and neglect, and that Lilia be given custody of Colin.

The birth mother had been notified and the petition published, and Lilia's lawyer told her the woman hadn't uttered a peep of protest. The hearing had been scheduled for today, and Lilia expected to hear from her attorney this evening. He had assured her that it was all very routine, and she shouldn't concern herself over this minor step in the process. She and Colin would still have a nine-month wait until the adoption was final.

All the same, Lilia had had a case of nerves all day—complicated by the phone call from Miles. Yet she knew she had to keep her focus on Colin and his needs. He ached for someone to trust, she felt, someone to hold on to for dear life. Even now his little arms around her neck were almost a stranglehold.

But the scars that had been formed in his infancy would take longer than ten months to heal. Colin still had terrible nightmares. He often developed stomach trouble, and food was a constant source of tension for him. Most significantly, Colin never spoke. Although many two-year-olds had a strong, early vocabulary, Colin said nothing. Not a word.

"Vervet monkeys," Miles was saying as they stopped at a glassed enclosure. "Have a look at these chaps, Colin. When I first met your mum, I was staying at a hotel on the beach in Kenya. These little devils were running about everywhere, trying to steal my breakfast right off the table, weren't they, Lilia?''

He looked at her, and again the shock of meeting her eyes sent a flame skittering through him.

"Every morning right after dawn," she told Colin, pulling her eyes away from Miles's face, "the vervet monkeys would start jumping through the trees around our house, swinging from branch to branch, and then scampering across our roof. *Boom-ba-da, boom, boom,* just like a drum, they ran around on the corrugated tin roof."

She laughed at the memory, and Colin joined her. Miles watched their faces—Lilia's beautiful smile, her son's tiny chuckle. Who was the boy's father? Was Lilia still involved with the man who had fathered her son? Why hadn't she married him?

"Will you have primates at your wildlife adventure hotels?" she was asking Miles.

He shook his head. Back to impersonal business. "It's tricky to keep primates enclosed behind a natural barrier. A monkey gets loose and people start worrying about rabies and such. Next thing you know, the local authorities will shoot it for sport. It's happened. No, we won't have any animals that can't be easily contained. Mostly gazelles and antelopes. Giraffes if we can get them. Zebras definitely. Ostriches, of course, and maybe even rhinos."

"Rhinos! How wonderful." Lilia walked beside Miles along the paved paths between exhibits. It felt oddly natural, moving along at his side. He was dressed as he had been at the coast—a light khaki shirt, a pair of olive trousers, suede safari boots. They might have been strolling down a street in Mombasa.

"Several places in Texas have been breeding rhinos with some success," he was saying. "But rhinos like to be left alone, you know. Plenty of room to roam about and a big mud wallow to lounge in. They're not sociable, even with one another, so it might be difficult."

"You already own enough land to support all this wildlife, Miles?" she asked.

"That was the difficult bit. That, and securing legal permission to keep exotics. I obtained records of David Hopcraft's experiment in Kenya to back us up as to the benefit these wild creatures can have on the land. You know, Hopcraft fenced half of a three-hundred acre test plot for cattle. Then he ran an equivalent herd of gazelles on the other half. After three years, the cattle enclosure showed significantly reduced plant species, and bare dirt tracks to and around the water hole. The native gazelle enclosure showed almost a third *more* grass cover and no bare ground.''

"That's because gazelles drink almost no water," Lilia observed.

"Exactly. Hopcraft proposed that if Kenya ever intends to hold back desertification, it must start wildlife ranches. The people could cull the game for food. He wanted to bring the idea to New Mexico as well, but everybody was outraged over it. Cattlegrowers, environmentalists, conservationists. The bill granting him authority never got past the first committee.''

"How did you pull it off, then?" They were strolling past the ostriches now, and Colin stared goggle-eyed at the large birds.

"We've purchased private land, for one thing. It's mostly barren desert that's much like East Africa, but is undesirable for cattlegrowers. Vast stretches with very little water. We won't allow any hunting whatsoever—not even to supply the hotels' restaurants. And we've obtained the cooperation of zoos, endangered species organizations and local exotic animal breeders. Habari Safari has offered to take in difficult animals. We've promised land for breeding programs. Most importantly, we've agreed to turn a portion of our profit over to preservation societies.''

"This is wonderful! I can just see it. You'll build natural barriers, so people won't even realize they're in a sort of zoo. You'll have water holes and native shrubbery, and the animals will feel perfectly at home. Of course they'll breed! It'll seem like home to them. Even the tourist buses will feel almost like Africa to the animals.''

Miles couldn't suppress a grin. Lilia's enthusiasm buoyed his confidence. She understood, as he knew she would. She had grown up among the animals, and she could see his vision for them as clearly as he did. "I'm even going to paint the tourist buses like they do in Kenya—with black-and-white stripes to resemble zebras, or brown patches for giraffes.''

Lilia laughed and hugged Colin. "What a crazy, wonderful idea! People who've never been to Africa will finally have the chance to see what it's really like. People who've lived there will feel like they're home again. It's great, Miles, really it is!''

"It should foster a lot of understanding and sympathy for the plight of Africa's wildlife. I hope to set up a fund for endangered species, once we make certain the project is profitable for private investors. The hotels are where we'll make the money, of course. Lodging, food, parties, conferences. I thought we'd construct each hotel differently to encourage people to visit all three. We might develop a sort of Salt-Lick Lodge effect—"

"So the buildings will look like enormous African huts on stilts? And you could put a water hole just outside the main lodge.''

"Every hotel will have a water hole. That's definite. We'll have sundowners on the veranda, toasting the survival of the wildlife as we watch the elephants file in for a drink.''

"What about designing another hotel with a Treetops theme? You know, the old British colonial *Out of Africa* look?''

"That's a great idea. Did you ever stay at Naro Moru on the slopes of Mount Kenya?''

"Of course. The icy stream nearly froze my toes off. That lodge is beautiful. The fireplace, white tablecloths and silver soup tureens, glittering crystal. Instead of the American concept of an African theme—green bamboo wallpaper and leopard-print bedspreads—you could recreate the actual ambiance of the old hotels in Kenya. Rich, polished woodwork, needlepoint pillows, firescreens, red-waxed floors, that smoky smell.''

"And I was thinking of a sort of camp. With tents.''

"Like Cottar's Camp at Maasai Mara! You could put up canvas walls and cots—but all with a luxurious feeling to them. Porcelain sinks, roll-down screens on the windows, hanging lamps.'' Lilia caught her breath. She was rambling, caught up in the vision. How could she have forgotten so easily that Miles had once betrayed her? Why should she be swept into this dream of his, when he had crushed hers once before?

She glanced at him. He was leaning over a rock wall and gazing down at a lion that paced back and forth in the small enclosure. His hair drifted in the breeze, fell across his forehead and over his collar. She set Colin on the ground and held his hand as he peeped into the lion exhibit.

But her own eyes were on Miles's bronzed arms, thickly roped with muscle and gilded with pale golden hair. He had become a man, hardworking, valuable to his company, reliable. Yet that didn't mean he had changed his basic nature. She couldn't count on him. Couldn't trust him. And the longer she was at his side, the more she knew she couldn't trust her own heart.

Chapter 3

"Colin, how would you like to ride on an old African elephant?" Miles asked, patting his own shoulders. "Give your mum a rest."

When the little boy made no response, Lilia smiled down at him. "Colin doesn't talk just yet," she said, more to her son than to Miles. "I always tell him that when he's ready to say something, I'll be ready to listen."

Miles mused on that for a moment. Odd that a child wouldn't speak. His sister's children had been babbling like magpies at Colin's age. A lot of it unintelligible, but definitely a stream of chatter.

"Right then," he said, acknowledging to himself that he was certainly no expert on children. "I'll swing you up, and you'll be nearly as tall as the giraffes. How's that?"

To Lilia's surprise, Colin took a step away from her. His sweaty little hand reached from hers to Miles's, and the next thing she knew, he was being hoisted through the air and deposited on Miles's shoulders. His deep chuckle turned the edges of her heart. She had to laugh as Colin buried his fists in Miles's hair, and Miles made an agonized face.

"Get a good grip there, boy," Miles instructed him, ignoring the tightening of Colin's fingers against his scalp.

"This old pachyderm's got a tough hide. Hang on now—you know elephants have a bit of a wobble to their walk."

With Colin squealing in delight, Miles assumed the stride of an aging elephant as he lumbered off down the path. Lilia gazed at them for a moment, the big blond Miles with his strong arms wrapped around Colin's skinny brown legs. What a mismatched pair.

Miles had never shown the slightest interest in the myriad children who had swarmed around her on the beach ten years before. In fact, he had almost resented her sandy, seaweedy little wards because of the amount of time they kept her away from him.

But she had loved the children. After Miles had asked her to marry him, she had told him she wanted to bear him half a dozen children. He'd laughed and nodded his acceptance, but obviously being her husband had been more on his mind than being a father.

And ten years later, he was still childless. If Miles had wanted a wife and family, Lilia thought, he'd have married by now. Yet she couldn't deny that with Colin he had been both kind and gentle. Never in a million years would she have dreamed of describing Miles Kane as a tender man. But as she observed him ambling down the path with Colin on his shoulders, she realized Miles was exactly that. Tender.

"It's the cheetahs!" he called from a distance, beckoning her with one free hand. "Come on, slow-coach!" Colin, fingers still tangled in Miles's hair, was spurring him like a horse, tiny heels digging into the massive chest. The boy waved at Lilia, his face bright with excitement.

She hurried toward them, then gasped with delight at the sight of the cheetah mother and her litter of nursing cubs. "Colin, that's the mommy with her babies!" she exclaimed. "They're drinking milk so they can grow big and strong."

"The Springfield Zoo's cheetah breeding program has had decent success considering the animals' limited enclosure," Miles told her. "I've been speaking over the phone with the director here about the possibility of Habari Safari participating in the program."

"That would be great!" Lilia smiled at the roly-poly balls of fur tumbling over one another. "Cheetahs have always been my favorite cats. I can't stand to think they're in danger of becoming extinct."

"You may not like zoos, Lilia, but they're probably the cheetahs' best hope for survival."

"But I read somewhere that cheetahs don't breed well in captivity."

"Breeders stand a chance of success if they keep the animals as individuals and in groups, and then mix the groups so sibling bonds don't form. But there are other factors as well. Cheetahs need large enclosures so they can exercise. They've got to be kept active, and their routines need to be changed regularly."

Lilia could hardly comprehend how Miles would run a hotel, accommodate tour groups and provide valuable programs for wildlife. As she covertly studied him, she saw the intensity in his blue eyes, and she knew he meant what he said—at least about the animals. He might have abandoned *her* once, but he was committed to *them*.

"The best thing we can provide at Habari Safari," he was explaining, "is the presence of natural prey right outside the cheetah enclosure. That's been proven to stimulate their reproductive functions."

"You've done a lot of study on this."

"I won't make mistakes." He set off down the path again, Colin perched on his shoulders, and this time Lilia kept up. "You remember my father wanted to send me off to England to university?"

"Yes," she said. "You didn't want to go."

"I had other plans at the time." He gave her a significant glance. "At any rate, once I recovered from that initial bout of malaria, I turned my interest in wildlife into a job at one of the game reserves. I got a better education there than I would have at some frigid university in England."

Lilia had fallen silent, and Miles wondered if she was recalling the way they had eagerly built their dreams as they wandered hand in hand down the beach. She had wanted to study, but she had agreed to take courses in Lusaka after they married and settled in Zambia. Miles planned to use the money his father had set aside for his education to buy them a small house. He would get a job. They could start a family.

Castles in the air.

"Look at these elephants now, Colin," he said, forcing his own thoughts away from painful memories. "These are Asian elephants. They're smaller than the sort your mum and I grew up with. See their ears? They're not much bigger than yours, are they?" He reached up and tweaked Colin's ear. The boy squirmed and giggled. "Well, maybe a little larger. Now, listen closely and I'll tell you a story about an African elephant I once met. Face-to-face, we were, right in the middle of the bush with only a skinny thorn tree between us."

Miles launched into a tale, embellished only slightly, from his days as a tour guide. As he toted Colin past one animal enclosure after another, he regaled the silent little boy with accounts of his adventures. Lilia joined in now and then, her own tales hardly less exciting. They had nearly reached the end of the zoo, when Miles felt Colin's warm little body drape around his neck and the boy's fuzzy head come to rest on top of his own.

"He's getting sleepy," Lilia said softly, reaching to stroke Colin's leg. He surveyed her through heavy lids. "I need to take him home."

They walked through the stone gate to her car. Miles reached over his head and slid Colin from his shoulders. As he set the little boy on the ground, Colin quickly took Lilia's hand.

"So, will you be working with Habari Safari, Lilia?" Miles asked. "I'd be pleased to have you."

She glanced away at the orange-streaked sky. Even the way he said her name sent a shiver through her. His voice was deep and lazy, and it made her name sound like an exotic hothouse flower. If she turned him away, she knew their paths would never cross again. But if she let him in, even on a business level, there would be pain. The old wounds would have to be opened, explored. And it had taken so long to heal.

"I don't know, Miles," she said, letting out a breath. "It's so hard. Everything seems sudden, unexpected."

"Think it over, then. I'll ring you later, and you can give me your answer."

"All right." She looked into his eyes. "I'll let you know."

He smiled . . . that familiar, heart-stopping grin. Then his focus dropped to the boy. "Colin, pleased to have met you, my young friend," he said. "You sleep well tonight, lad."

"Say goodbye to Miles," Lilia whispered.

Colin held up his little hand, and Miles shook it gently, then placed a hand on Colin's head. With the other, he took Lilia's hand. The touch jolted through her, jarring her heartbeat into a crazy dance.

"Goodbye, Lilia," he said. "I've enjoyed spending the afternoon with you."

He shook her hand once, lightly, and then let it go. His blue eyes met hers, lingered a moment, then he turned and walked away.

"Goodbye, Miles," she called after him. As she bent to open the car door, she heard the faintest whisper.

"Bye, Mice." It was Colin.

Lilia drove home in a purple haze of confusion and dismay. Miles Kane had come back into her life, disrupted her orderly world, thrown her emotions into havoc. Colin had spoken for the first time in his life. And Miles was the one who had drawn her son out of his silence.

She pushed open the front door of her large old Victorian home, and Colin scampered into the foyer. She knelt to give him a hug.

"I'm so proud of you, Colin," she murmured. "You said some big words today, didn't you? I think you really liked Miles."

Colin grinned and nodded.

"I'm going to warm up our stew and make some cornbread for our supper. After we eat, you can hop in the bathtub and play with your boat. Now, where's Tembo? Do you think your elephant is waiting for you up in your bedroom?"

Lilia watched the dawn of realization light up Colin's face. She had given him the soft, stuffed elephant the first night they had spent together. Now, whenever they were at home, Colin and Tembo were inseparable. After giving her neck a tight squeeze, he tore across the foyer and headed up the long staircase.

Lilia watched him, her heart aching with tender love for the little boy. When his legs vanished from the landing, she stepped into the office that had once been a small bedroom. The red light of her answering machine blinked at her. As usual. She dropped her keys into her purse and pushed the play button.

"Lilia, this is Jenny," came a breathless voice. "I hope I catch you before you do something rash! Miles Kane was just here in the store and I didn't have any choice but to let him call you. He was so persistent and determined! Wow, what a great-looking guy. Listen, that man is a keeper. I've never seen eyes so blue. And his accent. It's to die for, Lilia! You've just got to do his project. Don't turn him down. Call me, okay? Okay?"

Jenny hung up, and Lilia sank into her plump desk chair. Oh, Jenny. Lilia thought of the young woman she had hired just out of college. How little Jenny knew of life. She was a dreamer, a bona fide romantic, who didn't have a clue that fairy tales rarely came true.

By this time, the tape had rolled forward. "Miss Eden," an unfamiliar female voice said. "I'm interested in a complete redecoration of my living room and dining room. I just bought this house, and everything's done in rust, gold and brown. But my furniture is maroon and navy! I'm desperate to change things, and you come highly recommended. Please return my call."

The woman left her name and number. Lilia scribbled them on her memo pad. Word of mouth had been the best advertisement for her design studio. Within months of buying the Creative Interiors franchise, Lilia's business had boomed. Now she was receiving large contracts—like the one with Habari Safari Hotels.

With a sigh, Lilia leaned back in her chair, already envisioning the wallcovering books and paint samples she would need for her latest caller's redesign project.

"Lilia," came the stiff but familiar voice of her attorney as the tape continued. "Lilia, this is Don Hanes. Um ... I need to talk to you about the hearing on Colin's case. Things didn't go exactly as planned. Give me a call."

A prickle ran down Lilia's spine. As the tape went dead, she grabbed the receiver and dialed her lawyer's number. He answered at once.

"Don, Lilia Eden here," she said. "What's going on?"

He cleared his throat. "Well, at the hearing this afternoon, Colin's birth mother showed up."

Lilia shut her eyes and tried to breathe. "Tell me this is a joke."

"I'm afraid it's not. She told the judge she has turned her life around and she wants her son back. She presented this incredible package—visits she made to Colin, a list of gifts she'd given him. Then she showed the judge a record of employment for the last five months, along with her boss's recommendation. She's engaged to someone who owns a nice house where she's been living. To top it off, she's been in a drug rehab program. She had records of all the times she's gone to meetings, and testimonials from her sponsor. The upshot of it, Lilia, is that the judge was swayed in her favor."

"What do you mean?" she whispered.

"Well, he threw out our petition."

"No..."

"I did everything I could. I asked him to call for a home study of the birth mother—just to make sure what she had said was correct. I asked him to postpone the hearing for three months. That would have left Colin with you during that time. But the judge wouldn't go for it. He stated that the birth mother had proven herself competent, and he awarded her custody of the child."

"The child! This is Colin we're talking about, Don! My son!"

"Family services is working on the situation, Lilia. But right now, there's not a whole lot anyone can do. You knew

Colin was a legal risk when you took him. Your home was still preadoptive, and when I petitioned the court, you knew the birth mother would be notified.''

''But she hadn't shown her face for eight months!''

''Lilia, I want you to remain at your house with Colin until your case worker from family services can come by tomorrow morning to discuss everything with you. Jean Banes said she'd be there by eight. Please try to understand, Lilia. I'll do everything I can. The court only wants what's best for Colin ... And I know you do, too.''

As the phone clicked off, Lilia's focus fixed on the gray machine. *What was best for Colin was her...his mother.* She had loved Colin from the moment she'd spotted him seated on a bench in the agency, skinny legs dangling and limp socks hanging around his ankles. His brown eyes had gazed up at her with a mixture of fear and longing that had nearly broken her heart. Within a matter of hours, he had begun to bond with her—clinging to her finger with his tiny fist, hanging on to every word from her mouth, gazing at her from a distance as she prepared dinner or ran his bath.

By the time a week had gone by, she felt as though Colin had always been a part of her life. His tears were her tears. His laughter brought a responding chuckle. Though he had never spoken a word until that afternoon at the zoo, Lilia had always felt a sense of communication with her son. As she spoke to him, she read his response in his small, trusting face—the turn of his cheek, the shrug of a shoulder, the glorious smile that lit up a room.

Lilia couldn't have felt more like Colin's mother if he had been conceived in her own body. And now, her son was being taken away from her. She slumped over on her desk, fighting tears. She couldn't bear it! She couldn't sit by and let them take Colin!

A gentle tugging on her shirttail made her lift her head. Colin was staring at her, a line of worry running across his forehead. ''Oh, Colin, honey,'' she said, scooping him up in her arms. ''Did you find Tembo?''

He settled in, wedging his warm body into the comfortable nest of her lap. He slipped his thumb into his mouth and hugged his elephant. Lilia laid her head on his. The cottony fluff of his hair formed a pillow for her cheek.

As they sat in silence, she swallowed again and again to keep the lump from forming in her throat. They were so comfortable together, just the two of them. She knew intimately the sweet smell of her son's skin, the silky texture of his fingers, the gentle sucking sounds he made when he was relaxing.

"I love you, Colin," she whispered.

He rubbed his elephant's trunk up and down her arm. His way of giving back to her what words could never say.

The shrill ring of the telephone jarred her. Before it could ring again, she lifted the receiver. Dread coursed through her. What now?

"Hello," she managed to say.

"Lilia. Miles here."

"Oh, Miles." She couldn't keep the relief from her voice. He sounded so strong, so sure of himself. A rock.

"Have you given it some thought—the hotel project?"

"Not really. Not yet." Colin had turned his head up and was gazing at her, eyes like depthless brown pools. "Miles, I don't think this is going to work out."

"Look, I want to see you again, Lilia. There are things we need to talk about. Things left unfinished between us."

"Oh, Miles, I . . ." She gulped. She had to hold back the tears. She couldn't break down in front of Colin, especially not while talking to Miles. "I don't think so, Miles. I can't."

"Lilia, don't push me away again. We were brought back together by some power larger than we can imagine. You can't deny that. The least we can do is talk."

"Miles, really, there's nothing to discuss." A tear trickled down her cheek, and she brushed it away. His voice was like a fortress. How easily she could run to him, hide her pain in his strength. But she had learned he couldn't be trusted. "I have other things . . . matters I'm dealing with right now. I'm sorry."

She hung up before he could respond.

Colin was staring at her. He touched her damp cheek. "Mice?" he asked.

She nodded.

"Bye, Mice," he said wistfully.

Lilia sniffled. "Come on, sweet boy. Let's have some supper."

There was nothing more fragrant, Lilia had decided, nothing more compelling or more endearing than the warm bundle of just-bathed little boy. Dressed in soft blue flannel pajamas with rubber-soled feet, Colin snuggled onto her lap as she sat in the rocking chair in his bedroom that evening.

She had decorated the room just for him—pale blue ceiling painted with white clouds, sheer white curtains at the long windows and a mural of rounded green hillsides, white sheep and apple trees on his blue walls. Lilia had painted the mural herself during hours and hours of sleepless nights while she waited for Colin's paperwork to clear.

Their favorite rocking chair had been a garage-sale find, covered with thick red paint. She had stripped it down to the bare oak, then oiled the wood and upholstered it in a gentle blue stripe. His closets were stuffed with toys that Lilia had bought for him. More outfits than he could ever wear out hung from small white hangers. Books jostled for space in his tall bookcase. His crib, a tumble of white flannel bedding, sat in the center of the room.

As always in the routine she had established for Colin, Lilia read her son a favorite bedtime story. On page after page of simple activities, they patted a furry bunny, peeked under a cloth, sniffed a bouquet of flowers, gazed in a tiny mirror. Lilia studied Colin's solemn face in the mirror, and it again amazed her that he had been classed as "hard-to-place."

It was true Colin was of mixed races, and also that he was not a newborn when he had been taken from his mother. In fact, when family services had removed the neglected baby from the empty apartment where his mother had abandoned him, Colin was almost ten months old. All the same, Lilia thought he was the sweetest, brightest, most desirable child ever offered for adoption.

"Colin," she said finally, struggling to form the words she had dreaded all evening. "Colin, there's something I need to talk to you about."

He held up his elephant.

"Yes, you and Tembo." Lilia tried to smile. "Tembo needs to hear this, too, since he loves you so much. Colin, today I found out that it might be time for you to go and live with...with your other mother again. In the morning, we'll talk about it some more. But tonight I want to tell you something very important. I want you to know, Colin..." Lilia felt the tears well up as she gazed at the solemn little boy. "Colin, I love you very, very much. No matter where you go or who you live with, I'll always love you. Will you remember that, honey?"

Colin hung his head. He rubbed Tembo's ear.

"Colin?" Lilia whispered. "If I could keep you here at my house with me, I would. But I'm not the boss of that."

Colin sank against her breast and slipped his thumb into his mouth. He stroked his elephant's trunk up and down her arm. Through the blur of her tears, Lilia tried to memorize his tiny, curled fingers, the smell of baby shampoo in his fuzzy hair, the rustle of his diaper, the damp curves of his little knees.

"I love you, Colin," she whispered. "Please don't ever forget that."

As the minutes ticked by, Lilia rocked. Colin's hand clutched her shirt, and he finally fell asleep. When she was sure he could hear nothing, she gave into her tears. Alternately, she sank into the depths of despair, then rose again with choking, broiling anger at the unfairness of it all.

On the one hand, she pictured herself spending the rest of her life in an aimless, meaningless existence without her son. On the other hand, she mentally wrote speeches which she shouted at imaginary judges and social workers; or she sneaked around in the dead of night and stole Colin away so they could live together in Africa, or Europe, or China. Anywhere.

Sometime in the night, it occurred to Lilia that she had grieved this way once before. It had been the loss of another love—the aching loss of her husband, Miles Kane—

that had so devastated her, she couldn't imagine ever recovering. But she had gone on, hadn't she? People did survive crushing losses, incredible pain, the senseless death of loved ones. Maybe she could live through each day without this little boy... but at this moment she couldn't see how.

Unwilling to let go of Colin even for a minute of their last hours together, she fell asleep in the rocking chair.

The doorbell brought Lilia wide-awake the following morning. A sense of dread curled into her stomach as she lifted the drowsy Colin onto one hip and started down the long staircase. She would fight for him, she resolved. No, he would be traumatized by such a scene. Then she would let him slip away peacefully. No, she couldn't do that, either!

Churning with tension, Lilia turned the brass knob and pushed open the door. Miles Kane was leaning against a porch post. His broad shoulders blocked the sunlight. His golden hair, thick and damp, had been combed back off his forehead.

"Morning, Lilia." His blue eyes softened as he took in the sleepy little boy and the woman in her nubby robe. "Hope I didn't wake you."

"We were just... we were sitting in the rocking chair upstairs." Lilia couldn't make herself accept that this was Miles and not the social services worker she had been expecting. She ran a hand through her tousled hair. She should have been up hours ago, showering, brushing her teeth, fixing breakfast. "Miles, I—"

A green van pulled up in her driveway. She recognized it at once. Jean Banes stepped out, briefcase in hand. Lilia backed into the foyer. Her arms tightened around Colin. Miles frowned.

"Lilia?" he asked. "Lilia, what—"

"Miss Eden, good morning." Jean Banes climbed the stairs to the porch. Her sharp eyes looked Miles up and down. "I'm Jean Barnes," she said to him, sticking out a stiff hand. "Family Services of Missouri."

"Miles Kane," he returned. "Zambia."

She blinked. Reddish eyes behind tortoiseshell glasses. "How interesting. If you'll excuse us, Mr. Kane, Miss Eden and I have business to discuss."

Miles turned to Lilia. One look at the frightened expression on her face told him this bear of a woman meant trouble. "I just arrived to discuss business with her myself, as a matter of fact. Why don't we all go inside?"

Lilia let out a breath. "Miles, please," she pleaded softly.

The two women stared at him, but Miles decided not to budge. Better to be a buffalo in some situations. This was one. "Carry on," he said. "Don't mind me. I'll wait my turn."

Lilia debated sending him away, but she knew she didn't have the energy it would take. The man was as stubborn as they came. She glanced at the agent. "It's all right, Jean. Miles is an old friend."

"Very well." The social worker shrugged. She surveyed Lilia for a moment, obviously assessing her, and then she took a deep breath. "As Mr. Hanes told you last night, Lilia, I'm afraid your situation has been reversed."

Lilia shut her eyes, a weight slamming into her heart.

"Colin," Jean said softly, taking the little boy's hand. He regarded her with solemn brown eyes. "Colin, I've come to tell you some news. Do you remember the mother you lived with before you came to stay with Lilia? Well, she wants to be with you again. She wants you to go and live with her. How about that?"

Colin began to pull on his elephant's ear. Lilia couldn't stop her trembling lip. "This will be a new adventure for you, sweetheart," she managed to say. "I won't be able to go with you, but Tembo can. You and your old buddy will be together."

"That's right," Jean went on. "Now, Colin, I want you to come with me."

When she reached for him, Colin threw his arms around Lilia's neck and buried his face in her shoulder. The elephant dropped to the porch.

"Well, now." Miles picked up the soft toy and nudged Colin's cheek. "I believe Tembo wants to go for a ride, Colin. But I know he won't go anywhere without you, lad.

Will you come along? You can show me the garden where you play.''

Colin peered at Miles for a moment. Then he stretched out his arms and leaned into Miles's embrace. Lilia turned away and vanished into the house before he could see her tears. Outside, Miles started off around the house with Colin perched on his shoulders.

''Lavender's blue, dilly, dilly,'' Miles began to sing, ''rosemary's green. When you are king, dilly dilly...''

''Lilia?'' Jean Banes followed her into the foyer. ''I'm so sorry this has happened. I know how attached you are to Colin.''

''Attached?'' Hot with frustration, she turned on the woman. ''I love him, Jean! Colin is my son!''

''I know you must feel devastated, Lilia. Try to remember that the birth mother's rights supercede the adoptive mother's. This is terribly difficult, but please try to be strong for Colin's sake.'' She pulled a file from her briefcase. ''We spent hours at the office last night going over your case, and we're going to do all we can to lessen your grief. We'd be happy to set up a counseling appointment for you, and of course Colin will be under a psychologist's care.''

''Colin needs more than a psychologist can give him, Jean,'' Lilia retorted. ''He came to me neglected and abandoned. To this day, he doesn't speak. The woman whose rights supercede mine left a ten-month-old baby alone for two days in an empty apartment while she went off in a drugged daze with one of her innumerable boyfriends. How can you say it's in Colin's best interest to put him in her hands again?''

''She's been attending group therapy meetings, Lilia. For two months now, she's been drug-free.''

''Two months!''

''That's better than she's ever done in the past. She has a daytime job, too.''

''Where?''

''I can't tell you that. Trust me, she's been going to work faithfully. She has a new boyfriend, and he seems to be stable. He is employed, and they're living in a nice home here in Springfield. Look, Lilia, she wants Colin back. He *is* her son."

"He's been *my* son for months and months! I've had him a lot longer than she had him. I've given him everything— not only materially, but emotionally. I love him, and he loves me. How can you say that woman deserves him any more than I do?"

Jean shook her head and flipped open the file. "There's nothing you can do to fight Missouri's legal system, so you might as well put this behind you, Lilia. You've already met the state's adoptive standards, and you've been wonderful to work with. You have a great relationship with family services, so you'll be at the top of our list to receive another special needs child."

"I don't want another child! I want Colin!" she sobbed. "He's my son. I'm his mother!"

Jean handed her a tissue. "Lilia, this kind of thing almost never happens. Most of our adoptions go through without a snag, but there's always a small risk. Next time, we'll try to make doubly sure the birth mother is going to stay out of the picture, okay? I promise you that."

Lilia couldn't speak. She buried her face in her hands, unable to stop crying. This was really happening! They were going to take Colin from her, and there was nothing she could do to stop them.

"Try your best to look forward," Jean said again. "Throw yourself into your work. Take a long vacation somewhere far away. Family services will be in touch to help you get through this."

"Colin...he gets ear infections, you know," Lilia said into the soggy tissue. "His shots weren't up-to-date. I've been taking him in.... And he's allergic to penicillin...."

"Yes, I know. We'll be doing regular follow-ups on his care. You won't have to worry about that. Now, Lilia, please go upstairs and pack his things. And try to pull yourself together. Be brave, now, for Colin."

Blinded by tears, Lilia stumbled up the stairs. She took down the little bag he carried to Miss Maddie's Playland each morning and began to stuff his clothes inside. She filled a canvas suitcase with toys and the rest of his clothes. She folded his flannel blanket and picked out a stack of his favorite books. But she couldn't stop crying. Nothing she tried would hold back the flood.

When she came downstairs, she set Colin's things in the agency van. She was refolding his blanket when Miles came around the corner of the house with Colin.

"I've been to London to visit the Queen," Miles chanted, bouncing with each step. "Pussycat, pussycat, what did you do there? I frightened a little mouse under her chair."

Miles stopped at the sight of Lilia standing beside the bear lady. Her face was swollen and streaked with tears. Colin dug his fingers into Miles's hair as they approached the van.

"Mr. Kane," Jean said, "would you please put Colin into the safety seat and buckle him up?"

Miles looked at Lilia. She nodded. Not for all the world would he willingly have given the boy to that woman unless Lilia agreed. In fact, he had almost decided he would abscond with the child no matter what the two of them decided. But seeing Lilia's miserably resigned face, he swung Colin down from his shoulders and placed him in the seat. As he began to buckle the child in, he felt Lilia move against him.

"Colin," she said softly. "You take care of Tembo, now. He needs you to be a strong, happy boy."

Colin hung on to the stuffed elephant as he looked at Lilia.

She leaned across him and kissed his cheek. "I love you, Colin. Please don't ever forget that."

Miles watched her turn and run up the stairs into her house. Colin blinked at him. "You remember what your mum said, lad. She once told me that, too. She said she loved me, and I wasn't ever to forget. I haven't forgotten . . . not for a moment."

Colin stuck his thumb in his mouth, but as Miles was pulling the van's door shut, he drew it out again. "Bye, Mice," he said.

Miles swallowed. "Goodbye, Colin."

He settled back in the seat and shut his eyes. But when the van started up and pulled away, Miles could see Colin's little head appear over the back of the seat. His brown eyes were wide, and his mouth formed words again and again.

"Mama!" Miles was sure he was saying. "Mama, Mama!"

Chapter 4

Miles opened the front door of Lilia's house. Inside, all was silent, except for the sound of soft weeping. He stepped through the wide arch between the foyer and living room. She was leaning on the fireplace mantel, head buried in her arms, shoulders shaking.

"Lilia," he said.

She didn't answer. He walked into the room as far as the sofa. Brought up in a family where the father had ruled with an iron hand, Miles had rarely seen emotion openly displayed. "Get a grip on yourself, young man," had been the curt response to childish tears or adolescent anguish.

Miles stuffed his hands into his pockets and shifted from one foot to the other. Getting a grip on something like this wouldn't be so simple. It was clear to him now how deeply Lilia loved Colin. She was devastated, and he knew neither his accumulated wealth nor his influence could put her son back in her arms. Worse, Miles was again stricken with the knowledge that he could never hope to give Lilia a child himself.

He was powerless. The feeling was not a familiar one, and Miles didn't like it. A man's strength ought to be able to correct an unacceptable situation like this. He knew what he *could* do—build a steel fence that could contain a rhino, lift the front end of a Land Rover out of an ant-bear hole, subdue an angry, blinded crocodile. But where Lilia was concerned, he felt helpless. He couldn't bring Colin back. And he didn't have a clue how to comfort Lilia, how to heal her pain.

Not only that, but seeing her this way had only confirmed how much he wanted her. Lilia had always been his, he realized, from the moment they had been drawn together on the beaches of the Indian Ocean. She could be his again, if only he knew how to reclaim her. Right now, inconsolable grief claimed her.

Feeling awkward and uncomfortable, he walked toward her. "Lilia," he said, laying a hand on her shoulder. At the touch of her softness, his doubt fled. He lifted her away from the mantel and wrapped his arms around her. "Lilia, oh, Lilia," he murmured. "I'm so sorry."

She clung to him, sobs breaking out anew. He smoothed his hand down her rumpled hair, drinking in the sweet morning scent of her skin. She felt so small and fragile against him, as though she might break in two at the slightest jar. He moved his hand down her back, vaguely aware of the fine curve of her spine and the gentle swell of her hips. There must be something he could do.

"Listen, Lilia," he said, suddenly latching on to his mother's favorite remedy. "You curl up in this chair, and I'll brew you a pot of steaming tea. How's that?"

"No." Her voice was muffled against his shoulder. "I can't."

"But tea...with milk and sugar?" He'd used his only resource.

What did a man do with a weeping woman? Buy her a stiff drink? Chuck her on the chin and tell her to buck up? He stroked her hair. Maybe if he offered to take her shopping, put her mind on other things.

"I can't stand it," she cried softly, her hands gripping the fabric of his shirt. "It hurts so much."

"I know. You loved Colin. You gave him all you had to give."

"Y-yes." She only sobbed harder. "Oh . . . this is unbearable."

Miles cursed his gross ineptitude. By trying to be sympathetic, he'd only made her pain more intense. It couldn't be good to cry this much. She'd be empty when she was through.

What could he do? Suggest a game of tennis? An outing in the country? A trip to the cinema to see the latest comedy film? Or . . .

"Lilia," he said, setting her away from him enough that he could look into her gray eyes. "Fly with me to Albuquerque tomorrow morning. I'll be driving south from the city to the site of Habari Safari's first hotel. It's a great place, just at the edge of a mountain range. We'll look things over, the two of us. You can give me your ideas for the interior design. It'll take your mind off things."

She stared at him. "What?"

"We'll go away together. You'll feel better."

"Feel better?" She brushed his hands from her shoulders. How could he even suggest that she would leave Springfield at a time like this? What if Jean Banes called her back? What if Colin needed her? What if . . .

Her heart stumbled. Of course that wouldn't happen. Colin was gone forever.

She looked into Miles's blue eyes, and her pain transformed into anger. "What do you think I'm made of?" she snapped. "Stone? You think I can just go prancing off to Albuquerque? You think I can shrug this thing off—like you thought I shrugged off what you did to me ten years ago?"

"No," he began.

"You expect to walk back into my life and have everything the same, don't you? You think I'll fall all over myself to be with you. That I'll drop my entire life just to grab on to whatever whimsy filters into your stubborn, selfcentered brain."

"No—"

"Well, I won't!" Her eyes flickered with a silver fire. "Ten years ago, we made a commitment to each other, Miles Kane. A lifetime promise. Did that mean nothing to you?"

"No—I mean, yes! Of course it did!"

"Oh, come on. If you really cared for me—if you loved me the way you said you did—why did you insist on ending our marriage? Can you explain that?"

"What?" He looked at her blankly.

"Because when I give my love to someone," she raged on, "like Colin . . . or *you* . . . I don't just sweep that love aside when things get a little difficult. I make my commitments for life, Miles!"

"So do I."

"Oh, I don't need this! Just get out!" She shoved her hand against the rock wall of his chest. The loss of Colin had brought back all the memories of her first great loss— Miles Kane. Now that he stood before her, she couldn't control the sense of devastation sweeping through her heart.

"I won't let anyone hurt me ever again!" She hurled the words at him as he started for the door, a look of bewilderment on his face. She could be cold, callous and indifferent, too, if that was what if took to barricade herself from this kind of pain. "Don't ever come back here!" she said, giving him a final push out onto her porch. "Don't ever set foot into my studio. Don't ever phone me again. I don't want . . . I don't want *you!*"

Miles stared at the old wooden door as it swung toward him and slammed shut. For a moment, he couldn't move. Lilia's words filtered through his brain. *If you really cared for me—if you loved me the way you said you did—why did you insist on ending our marriage?*

But he hadn't ended their marriage! His father had clearly told him the hard truth that afternoon in the hospital: *Lilia* had asked for an annulment. *She* had wanted to go to college, to date those American boys, to get on with her life. *She* was the one who had ended it all. Not him.

He stared up at the windows on the second floor of her house. "Fine then, if that's the way you choose to remember it," he shouted at the top of his lungs. "To hell with you, too!"

Miles took an early flight to Albuquerque. Anything to get out of that gray city, with its lines of cars and interminable neon signs. Anything to put Lilia Eden out of his mind.

The site of the first Habari Safari Hotel to be built lay south of Albuquerque, New Mexico, not far from the little oil and farming town of Artesia. A commuter airline would fly guests into Roswell, and tour buses would take them to the hotel.

The land Miles had purchased nudged up against the Lincoln National Forest. The Peñasco River trickled through, providing enough water to run the hotel and fill small reservoirs for the animals. It was a dry country—warm enough most of the year to sustain equatorial wildlife—and covered with long, pale silver grasses and clumps of mesquite. If there had been a few thorn trees and some giraffes wandering past, Miles would have sworn he was in East Africa.

He spent three days on the site. In the evenings, he stayed in the home of a family of cattlegrowers from whom he had purchased most of the hotel's acreage. His hosts were people whose families had ranched in the area for nearly a century. The rancher and his wife were discouraged by government control of their lands and the generally poor price of beef. Although they were aggressively involved in promoting the cattle industry, they listened with interest to Miles's explanation of the David Hopcraft experiment in Kenya and the value of repopulating the land with wildlife.

"Grass out here in the Peñasco Valley used to be belly-high to a horse," the rancher told Miles. "A hundred years ago, every river, stream and gully was flowing. This place was the Garden of Eden—thick with fruit orchards, pecan groves, fields of cotton and alfalfa."

"You wouldn't know it today," his wife chimed in. "We blame the decline of the land on years of drought and the lowering of the artesian water table. But I guarantee we'll be watching your little spread to see what happens. If we could bring back the native grasses and choke out pests like turpentine weed and greasewood, we might consider making a few changes in the way we run things. Of course, *African* animals . . . now that's an odd thought."

Miles's heavy heart lifted at the thought of opening the back end of a trailer and setting a pair of zebras free on the land. During his three days on site in New Mexico, Miles and a contractor who had worked with zoos surveyed the terrain and discussed the types and placement of natural and artificial barriers around the hotel.

Miles had already been negotiating with wildlife parks and zoos in the United States to secure a flock of breeding ostriches, a pair of endangered Grevy's zebras, and small herds of Thomson's gazelles, impalas and wildebeests. It would be almost two years before he could start to stock this land, and a year after that before the hotel would open. But Miles had been assured of obtaining oryx from the nearby White Sands Missile Range where they had been roaming wild, and he was in the process of contracting for a pair of rhinos, some sable antelope, two eland and the Missouri cheetahs.

More than anything, he wanted giraffes and elephants. Their silhouettes on the horizon would ensure an African image for the busloads of tourists. Of course, the ambience of the hotels themselves would be a vital factor in their success or failure—and that necessitated the services of a talented interior designer.

Miles's thoughts swung to Lilia, and just as quickly he snuffed them. He couldn't think about her. Wouldn't. She obviously didn't want him to be a part of her life—not in any way. Besides, she had Colin to think about. To grieve.

As he drove back to Albuquerque for a round of meetings with contractors who wanted to bid on the hotel project, Miles tried again and again to put Lilia out of his thoughts. Maybe they had been brought back together to finally seal the wall of separation between them, he reasoned. Maybe their meeting was fate's design for closing the door to his memories of her forever.

But if so, why couldn't he forget her? Every time he shut his eyes, Miles saw Lilia's beautiful face, her sad gray eyes, her porcelain skin, her long legs, her compelling lips. At night when he tried to sleep, he could hear her voice like a melodic echo running circles inside his head. He had barely touched her—shaken her hand, held her for a brief moment. But he swore he could physically feel the silky texture of her hair. He knew every curve and hollow in her back. The tantalizing pressure of her breasts against his chest haunted him.

But she didn't want him! She'd shouted out her rejection. She had pushed him out of her house, out of her life. She blamed Miles for the rift that had ended their marriage.

Her accusations lingered, tapping like an insistent hammer to the beat of his pulse. *He* had asked for the annulment, she'd claimed. *He* had wanted to sever their wedding vows.

But Miles knew that it was a lie. His own father had told him . . . his own father had said . . .

Miles conjured up the white-haired man who had tried to dominate his life for thirty-one years. William Kane had wanted to send his son to boarding school, and Miles had gone. The father had wanted his son to wear small gray suits with blue neckties, and Miles had worn them. The father had wanted Miles to befriend the sons of his executive associates, and Miles had obeyed. And William Kane had wanted Miles to end his marriage to Lilia Eden—"that wild American girl."

For the first time in his life, Miles had stood up against his father's will. Weak with malaria, exhausted and feverish, he had fought for his young love. "Telephone her," Miles had pleaded with his father. "Ring Lilia and tell her I'm all right. Tell her I love her. Tell her I'll return for her as soon as I can travel."

And then that afternoon in the hospital, Miles's father had come with the news. Lilia was off to her university in America. She hadn't waited for him. She was studying, making wonderful grades. She was dating American boys. She wanted an annulment. Of course she did—she wanted to get on with her life.

Miles had broken, succumbed. What else could he do? He didn't have the money to fly to America and force her back. She didn't want him anymore. His father had said so.

His father had said so.

Miles recounted the ways he had stood up against his father's will from that time on. He hadn't gone to university in England. He hadn't worked a single day in the Zambian copper industry. He hadn't married any of the score of young ladies his parents had fawned over at parties. "You've gone wild, Miles," his father had shouted at him more than once. "You roam about in the bush like a native! You've gone wild."

Miles had felt wild. Wild. Free. Angry. He had shed his father's domination. But now, as Miles drove across the flat, dry land of New Mexico, he began to think about that afternoon in the hospital in Lusaka. He began to wonder. And he began to doubt.

Lilia's entire world shut down after they took Colin away. She couldn't eat. Couldn't sleep. Couldn't even think. Jenny handled the shop, putting customers on a waiting list and taking orders by phone. Lilia sat on her couch and stared at the ashes in the empty fireplace.

On Sunday morning, Jenny dropped by as usual. When she saw the depth of Lilia's despondency, she flew into a flurry.

"You can't sit around like this, Lilia!" she ordered. "Come on. Get dressed, and we'll go to church."

Lilia had first met Jenny when the younger woman was a student at Southwest Missouri State University. They had attended the same church for years, but had never really known each other until someone in the congregation put two and two together—the successful interior designer with the young art major who had a penchant for redecorating houses. Since that time, Jenny had practically worshiped Lilia as advisor, mentor and friend.

"Lilia, I'm not going to let you drift away like this," Jenny warned as she took Lilia's arm and led her up the stairs. "You get in the shower this instant. I'll pick out a dress, and then we're going to church."

It turned out to be the tonic Lilia needed. The activity of bathing and eating food, the swarms of people who thronged to express sympathy and love, the sermon filled with hope—all brought Lilia back from the brink of despair. She managed a smile or two. She noticed a pair of blue jays squabbling on a branch outside the window. She joined a hymn of praise.

People did survive, she admonished herself. She could, too.

She went back to work the following Monday. Blots of black grief alternated with the busyness of taking phone calls, meeting with clients, making decisions.

"Where's Miles these days?" Jenny asked one morning near the end of the week. "You haven't mentioned the Habari Safari project, and I noticed you've been scheduling clients during the time we blocked off to work on the hotel design."

"Oh, I canceled that deal," Lilia retorted. She was searching wallcovering books for a floral border in mauve and teal.

"Canceled Habari Safari? Lilia, are you crazy? That was going to be our big break! We were going to make enough money to open the loft upstairs and start carrying furniture. Remember? Decorative gifts? Flower arrangements? All our dreams!"

Lilia lifted her head. Jenny had left her desk and was staring at her, obviously expecting an explanation. "I changed my mind about it, that's all," Lilia said. "We don't really need the extra work and time the loft would have required."

"But you were looking forward to it! You said we'd be the top-flight design studio in town. You said—"

Lilia slapped her palm down on her desk. "It doesn't matter what I said! I told you, I changed my mind."

Jenny's face fell. "Gosh, Lilia, we turned down a jillion projects just to leave time to work on the hotel design. You were so excited about it. I only thought..."

"I'm sorry, Jenny." Lilia flipped the wallcovering book shut. "I didn't mean to snap at you. You're right, I was looking forward to the hotel deal, and I had made big plans for the extra cash it would bring in. But after thinking it over, I decided I didn't want to do it."

"Miles Kane, right?"

"I suppose he played a part." Lilia sighed. "Okay, I'll admit he's the reason I decided to cancel. I can't deal with the man."

"I thought he was wonderful. It's not every day someone that great-looking walks in here, you know. I mean, just the sound of his voice could melt your heart. And those gorgeous blue eyes—"

"Jenny, do you mind?"

"Sorry, Lilia. But you're being awfully stubborn. It was clear to me the minute I saw the man that he's still in love with you. The way he talked to you on the phone. The way he tracked you down."

"He didn't track me down. Our two companies put us together. The whole meeting was an accident."

"But don't you get it? It's cosmic!" Jenny spread her arms as if to embrace the universe. "It's a heavenly design!"

"Oh, Jenny!" Lilia had to laugh. "Believe me, there's nothing the least bit ethereal about Miles Kane or anything he does. In fact, there couldn't be a man more earthy."

"You can say that again. He reminded me of a big, tawny lion. You should have seen him take control in here. And that shaggy blond mane of hair—"

"Jenny!"

"He's a hunk, Lilia! I can't believe you let him get away."

"I didn't let him get away. I shoved him out the door and then slammed it in his face."

"You're kidding." Jenny's mouth dropped open. "You mean that's that? You're never going to see him again? The man you married? The man you *loved?*"

Lilia stiffened against the call of her heart. "I might have loved Miles once, Jenny. But not anymore. There's too much water under the bridge. Too much pain."

"The pain is coming from Colin. That's where you're hurting the worst. Are you sure you didn't take out your frustration over Colin on Miles?"

Lilia pondered the question. "I think it was the other way around. The pain Miles caused me ten years ago came out all over again when I lost Colin. It made giving Colin up a thousand times worse. And it made my anger at Miles equally hot.''

Jenny sat down beside Lilia. "Maybe you haven't lost either one of them. You could call up Habari Safari's main offices and find Miles again. You could call family services—"

"I already did." Lilia gave a dry laugh. "About fifteen times. Jean Banes informed me that I can have no contact with Colin. He's completely off limits to me. In years to come, I won't be allowed to know what's happened to him. If I pursue the case, his birth mother can even take out a restraining order against me."

"No!"

"Like I'm some kind of witch lurking around to ruin Colin's life. Jean Banes has told me over and over to put the situation behind me and focus on the future." Lilia swallowed, forcing back the tears. "I'm trying, Jenny, I really am. But I can't stop thinking about him, wondering if he's all right. It's okay during the day while I'm at work. At night, though…in that empty house with his big room and our rocking chair…and his shampoo on the edge of the bathtub…and his sipper cups on my shelf…"

"Oh, Lilia!" Jenny threw her arms around Lilia's shoulders.

"I'll be in the grocery store," Lilia sobbed, "and I'll reach for the bananas because Colin loved them. And then I realize I don't even like bananas."

"Oh, Lilia…"

"I get so mad. I'm furious at myself for ever starting that adoption thing, for ever thinking I wanted a child of my own. Then I start feeling so guilty about what effect all this might have on Colin. I know he felt my uncertainty and uneasiness—especially at the end. And then I fly into a rage at Colin's birth mother for taking him away. I contemplate crimes against poor Jean Banes or my attorney, who were just doing their jobs. Isn't that crazy? But you know who I'm angriest with?"

"Who?"

"Miles." Lilia sat up and sniffled. "Miles Kane. Why? Why am I so mad at *him*, Jenny?"

"Because you lost him just like you lost Colin," Jenny said softly. "Because you love Colin. And because you still love Miles."

It wasn't true, Lilia decided Friday afternoon as she was clearing up before the weekend break. Jenny had been dead wrong about Miles. The whole reason she couldn't get Miles out of her mind, Lilia realized, was because of the grief and the transition she was going through.

Miles had come back into her life during a difficult time, and his presence had opened up some memories. Somehow those memories had fused with her grief over the loss of Colin, and that was why she couldn't stop thinking about Miles.

In fact, Lilia deduced as she set a stack of wallcovering books back onto the shelf, the reason she kept remembering her earlier life with Miles was that the memories offered an escape. Her years as the daughter of missionaries had been wonderful. She had loved growing up near the Portuguese and Arabic town of Mombasa on the Indian Ocean. Miles was simply a part of those memories. That was why she regularly found herself replaying the moment they had met, the hours they had spent strolling the beaches hand in hand, the times they had swum together in the salty water, the evenings he had held her beneath the glimmer of the Southern Cross.

So, that was that. Memories were a comfort, nothing more. Lilia dusted off her hands and checked the rack of paint chips. She slid a strip of purple shades into its slot. Then she scanned the books from the furniture companies, the ringed collections of upholstery swatches, the flip-stands of vinyl floor coverings. Everything was in order.

As she picked up her purse, she scanned the calendar. Checking off another day, she congratulated herself on having made it through twenty-four hours without calling family services to see if there was any news about Colin. There never was.

All the same, life was looking better. Maybe she would take herself out to dinner to celebrate this small victory. She dug out her keys, slung her sweater over one shoulder and headed for the front door.

Miles Kane was leaning against a lamppost.

Lilia came to a stop inside her studio, her heart slamming into her ribs. She could turn around and go out the back door. She could walk past and ignore him. Oh, but he looked good. His khaki-colored shirt was rolled up at the sleeves, and the sculpted muscles of his arms seemed even more deeply tanned. His hair had slid over his forehead. His eyes, like a pair of crackling blue flames, held her.

She walked to the door. Pushed it open. Stepped outside.

"Lilia," he said, "there's one item we should clear up."

She met his frank gaze. "Hello to you, too, Miles."

"Thought I'd better be blunt about what I have to say before you drive me away again."

"I apologize for that scene, by the way. I could have used a little more tact."

"Well, you got the message across."

"Apparently not. You came back, didn't you?"

He smiled. "But I didn't set foot in your shop. Didn't go to your house. Didn't ring you on the telephone. The only way I could reach you was to fly back here to Springfield and wait outside on the street until you showed up."

"You always were persistent." She started for her car. "So what's this we need to clear up? As far as I'm concerned, there's nothing to discuss."

He was striding beside her, his long legs easily keeping pace with hers. "Something you said has been haunting me."

"I told you I wasn't really all together that morning, Miles. You shouldn't have taken anything I said too seriously."

"Then it *was* you who called off the marriage?"

"What?" She swung around.

"Ten years ago. While I was recovering from malaria, you decided you didn't want to be married to me, after all. You wanted to get on with your life. You wanted to annul our marriage."

Lilia stared at Miles. She couldn't believe he was saying this. But there he was, larger than life, looking straight into her eyes and wanting her to take the blame.

"Don't try to change the facts, Miles Kane. I *never* wanted to annul our marriage!" she said. Then she stuck her finger straight into his chest. "*You* wanted it over. *You* wanted to get on with *your* life!"

"What life? I was nearly dead from malaria. My entire future was wrapped around you. And you dashed it to the ground."

She wanted to laugh, but his blue eyes were deadly serious. "Is this some kind of joke, Miles? Because I don't think it's very funny."

"It's not a joke, and I don't think it's funny, either." He took her hand and pulled her toward him. "Look, I'm flying to Kenya in a few hours' time. I'll be away for two weeks, and I'm not going to spend that time wondering what happened between us ten years ago. When you shoved me out of your house the other day, you accused me of ending our marriage."

"That's right." Her gray eyes went silver. "You'd better not try to deny it, either. Your father talked to me on the phone from Zambia, Miles. The connection was terrible and we were both shouting to be heard, but I remember every word he said. You were fine. Completely recovered. No ill effects whatsoever."

"He said that?" Miles hissed.

"He told me you had decided to go to college in Lusaka instead of England."

"But I never—"

"And he said you wanted to get on with your life. He told me you had asked for an annulment of our marriage."

"I didn't!" He took her shoulders, shaking her as if he could erase what she was saying.

Her lower lip began to tremble. "Yes, you did! Your father told me you wanted to get on with your life."

"No! *You* wanted to get on with *your* life!"

"Miles, I was waiting in Kenya for you. I was waiting for you to get well and come for me, like you promised you would."

"But you had already gone to college in the States by the time my father phoned Kenya. He talked to your parents, not to you."

"No, I was still there. Why would I leave? We were going to live in Zambia, Miles." Lilia shook her head. She didn't understand. What was he trying to say? "We were planning to buy a house. We were going to have children—"

"Lilia!"

"You're crushing my shoulders, Miles!"

"Oh, Lilia," he exploded, catching her fully against him. "I'm sorry. I'd never hurt you. Never."

He paused for a moment, breathing hard, trying to sort through the tangle of thoughts and feelings. Suddenly a thread of an idea came loose, presenting itself with startling clarity. "Lilia," he said impulsively, "come with me to Kenya. I'll buy your ticket."

"You're crazy." She couldn't hold back the welling of emotion. He smelled the way he always had, of coarse cotton khaki, of sunburned skin, of fresh air. She could feel his hands on her back, molding her against him, holding her so tightly she could hardly breathe.

"I'm perfectly sane, Lilia. You need a break. We both need time to talk, to sort this out. Look, I'll be staying at five hotels in Kenya—two of them at Diani Beach where you grew up. Meetings with management and that sort of tripe. But, Lilia, you'd have every reason to come with me if you're working with Habari Safari. You could study the hotels' designs. You could research the project and develop a portfolio. It makes perfect sense. My company would pay for the trip—I'm sure of it."

"Oh, Miles."

"When was the last time you went home?" He set her away from him, forcing her to meet his eyes. "When, Lilia?"

"Ten years ago," she whispered.

"Lilia, don't turn me away. Not this time."

"Miles, I just—"

"Think of the Indian Ocean, Lilia. The reef, the white sand, the palm trees. Remember the narrow, winding streets of Old Town Mombasa? You can go there again. You can visit Fort Jesus. You can see the house you grew up in. Talk to your old friends."

Lilia drifted into his words, losing herself in the beauty of his vision. How homesick she had been when she'd left Kenya. It had seemed unthinkable that she would never return. Never go home again. But the years had passed, and the unthinkable had become a reality. Home was ten thousand miles away—too far and too costly for a struggling college student and then a small business owner.

She had put her dreams of Kenya away forever... along with her memories of Miles. She had replaced them both with the goal of building a new future. A future that had included Colin.

"Do it, Lilia," Miles whispered against her cheek. "Say you will."

She felt like a puppet, jerked by the hands of fate. But whispers of common sense drifted into her scattered thoughts. *Take a long vacation somewhere far away*, Jean Bates had said. *Try to put this behind you, Lilia. You have to look forward now.* And Jenny— *You were so excited about the hotel project. You had such big plans!*

And Miles, holding her close, offering her a gift too precious, "Come home with me, Lilia. You'll be healed."

She could almost feel the white foam tickling the tips of her toes. She could almost taste the sweet juice of a ripe mango. She could almost smell the seaweedy fragrance of the moist, heavy air. She could almost hear the rush of waves, the cries of fishermen, the plop of ripe coconuts on the sand. On her tongue, she tasted the salty water of the sea... or were those her tears?

"All right," she whispered. "All right, Miles. I think it's time to go home."

Chapter 5

Lilia had one hour to pack. The whole time she was throwing blouses, jeans, skirts and sandals into her suitcase, she was telling herself she was crazy. Absolutely nuts.

A week ago, she had been building a wonderful future for herself and her son. Now Colin was gone. So was her sanity. Miles Kane had bulled his way back into her life, overturned the neat and orderly pattern of her world, thrown her heart into havoc and convinced her to go to Kenya with him! This evening!

She turned her heavy suitcase on its side and slid it down the long, carpeted staircase. Following her luggage down, Lilia counted every reason she should back out. Number one, customers expected her to work with them personally on their redesigns. Of course, Jenny could handle the studio. She was perfectly competent. Lilia had trained her well. And it was true they had more or less cleared the calendar in order to work on the Habari Safari project.

Well, maybe that reason wasn't quite valid. But number two certainly was. Lilia needed to be available in case Jean Banes called to say Colin needed her. Of course, that hadn't happened yet. And she had to acknowledge that it wouldn't happen. What better way to start dealing with the truth than by distancing herself ten thousand miles from the situation?

Even though the studio could stay in business and family services wasn't likely to phone, Lilia knew she should never go anywhere with Miles Kane. The man had been trouble from day one. He was just as stubborn, just as persistent and dogged as ever.

And what was all this business about *her* having wanted to end their marriage? She couldn't fathom what he had been blathering about on the sidewalk that afternoon. The man was clearly unstable—an unreliable, backtracking, rationalizing...handsome devil if there ever was one. Just being around him made her feel off balance, dizzy and totally young-at-heart, full of hope, almost happy!

But it could end in disaster. If Miles somehow managed to knock holes in the careful wall she had built around her heart, he could get inside and tear her to pieces. She couldn't let that happen. She was already far too fragile.

Shoving her suitcase across the foyer to the front door, Lilia made up her mind. This trip was for *her*. Miles Kane was simply the convenient catalyst who had put it together. Nothing more.

Lilia hadn't been home in ten years and by golly, she was going to make the most of every minute of her two weeks in Kenya. She would do the things she wanted to do, go where she wanted to go, visit the people she wanted to see. The journey home would help her to reconnect with who she was, and who she had always longed to be. She would let her homecoming heal her.

Unable to suppress the bubble of excitement that welled up inside her, she practically skipped into her office. But practical matters sobered her as she picked up the phone to dial Jenny.

"Guess what I'm doing tonight?" she said when her assistant answered. "I'm flying to Africa."

"Africa? Lilia, are you all right?"

"I think so." She couldn't help but laugh at the absurdity of it. "I'm going to Africa with Miles to work on the Habari Safari project. I'll be away for two weeks. Think you can handle things at the studio?"

"Sure, but Lilia—"

"Now listen, Jenny. Mrs. Keane has changed her mind about the tartan plaid. She wants paisleys. You'll have to search the wallcovering books and fabric samples. And John Talbot has decided on a neoclassic theme for his entertainment room. Pillars, Greek pediments, the whole bit. He wants a statue of Apollo."

"Okay." Jenny sounded a little lost.

"Don't forget that Millie Beaton wants to go Victorian, after all. She completely changed her mind about the whole Southwestern look we worked up for her. I mean, the geometric border, the Mimbres pots, the soft cactus sculptures, everything. They're out. You'll have to start looking for crocheted doilies and teapots, okay?"

"Lilia, a couple of days ago you told me you weren't going to do the hotel project. You said Miles Kane—"

"I guess I changed my mind, too. Not about Miles—about the project. He's flying me to Kenya to study five hotels there."

"Where's he going to be while you're looking at the hotels?"

Lilia slipped one hand into the pocket of her skirt and fiddled with a bead of lint. "Well...he'll be in Kenya, too. But not with me. Not really, anyway. I mean, we *will* be traveling together and all, but he'll be in meetings with management. We'll hardly see each other."

"Oh."

"So anyway..."

"Golly, Lilia, it sounds to me like you two are—"

"We're not. Definitely not!" Lilia tucked a strand of hair behind her ear. "So, will you handle things for me? You can contact me through Habari Safari. They'll know where I'm staying at any time during the two weeks, and you have the phone number in their file. Okay, Jenny?"

"Okay. Sure."

"See you soon."

Lilia hung up and made another call. "Jean? Jean Banes?"

"Lilia, is that you again? I've tried to tell you that I can't give out any information about—"

"Jean, I'm calling to let you know I've decided to take a vacation, after all. Sort of a busman's holiday."

"A what?"

"I'm going home—to Kenya. I'll be away for two weeks, but Jenny has the phone number if you need me for *any* reason...."

"Lilia, you know I won't be calling you about Colin."

For a moment Lilia couldn't make herself speak. Just the sound of that sweet name sent a knife slicing through her heart. "Is he all right?" she whispered.

"He's all right."

"What's going on? You sounded a little tentative, Jean. Is something the matter with Colin?"

"Lilia, stop hanging on every inflection of my voice. Colin is all right. I told you we've been checking on him and we won't let anything happen. You *do* need to get away. Try to make the break, Lilia. Focus on the future, okay?"

Lilia nodded. "I'll be back in two weeks."

"You can call me then." Jean paused a moment before speaking again. "And Lilia—have *fun.*"

"I'll give it my best shot." She was hanging up the receiver just as the doorbell rang. Dismay, excitement, a thousand emotions skittered down her spine as she hurried across the foyer. Miles was waiting on the porch, a smile on his face. In the driveway, a yellow taxi idled.

"We're off then," Miles said. "Back to Africa."

"Back to Kenya. Back home."

Meeting his smile with one of her own, Lilia stepped out into the warm night air and locked her door behind her. As she lifted her head, Miles picked up her suitcase.

"Back to where we met," he said, and gave her a wink.

No adventure in all the world could quite compare with the thrilling, mind-boggling, exhausting experience of flying from the United States to Africa. Lilia and Miles boarded a small airplane, which took them from Springfield to Chicago, with a short stop in St. Louis.

In Chicago, they transferred to the immense, crowded hubbub of a 747 jumbo jet filled with groups of students and families of American, Asian, Oriental, European and

African descent. The babble of Hindi, German, Spanish and Chinese filled the air as passengers shoved their bags into overhead compartments and tried to figure out how to adjust their seat belts. Babies wailed. Toddlers ran up and down the aisles, tangling the feet of incoming passengers.

Lilia and Miles found their seats in the long center section. A Nigerian university professor who had been on a leave of absence studying the effects of television on American children sat beside Miles. A British horticulturalist specializing in rare nineteenth-century roses more than filled the seat next to Lilia.

There was little time for introductions, however, as the jet swooped into the sky and flight attendants began serving soft drinks and honey-coated nuts. Before long, tray tables descended and the passengers began to partake of their first of many bland airline meals. Between bumps and jolts, and her neighbor's long discourse on various species of tube-roses, Lilia managed to down most of a slab of chicken breast, a few lukewarm peas and some sticky chocolate pudding.

Miles requested blankets and pillows, but before he and Lilia could settle in for the night, the passengers in their row began the long back-and-forth trek to the bathrooms.

"I'll be damned," Miles muttered, wincing in pain. "If someone treads on my toe again, I'll not be responsible for what I do."

Lilia grinned. In spite of it all, she felt lighter and freer than she had in years. This awkward spawning ground for claustrophobia felt like a second home to her. How many, many times as a child had she climbed aboard one of these huge airplanes and flown uncountable hours across the ocean? She relished the sight of the little plastic flip-down tray tables, the white paper headcloths, the buttons that controlled the seatbacks, the tiny vent that turned a stream of cool air on or off overhead. She even liked the bathrooms.

"When I was a little girl," she confided to Miles, just as the heavyset rose scientist was mashing Miles's toes into the floor, "I loved to go to the bathroom on airplanes."

He formed his hands around an imaginary neck and wrung it with great enthusiasm. As Lilia giggled, he shook his head. "It's only by divine miracle that my aim ever hits the blinking toilet. There's hardly room to turn around."

"Not for someone with shoulders like yours. But I always loved it. Everything fit into those neat little built-in compartments. The tissues in one slot, the soaps stacked in another. Then when you flush—*whoosh*—all the blue water gets sucked straight out into the sky."

"Into the sky!" Miles laughed out loud.

"Well, that's what I always thought when I was a little girl. I used to run for cover when I saw a plane flying overhead."

Chuckling, Miles met her eyes, and a sense of wistfulness settled over him. He had once loved that little girl who scampered away from leaking airplanes. Lilia hadn't been much more than a child when they'd met—still so young, so naive, untouched by the harsh hand of reality. She had grown up in a bubble, a world protected and nurtured by her missionary parents. She'd known nothing of divorce, alcoholism, drug abuse, the sorts of things that plagued American families. Her parents had been stable and loving.

But Lilia, like himself and every child brought up in the Third World, had seen a different sort of pain. Beggars in rags, old women eaten up with leprosy, children starving. He wondered how well she remembered her beloved Africa.

"I used to think there were fairy cities in the clouds," she was saying softly, more to herself than to him. "We would blast through a gleaming white mountain of cloud, and I'd get so worried that we were smashing into a fairy town. I'd envision all the fairies in a panic, diving into the soft cotton. And then the plane would roar past, leaving a big hole where their homes had once been."

"I suppose it came out of your fear of losing your own home." Miles slipped his hand around hers. "You told me your parents were transferred often, moving inland and then back to the coast."

"Yes, and furlough. That was the worst. Every four years we would have to pack up and leave our house and all our friends. We'd fly to the States, and I would try to fit in. It was hardly worth the effort. In a year, we'd be back on a plane headed home to Kenya."

"I never could imagine you in America. After I'd lost you, I used to try to picture you at some university—leaves turning orange on the trees and a nip in the air. I'd mentally put you into a plaid, pleated skirt with those sorts of shoes with coins in them."

"Penny loafers."

He chuckled. "That's it. But I couldn't hold the picture. You always came rushing back to me in your long white kanzu shift with the sleeves billowing and your hair flying out behind your back."

Lilia looked down at their entwined hands. Miles had slipped his fingers between hers. His skin was golden brown against her pale, almost translucent hand. She hadn't even noticed that he was leaning against her, their shoulders pressing together and their faces so close she could see the gilded sheen of his stubble. It had happened so easily, so naturally.

Fearing the start of something uncontrollable, she pulled her hand away and began tucking her thin airline blanket around her thighs. "Miles, you said something a minute ago." She kicked off her high heels and studied her wiggling toes. "You said, 'After I'd lost you.' I hope you know I don't believe you *didn't* ask for the annulment."

"You can believe whatever you like, Lilia. But I didn't ask for it."

She turned. "Your father told me—"

"My father lied."

She caught her breath. "No, he didn't."

"Yes, he did." Miles glanced at the Nigerian professor, who was listening in with undisguised interest. "Do you mind? This is a private conversation."

"Sorry." The Nigerian gave a polite smile. Then he added in his thick accent, "Based on my observation of this interchange, I would conclude that the gentleman is speaking honestly. I believe his father did conceal the truth."

"Thank you very much," Miles returned.

"Not at all." The Nigerian tipped his head politely, then shut his eyes and leaned back on his headrest.

Miles rolled his eyes, but Lilia was too distraught to accept any humor in the situation. "Look," he said. "All I know is that my father came into my hospital room one afternoon, sat on the end of my bed and told me that he'd spoken with your parents by phone."

"He spoke with *me!*"

"And they told him that you'd already gone off to college. You were having a lovely time, making wonderful marks in school and dating lots of American boys."

"I was not!" Rage blossomed inside Lilia's chest. "I'd just gotten married to you, for heaven's sake. I'd have felt like I was committing adultery, or something. Even after I knew it was all over... after years... I couldn't make myself... I didn't feel comfortable...."

"Nor did I." Miles was looking into her eyes, his own a deep indigo. "I'd married you, and that seemed to seal it for me. At any rate, since my father had told me you wanted to get on with your life—"

"I never said that! That's what he told me *you* wanted to do."

"It is what he wanted both of you to do," the Nigerian put in, opening one eye. "It is quite apparent that the father was not pleased with this marriage between his son and the young lady. So he arranged to end the relationship. Each of you would feel betrayed by the other. The father knew that anger is a great healer. It is much easier to forget someone who has cheated and deceived you, than to forget someone whom you love deeply enough to marry."

Lilia didn't know whether to chastise the man for being such an intolerable buttinsky. Or thank him for his insight.

"How long has it been since this dreadful experience?" the rose expert asked, leaning into Lilia. "Not too late to correct it, I hope!"

"Ten years," Lilia answered.

"Yes," Miles blustered. "And if the two of you don't mind..."

"Look, the movie's starting!" Lilia laid a calming hand on his arm. She could feel his tension throbbing like a rocket about to blast off. "Miles, did the flight attendant hand out earphones?"

The tips of his ears had gone red—a bad sign. But he kept his thoughts to himself as he rummaged in the seat pocket. Handing Lilia a plastic bag with an orange headset inside, he glared at the Nigerian.

"You might like to analyze the film for a change of pace," he said, setting his own headset on the man's knee. "And I'll thank you to let me and my wife work this situation out on our own!"

Lilia gasped. "I have not been your wife for ten years, Miles Kane. And I'm not your wife now!"

"Damn!" He exploded up from the seat and shoved his way down the aisle.

Lilia raised her head over her own seatback to watch him stalking toward the back of the plane. When she sank down again, the Nigerian and the horticulturalist were staring at the movie, orange wires dangling from their ears. Lilia let out a breath. He probably hadn't meant to say it. All the same, she didn't like the thought that it had just slipped out.

She pulled her blanket up around her shoulders and nestled her head into the miniature white pillow. An annulment meant their wedding had never happened. They'd never been married at all. She hadn't been a wife. She certainly wasn't a wife now. Was she?

So maybe Miles's father *had* engineered the whole thing. Maybe Miles had wanted to stay married. And maybe she had, too. But that was all a long, long time ago.

The 747 landed at Gatwick Airport at four in the morning, Missouri time. Of course, in London it was already ten a.m. and the great city was in full swing. Lilia and Miles crowded out of the plane along with the other bleary-eyed passengers. Dragging children, carry-on luggage, torn sacks of duty-free gifts, they all made their way through the long line at the customs desk.

Miles felt a mild concern over what lay ahead. He had barely had time to purchase Lilia's ticket in Springfield. Then he had wired Habari Safari to secure her Kenya visa. He felt sure that because the London stop was considered a layover, she could legally visit the city for a few hours. They approached the desk, the blue-suited customs official gave their passports a perfunctory stamp and they ventured out into the large open hall.

"That was easy enough," Miles commented. "And I don't imagine we'll have much difficulty when we get to the Nairobi airport."

"Ah, the power of an international business conglomerate," Lilia said, thankful Miles was talking to her again. Throughout the latter part of the journey, he had remained almost totally silent, sleeping most of the way and eating his breakfast with a taciturn expression on his face.

"Our Nairobi flight leaves from Heathrow Airport at ten o'clock tonight," he was saying as he reset his watch. "Would you like to have a peek at the sights of London?"

Lilia studied him for a moment. He looked all rumpled and rough around the edges—and totally huggable. His khaki bush jacket was wrinkled; his jaw sported a thick golden stubble; his hair was tousled; his tattered ticket hung askew from one pocket. She couldn't help but smile.

"I've seen the Tower of London so many times, I used to know the beafeaters' names," she informed him. "Unless you're set on viewing the crown jewels, why don't we go to Brown's Hotel for tea? You can tell me your plans for the hotels, and I'll start building my portfolio."

"Business as usual, is it?"

At his stiff tone, her spirits sank. "Miles, I'm sorry I jumped on you about what you said in the plane."

"It was a slip of the tongue."

"I know. But I do want to keep a distance during this trip." She dug her hands into her skirt pockets. "Even if your father did lie ..."

"He had to have."

"Okay, but that doesn't change what happened. Ten years have passed, and I *have* gotten on with my life. So have you. I'm not interested in turning back the clock."

"Then why did you come on this trip?"

"To work on the hotel project."

"Bunk."

"Okay, to see Kenya. It's my home."

"And that's not turning back the clock?"

"Miles, don't be difficult. I'm not willing to pretend that you and I are starting up where we left off. I've changed. So have you. Everything's different now."

"Right," he said. He looked away from her and gave a brief wave at the Nigerian and the horticulturalist, who were wheeling their luggage down the hall. "You don't want to take a risk then, is that it?"

Lilia felt her hackles rise. "I've never been a coward, but I know when something feels right and when it doesn't."

"And how do you feel when you're with me?"

"How do *you* feel when you're with me?" she countered.

"Confused. Angry. Frustrated."

"Exactly."

"Intrigued. Stimulated. Hungry."

"Hungry."

"A man lives without his wife for ten years, it leaves him famished."

"I am *not* your wife!" Lilia grabbed her purse strap. "All right, that does it, Miles. I'm getting on the next plane back to the States."

"Calm down, Lilia." He took her arm and pulled her back to face him. "I've never been one to mince words. You know that. But I'll try to be the model of proper British decorum if you'll feel more comfortable. Come on, let's go take tea at Brown's Hotel. We'll nibble a scone with clotted cream and strawberry jam. And we'll discuss the interior design of Habari Safari's latest hotel project."

Lilia crossed her arms. "We're going to set some rules right here and now, or I won't go another step with you."

"Rules?"

"Number one, you will stop calling me your wife. Number two, there will be no further discussion of the past. Number three, you will treat me as a business associate and nothing more. Agreed?"

"Agreed." He nodded seriously. "Come along then, Mrs. Kane."

"Miles, that is not funny!"

"Oh, Lilia, it's you and me here in Gatwick Airport, for heaven's sake. You know damn well I'm not the sort of man to be tied up with rules and regulations. I'd feel like a lion in a cage if I had to force myself to act a certain way. I've always done exactly as I pleased. Whatever I wanted, I fought for until I got it.''

"And just what is it you want?" she snapped.

"I want you." His blue eyes flashed with fire. "That's what I want. That's what I wanted from the moment I saw you running down Diani Beach ten years ago. And it's what I wanted the minute I heard your voice on the telephone in Springfield, Missouri."

"Well, you don't have me!"

"And that's bunk, too."

"All right, I'm leaving. I don't need this." She turned on her heel and started marching down the corridor toward the ticket agents. She *didn't* want him! She hadn't asked for him back in her life. She wasn't going to Kenya to be with him, or to relive any faded memories from her past.

Tears sprang to her eyes as she found the line for purchasing tickets. Her credit card would barely cover the cost of the return ticket, but she didn't care if she had to scrimp from now to eternity. Miles was just as stubborn and bullheaded as he'd ever been. He was impossible! They had nothing in common—not a single thing! She couldn't imagine what she'd ever seen in the man in the first place.

Oh, great. He was walking toward the ticket desk, no doubt gearing up to cause another huge scene. He looked exactly like a caged lion, with his tawny hair, his enormous shoulders and a stride like a cat's.

She gripped her purse strap. "Miles," she warned as he approached.

"Miss Eden, will you please accept my apology for my unforgivably rude behavior?" he asked. "What I said to you was unconscionable. If you would be so good as to join me for tea, I'm certain we could begin our business association on reasonable terms."

Lilia glanced at the sharply dressed Englishman who was eyeing her over his *London Times*. She glared at him until he raised the newspaper over his face.

"You agree to abide by the rules?" she demanded in a low voice.

"All of them."

"Okay." Her shoulders sagged, and she suddenly felt exhausted. What time was it in Missouri now? Five a.m.? Colin would still be sleeping, his little thumb tucked in his mouth, his arm tightly clutching his cloth elephant. A wave of sadness and defeat washed over her as she stepped out of the line.

"We've been acting like children," she said.

"Jet lag." He took her arm, and they walked together toward the exit. "It'll only be worse when we get to Kenya."

"I'll try to be patient."

"I'm a very patient man." He hailed a taxi, and Lilia forced herself not to read anything into his words. They climbed into the cab. Lilia seated herself at the far end of the seat, and Miles reluctantly positioned himself near the opposite door.

As they pulled out into the busy traffic, he tried to focus on the sights and smells of this familiar city. It took little more than a minute to adjust to riding on the left-hand side of the street. Zambia had once been a British colony, and the budding nation had inherited many English laws—not all of them well suited to the life-style of its native citizens.

Gatwick lay a safe distance from London proper, and the taxi sped down narrow streets past rows of houses, each with a lovely garden and a chimney pot on the roof. Miles rubbed a hand over his eyes. He had to concentrate, stay under control. As tired as he was, he couldn't be certain of maintaining that detached decorum he'd promised.

Just one glance at Lilia made him uncomfortably aware that what he had told her was the truth. He did want her. She was leaning against the window, her pale cheek outlined with sunlight and her gray eyes as soft as a rainy afternoon. Her hands lay folded on her lap, half-buried in the billow of her cotton skirt. Long legs, made silky by her stockings, stretched across the open space. She had slipped off her shoes, and it was all he could do to keep from lifting her feet onto his lap and massaging her toes.

But she wouldn't like that. How many times would she have to say it before he finally believed she really meant it.

She wasn't his. She didn't belong to him. They weren't married anymore. It was over.

Maybe it was the jet lag, but he felt like a rutty boy again. He could almost feel his hormones kicking into place, rushing to man the abandoned posts, charging forward with renewed vigor. Again he glanced across the taxi at Lilia's face, her long eyelashes, her full mouth. He supposed it was her lips that had first catapulted him toward her with reckless abandon. Never in all his life had he seen such a smile—not that he'd caught a glimpse of it lately.

But when Lilia smiled, it was like the African sunshine after a long rain. Brilliant. Lighting up the whole world. She fairly gleamed.

At twenty-one, he couldn't wait to kiss those lips. In fact, he'd caught her off guard the first time. They were just coming out of the water after a swim. She was dripping wet, that white bikini of hers nearly translucent and driving him mad with desire. He had simply grabbed her and planted a grand, hard kiss right on her lips.

Miles couldn't help but chuckle now, as he recalled the way she had gasped in utter shock. She'd torn out of his grasp and fled down the beach as fast as her long brown legs would carry her. Of course, he had followed, caught up with her beneath the scanty shade of a palm tree, and in spite of his best intentions, he had kissed her again.

This time—her breath coming in tiny pants—Lilia had responded. She leaned into him, slipped her arms around his damp body and pressed those magnificent little breasts straight into his chest. He had thought he was going to die.

"What are you grinning about over there?" she asked, cutting into his thoughts.

"Who me? Oh, nothing. Nothing at all." He pushed his fingers through his hair, hoping to draw her attention away from the rather obvious result of his memories. "Enjoying the sights of London?"

"I love this city." She gave a big sigh and turned back to the window.

His eyes dropped to her bosom. Interesting, the magic womanhood could work on a young girl. The V of her creamy blouse revealed the shadow of cleavage. Ten years before, she hadn't had a trace of such mystery. In fact, as he recalled it, she had barely filled up her bikini top.

He clearly recalled the moment she had first permitted him to slip his hand over the soft, peaked mound of her breast. She had gasped then, too, and shuddered with uncertainty. But when he had flicked apart the clasp, and her bra lay on the white sand, she had been more than pleased with the stroke of his fingers on her flesh and the caress of his tongue across her pink nipple.

"What are you smiling about?" she demanded again as the taxi pulled up in front of the imposing facade of the hotel. "You're sitting over there grinning like the Cheshire cat. What's going on?"

"Oh, nothing." He tried to put on a poker face without much success. "Just happy to be alive on such a lovely London morning."

She gave him a skeptical glance as the door swung open. Miles climbed out, then reached back in to give her a hand. As she emerged, he took the opportunity to further inspect the silken valley between those two majestic peaks beneath her blouse. Yes, indeed. He did like what womanhood had done to Lilia.

"A lovely, fresh English morning," he said behind her as she walked into the hotel lobby. Her hips swayed with just the right beckoning lure. "Lovely, lovely, lovely."

Lilia frowned. "Miles, would you just get in here and order us some tea?"

Miles laughed aloud. It was going to be a wonderful two weeks.

Chapter 6

Tea at Brown's Hotel was a grand affair. At least, Miles felt certain it was meant to be. Lilia *oohed* and *ahhed* enough to convince him of that. The tearoom itself certainly warranted admiration.

A liveried young man escorted Miles and Lilia to a pair of high-backed, velvet armchairs with a small polished table set before them. Other tea-takers filled cozy groupings around the room. Miles noted a Japanese businessman and his extended family in one corner. In another, two men—one of whom Miles thought bore a close resemblance to Dracula—conversed intently over their tea. Snippets of conversation about a well-known female rock singer drifted by as Miles and Lilia were led past them.

Miles felt awkward amid the posh assemblage, but once settled, Lilia leaned back in her chair and let out a deep breath.

"Oh, I wish John Talbot could see this!" She sighed.

"Who?" Miles suddenly had the crushing thought she had a lover and hadn't told him. "Who's John Talbot?"

"He owns a successful printing business. That's how we met, as a matter of fact. He printed some brochures for me.

Anyway, he's just decided to go neoclassic in his entertainment room. He would love the ambience in here!''

"Oh, he's a client." Relieved that there was no handsome skeleton in Lilia's closet, Miles studied the room more closely and tried to get a feel for the ambience himself. As a matter of fact, he wouldn't know neoclassic if it hit him in the head, but he didn't want to tell Lilia that. He already felt like a Cape buffalo—big, muscular and unrefined—in this fragile room with its delicate chairs, stained-glass windows and beveled mirrors.

"Have you ever seen such intricate ceiling medallions?" Lilia exclaimed. "They're classic Georgian. And the fireplace in red and light pink marble—I'll have to remember that. John is dying for a fireplace."

"Very tasteful indeed."

Lilia glanced at him and couldn't suppress a chuckle. "Oh, Miles, you look so uncomfortable. Dressed the way you are, you might be just in from a safari."

He cocked one eyebrow and surveyed his khaki jacket and olive green slacks. He'd never worn any other sort of clothing. Hadn't even considered the possibility. Cotton shirt, heavy bush trousers, thick knitted socks, suede boots—the sort of clothing that camouflaged a man who might be tracking a leopard through high brush.

"I'll never be much of an English gentleman, that's for certain," he informed Lilia. "I might speak with the Eton accent my father passed along to me, but I'm all African. Put me out in the bush with a campfire, a canvas tent and a tin of beans. That's the sort of ambience for me."

"It sounds pretty good to me, too." Lilia gave him the kindest look he'd had from her since he had managed to offend her in every way possible at the airport.

"You know, I used to think I'd never get over Africa," she mused. "I missed the palm trees outside my bedroom window and the vendors roaming the shores with their bags of seashells. Every morning monkeys would play on the roof, and someone would knock on our back door to see if my mom wanted to buy a fresh lobster or an octopus."

"Octopus!" Miles realized he'd half shouted the word at the moment the waiter arrived to serve their tea. The young man gave him a slight frown, as if to warn him against such coarse impropriety.

"I wasn't crazy about octopus myself," Lilia was saying. She dropped two cubes of sugar into her Darjeeling tea, then carefully poured in a dollop of thick milk. "It was the mangoes I probably grieved over the most. There's nothing like a mango to start off the day."

Miles smiled. "I can't imagine giving up Africa forever. It's too close to my heart."

"Sometimes a person has no choice." She stirred her tea around and around, staring down at the swirling caramel-colored drink.

"You always have a choice," Mile said. "When you love something, you don't give it up. At least I don't."

Lilia looked up at him, and he knew what she was thinking. He had given her up, hadn't he? He certainly hadn't fought for her like the knight in shining armor she had wanted him to be. She probably wondered if he'd ever loved her at all.

But Lilia didn't understand everything that had gone into his accepting the annulment. As he'd lain in his hospital bed, his father had convinced him that Lilia had shut him out of her life. And his very soul had been cut in two.

An equally important factor in Miles's decision not to deny the end of the marriage was the knowledge that the malarial fever had destroyed his chances of fathering Lilia's children. She had known nothing about that. As a matter of fact, he wasn't keen to tell her about it even now.

So how could he have gone racing to the United States to claim her—only to face her rejection, only to have to tell her that their beautiful dreams could never come true?

The sad look in her eyes tugged at his heart. What wouldn't he give to erase those ten years? He still could hardly believe that his father had lied—ruined their young plans, their blossoming love—out of his own selfish ambition for his son.

One man had wreaked such havoc. How could another man hope to repair the destruction? Miles pondered the question as he gazed at the silver cake stand. Not by shouting and demanding, as he had in the airport. Not through fear and stubborn coercion.

Rebuilding what he and Lilia had lost would take a gentle touch. Kindness. Patience. All of which were in short supply when it came to the personality of Miles Kane. Perhaps it was time for a change. At least he could make the effort.

"Scone?" he asked, handing her the patterned china plate with its arrangement of thick triangular breads. "Strawberry jam? Clotted cream? Marmalade?"

Lilia gave him a grateful glance. It felt wonderful to finally relax with Miles. And she had to admit she was getting a kick out of watching him try to squelch his rugged nature and fit into the polite mold she had required of him. She knew his efforts were all for her benefit. Though she didn't expect his transformation into Laurence Olivier to last for long, it touched her that he was trying.

She scooped a spoonful of strawberry jam onto her scone. "Nowhere but in England!"

Miles watched her face suffuse with utter bliss as she nibbled the confection. He grunted. Nowhere but in England would a man be faced with sandwiches the diameter of small zebra droppings. Sandwiches lightly spread with egg salad or limp cucumber slices. He took a bite of something unrecognizable.

"Damn!" he muttered, wincing in distaste. "What the hell is that meant to be?"

"It's paté. Liver."

"Ought to come with a warning label."

Lilia couldn't keep the grin off her face. She watched as Miles jabbed his fork into a sandwich and caused tomato aspic to seep out between the slices of bread. An exasperated grimace crossed his face. Opting for more familiar territory, he moved on to the torte. He took a bite and gave a grudging nod.

"Tastes like American peanut butter," he said. "Not bad. But what you really want to have a go at is my mum's tea."

"It's different?"

"My mum can make a proper farm tea, the best in the world. A loaf of bread—fresh-baked, steaming hot and dotted with currants. A mound of yellow butter straight from the dairy. Here's the proper method for taking tea Zambian-style. Slather your butter on thick until it melts and drips through the holes in the bread. Take a big bite. Grab your cup of tea and wash it down in one grand swig. Burn your throat all the way to your stomach and don't even notice. By the time you've finished off the loaf, there'll be sweet cakes covered with crusty sugar and laced with cinnamon."

Lilia groaned. "Sounds wonderful!"

"Now that's tea." Miles set his thin porcelain cup in its saucer and leaned back. "But this is very lovely. Don't get me wrong."

"Lovely, lovely, lovely," Lilia teased.

Miles grinned. "As I recall, you were rather fond of marmite."

"Oh, no!" Lilia screwed up her face. "Did you have to remind me? I despised that stuff."

"All those lovely, lovely vegetables duly seasoned and then ground up into a thick brown paste. As a matter of fact, this very sandwich seems to be filled with..." He took a sniff. "Yes! It is. Wouldn't you like a bite, Lilia?"

She gave a muffled shriek as he swung the sandwich closer to her mouth. Laughing, they tussled for a moment, the odorous treat drifting back and forth between mouth and tray. Finally, Lilia grabbed Miles's hand and wrestled away the sandwich. As she set it back on the plate, his fingers laced through hers.

"This is how we used to be, Lilia," he said when he had caught her eyes. "We enjoyed each other."

Her heart dancing against her ribs, Lilia glanced at the waiter who was frowning at them from his post by the door. "We got into trouble back then, too. I think we're a little old to be causing scenes, Miles."

"I don't. I'm in the habit of shaking things up. 'Oh, no,' my boss always says when he sees me walk into his office. 'Here comes Kane. Here comes trouble.'" He shrugged. "Life's not much fun if you always play by the rules, now is it?"

"It goes more smoothly."

"Smooth is boring."

"Well, you're certainly not boring, I'll give you that."

"Nor are you, Lilia."

She moistened her lips. Already they were back on dangerous ground. She could feel the heat in her breath. Her pulse hammered in her throat. She looked into those blue eyes, and she was almost sure he was going to kiss her. Right here in Brown's Hotel. And she was almost sure she would let him.

"So, tell me your vision for Habari Safari," she said, jerking her hand from his and reaching for the attaché case beside her chair. "I'm thinking wood floors and huge fireplaces, but I won't go for mounted animal heads hanging over the mantel."

"I'm with you on that." Miles reluctantly settled his shoulders back into the chair. "But what would you put over a fireplace? It's got to be something special, something totally African."

"How about a framed piece of fabric—a kikoi or a kanga—with wonderful ethnic patterns in orange, green, red and black?"

"Not bad."

"Or a David Shepherd painting? His wildlife scenes are magnificent." She flipped open her file and began to take notes. "We could always do a batik. I've seen them mounted with lights behind. When they shine through, the batik looks almost like stained glass. Brilliant!"

"What about hanging up a Maasai shield with a couple of spears?"

"Oh, now that's an idea! We could tie the whole theme together with the red, black and white colors in the shield." She was lost to him now, her visions pouring onto the page. "Or carvings of African masks. I can't wait to start searching for artifacts when we get to Kenya. Will Habari Safari pay for shipping costs?"

"Of course." Miles watched her write. She had come alive again, beautiful and vibrant. It was almost as though the farther they got from Missouri and her loss of little Colin, and the closer they came to Kenya, the more life suffused her face. Even the way she spoke and moved reminded him of the Lilia he had fallen in love with ten years before.

Could it be that he was still in love with her? Would she open to him completely once they were back in Africa? Would she turn away from her American life and become his again? And what might happen if she did?

Another marathon flight—eight hours—lay ahead of Miles and Lilia as they boarded their second 747, this one bound for Nairobi. After tea, they had walked through downtown London—Oxford Street, New Bond Street, Old Bond Street and St. Christopher's Place. Ultrafashionable shops beckoned Lilia. Miles seemed buoyed by the experience. He hauled her into the boutiques of Pierre Cardin, Luis Vuitton, Gucci, Wedgwood, Laura Ashley, Fortnam and Mason, Chanel, Llandro, Christies, Sothby's.

At Penhaligon's, he bought her a flagon of fragrant perfume that had been concocted from a Victorian recipe. She returned the favor by purchasing for him a denim jacket at the Ralph Lauren shop. "Just for a break from khaki," she had told him. But when he had slipped it on, she acknowledged to herself that she had really bought it for the way it lit up his eyes.

By the time they had taken a train from Victoria Station to Heathrow Airport, Lilia was exhausted. Memories of Colin washed through her mind without warning. Jet lag, shopping, planning the hotel design, all had left her vulnerable. She feared yet another scene like that of the morning.

But Miles was solicitous and kind as he followed her into the airplane and helped her settle their growing numbers of bags. The jet roared out of the airport precisely at ten that evening, as prompt as only the English can be. A movie followed dinner, but Lilia could hardly keep her eyes open even through the other passengers' bathroom trek.

When the plane's lights dimmed, she sank into her pillow. Drifting, she saw visions of Trafalgar Square, St. Paul's dome, the houses of Parliament. She saw leather luggage, vials of perfume, Irish handknit sweaters, ivy-patterned china plates.

And then her head slid over onto a strong, warm shoulder. Someone tucked a wool blanket around her chin. An arm like a comforting shelter slipped around her shoulders. She breathed deeply, the haunting scent of male skin, well-worn cotton, herbal shaving cream. Gentle lips pressed against her forehead; fingers smoothed her hair.

A male African lion, sleek and golden, lounged beneath a tall acacia tree. He beckoned, lured her toward its shade. The hot breath of a Saharan wind blew across her cheek. Fluttering like a malachite kingfisher in a shimmery display of purple and gold, she danced toward the shadows... where she knew she could rest.

It was midnight in Springfield, Missouri—but eight o'clock in the morning in Kenya—when the jumbo jet glided past Mount Kenya on its descent into the Nairobi airport. The craggy mountain, dusted with snow, gleamed as if to boast of its prominence in African myth and legend.

Lilia stared out the window, drinking the sight of vast yellow plains and fertile highlands. "Tea!" she cried, grabbing Miles by the collar and hauling him to the window to admire the sea of pale green bushes.

"You're sure it's not coffee?"

"Coffee's much darker. Forest-green with red berries." Lilia's breath hung in her throat. "There's the Rift Valley. What memories I have of my boarding school there."

"Not particularly pleasant ones, as I recall." Miles was enjoying the proximity of Lilia's body pressed close to his as they strained to see out the same window. "Something about uniforms and strict regulations?"

"It was unbearable. The food was pathetic. The rules stifled us to the point of suffocation. The entire campus turned into a sea of mud during third term—Kenya's rainy season. I was miserable. But... I understand things have changed a lot since my time."

"You talk as if you're an old lady now. Ten years isn't that long."

"A lot can happen in ten years, Miles. Too much." She caught his eyes and hoped he understood what she was trying to tell him. *They* had changed in ten years.

"Sometimes the passing of years can bring good things, Lilia," he said. "I certainly approve of the way time's hand has touched you."

"Thanks, but I know I'm not the young girl I was back then." She had to smile. "I don't wear white bikinis, for one thing."

"Too bad. I was looking forward to that."

"I'm as pale as a ghost. Those Missouri winters and the lack of sunshine have just about faded me away. I've cut off my hair, too." She couldn't help glancing at him to read his reaction. Miles had loved her long hair.

"Your hair suits a grown woman. As does your body."

Lilia flushed at the glow of bold admiration in his blue eyes. How long had it been since she had let a man get this close? She had dated quite a lot as the years has passed. But something always held her back from intimacy. She couldn't bond. Couldn't commit. Any male comment about her body had thrown walls up around her to protect, barricade. After all, she had given away her body once. And been betrayed.

"Miles, please don't push me," she said softly. "I don't want you to get the idea that things can be the way they were."

"At the moment, Lilia, my mind is completely free of ideas. I'm simply enjoying the rediscovery of Africa with you." He paused, remembering the way she had unconsciously snuggled against him in the night while she slept. "But I will tell you this. If we were meeting now—on this airplane—for the first time, I would feel exactly as I do."

She was afraid to ask.

"I would be drawn into your gray eyes," he said, giving her his answer. "I would be charmed by your laughter. I would be intrigued with your intelligence and creativity. And I would be stirred by your body."

Lilia wanted to clap her hand over his mouth. He shouldn't say such things. They flew against the rules she had set up for a professional relationship. Yet somehow, Miles's acknowledgement of his attraction to her forced Lilia's own feelings to the surface. How could she deny that she coveted his approval? From the moment they had been reunited at the Springfield zoo, she had longed to know that he was still captivated by her.

And she was enthralled with him. She couldn't lie to herself about that. Miles was, if anything, more handsome, more virile, more stimulating than he had been at twenty-one. He was mature now, certain of himself and relaxed in his own masculinity.

As a young man, he had been persistent in his pursuit, but awkward and untested in his actual courting of her. Their lovemaking the night of their wedding had been wild and spontaneous with all the uncontrolled zest of adolescence. Now, Lilia felt sure Miles was even more stubborn in the quest for what he wanted. Yet she also sensed that a sensual gentleness would accompany his loving. Steely control would let him lead her to untested heights of passion. His body would tantalize hers in a dance of erotic ardor.

Lilia shivered. What on earth was she daydreaming about? She and Miles weren't lovers anymore. She didn't even want them to be.

"If we'd only just met," Miles was saying, his mouth barely an inch from her ear, "I would go after you with the same determination I had when you were eighteen years old."

"And I would run," she said. "Just as I did then."

"But I captured you, didn't I?"

"Yes, and you let me go."

He caught her arm, forcing her to continue looking at him. "Lilia, you can no longer believe I wanted that annulment. Admit it. Either my father was lying to both of us, or I'm lying to you now. Which is it?"

She studied the intensity that burned in his eyes like a tin roof on a summer day. No lie would pass through the refining heat of those blue eyes. "I believe you," she whispered.

"Thank God for that."

"But that doesn't mean the hurt never happened. It doesn't mean we can ignore the passage of ten years and the ways we've molded our separate lives. It doesn't mean I'll drop my dreams for yours, Miles. I'm not that naive child any longer."

He didn't care. As long as she believed him, they had a base. Something on which to build. They could acknowledge that they had loved each other once, and that neither of them had wanted their love to end. For now, that was enough for him.

"There's a gazelle," she said softly as she gazed out the window. "It's grazing right next to the airstrip."

"An impala. We'll have a herd of those at each of our hotels. With proper care, they should thrive even in winter."

And the spell was broken. They were back to business. The plane landed, taxied down the runway, came to a rest on the airport apron. The doors opened with a rush of warm, dry air. Lilia grabbed her bags, and Miles thought for a moment she might climb straight over the other passengers in her eagerness to be out.

But they waited through the long line. A second long line took them through customs. Then they set off to collect their baggage.

"*Jambo!*" Lilia greeted the official at the gate. "*Habari gani, bwana?*"

"Oh, you speak Kiswahili! You're not a tourist?" The man spoke in perfect English, albeit heavy with a rich accent.

"I grew up in Kenya," Lilia informed the stranger. "In Mombasa."

He beamed. "Welcome home, madam."

Lilia felt as though she were floating through the airport. Everywhere she looked, Africans manned desks, pushed luggage carts, inspected bags. She was the minority race here, and she was thankful for it. These people managed their own country—managed it very well, in fact—and she felt totally comfortable in their presence.

But when Lilia spotted a small ebony-skinned child seated on a bench beside the ticket counter, her spirits flagged once again. The boy had dark brown eyes just like Colin's. He regarded her solemnly, his gaze almost depthless. She fought the sudden urge to crouch beside him and wrap her arms around his little shoulders. The physical ache that the image of her missing son evoked left her fighting back tears.

She forced herself to turn away from the child and step up to the Kenya Airways desk to ask about their flight to Mombasa. *"Tunataka twende Mombasa,"* she told the ticket taker.

"You do that very well," Miles complimented her.

His smile warmed her. "I thought I'd forgotten every word I'd ever learned, but the minute I saw all the Africans, my Swahili came flowing back into me," she said, renewing her determination to put her pain behind her and find happiness in the present moment.

While they waited for the plane that would take them to the coast, she summoned her Swahili to chat with a pair of schoolboys, a stern businessman and two women bound for a women's rights conference in the States. By the time they boarded the plane, Miles commented that he thought she might have forgotten English.

The short flight took them high over the road they would later follow by land. It was a healing journey. Beneath them passed vast savanna grasslands, the Tsavo game park and finally the pale stretch of Kenya's coast. Palm trees. Crystal white sand. And the endless expanse of turquoise water, the Indian Ocean.

"Oh, Miles!" Lilia could hardly sit still as the plane bumped onto the ground. "Miles, I can't believe it. This *is* Mombasa, isn't it? Tell me I'm not dreaming."

He leaned over and kissed her flushed cheek. "You're not dreaming, Lilia."

She looked into his eyes, breathless, suddenly wanting more. She had to grip her seat cushion to keep from throwing her arms around his neck and kissing him. The place where his mouth had touched her cheek burned. Her mouth felt dry, her breath hot. She moistened her lips, aware that he was staring at her, aware that his body was only inches from hers, aware that her breasts had tightened with excitement. To her shock, she suddenly pictured herself sliding into his lap, pressing the tingling tips of her bosom against his chest, crushing their mouths together...

But, thank heaven, the plane jolted to a stop and the flight attendant's droned instructions broke the spell. Shaken, Lilia tucked a strand of hair behind her ear and stood to dislodge her bags from the overhead bins. Miles rose beside her, his tall form more than filling the tight space between her and the passengers filing toward the door.

His shoulders brushed hers. His hand covered hers when they reached for a bag at the same time. To her relief, he was talking about something, unconscious of her sudden arousal.

"Home's always been Zambia to me," he said as they wormed their way into the aisle. "But not Lusaka, though my family lived there during the school term. Home will always be the country house where we spent the holidays. My brother Peter lives there now with his wife and four kids. You've been living in Missouri ten years now. Do you call it home?"

Lilia turned her thoughts to the large old Victorian house she had so lovingly restored and decorated. "Springfield is my adopted home. But I remember how I felt in college when my friends were always talking about *home*. They went home for Thanksgiving. Christmas. Easter. They visited family and old friends. They went home for the summer. Home for them was twenty miles away. Or a two-hour drive. Home was not so different from where they already were."

"But you didn't feel you could go home, did you?" Miles asked. "*This* was your home."

He stood beside her on the platform at the top of the rolling steps. Her heart thundered against the packages she had clutched against her breast. For a moment, she couldn't move. She sucked in a deep breath of salty air. Tears rolled down her cheeks. Sunlight danced across her skin.

And then, from the bottom of the stairs, an African airline employee beckoned. "Come now, *memsahib*. Come down and greet Mombasa."

Chapter 7

A small bus dispatched from the Two Fishes Hotel on Diani Beach met Lilia and Miles at the airport. Tourists began to file onto the bus, and Lilia managed to claim a window seat. Miles wedged in beside her. He knew she was awash in memories of this country, but he was having a little trouble concentrating on the glories of the East African coast.

For one thing, it was hot. Hot and humid. The April rainy season had just ended, leaving the coastline a steaming greenhouse. Pleasant recollections of his family's month-long holiday in Kenya mingled with Miles's painful memory of the day his temperature began to soar. As the mini-bus traveled down streets lined with coconut palm trees, crimson hibiscus shrubs, exotic Bird of Paradise flowers and climbing magenta bougainvillea, he recalled the afternoon he had broken into chills and sweat and had begun to realize he was dangerously ill.

Even now, Miles was thankful for the antimalarial drug he had ordered delivered from a Nairobi chemist's shop while he and Lilia had waited at the airport. He still had occasional recurrences of fever, as malaria never truly left a human host, and he didn't relish the thought of contracting a brand-new case.

Not only were the heat and the dread of malaria making Miles uncomfortable, he realized. The proximity of Lilia Eden brought back a flood of emotions. As the minibus started across the bridge on to Mombasa Island, Miles became aware that he associated the smell of the sea with Lilia. And he always had.

There was something about the heavy air, the languorous vapors, the stimulating aroma of exotic spices and tropical flowers that evoked her in his mind. Zambia had no coastline, and all the Kane family holidays except the one in Kenya had been spent in their native country. Now that he was again under the spell of the Indian Ocean, Miles sensed the same heady aura emanating from Lilia herself. She *was* Africa to him—the sea, the salty breezes, the rush of waves that had swept him away.

"Old Town Mombasa," she whispered, her gray eyes reflecting the crumbling Arab houses that lined the narrow streets of the historic center of the city. "Persian carpets, spices, brass coffee urns . . ."

"We'll shop for the hotels' decor here if you like," Miles said. "I've scheduled a buying trip for our third day on the coast."

She turned to him, her face aglow. "Miles, thank you. I didn't realize how much I needed this."

His lips formed a half smile, and he nodded. She needed Kenya, but he needed her. Yet he knew he could never tell her what she had meant to him—what she meant to him now. She was too far away from him. Her thoughts were on this place, on the eighteen years she had called this island and the nearby white beaches home. Miles realized that Lilia's memory of him filled only a tiny niche in the vast panorama of recollections she held about this place.

But for him, Mombasa meant only one thing. *Lilia Eden.* Love. Passion. Ecstasy. Dreams. Loss.

The minivan stopped in the newer section of town to let its passengers have a quick lunch. Miles felt dead-tired; Lilia was obviously running on pure adrenaline. She ordered her favorite Indian food—spicy beef-filled samosas, a plate of

rice and chicken curry—and bottles of orange drink to wash
it down. Some of the passengers elected to stay in Mombasa to shop. But Lilia and Miles both were anxious to arrive at their hotel and do some swimming.

"There's the ocean!" Lilia cried as the minivan drove
along the coast of the island. It was her first sight of the vast
blue-green sea. "Oh, Miles...there's Kilindini Harbor. Have
you ever seen so many huge ocean liners? Naval vessels from
all over the world. Tankers. Cargo ships. When I was a girl,
my friends and I would stand on the beach and watch the
ships' lights just beyond the reef. I used to think of them as
wedding cakes all lit up for a Christmas celebration."

Miles smiled at the image. Of course, Lilia had never had
a wedding cake of her own. Or a ring. He looked down at
her bare hand lying on his arm. If only he had stayed healthy
long enough to make the trip into Mombasa Town to buy
her a gold ring at one of the Indian-owned jewelry
shops...maybe then she would have known of his commitment. Maybe she wouldn't have believed a lie so easily.

"Here we are at the Likoni Ferry," she told him. "The
ferry itself is motorized now, but I remember when African
men pulled it across Kilindini Harbor using the thick hemp
ropes stretched from shore to shore. I loved that. The fer-
rymen chanted and sang all the way."

"Songs you knew?"

"Oh, no. The men would ask your name, and then they'd
make up a whole ballad about you—one man singing out
the story and the others chiming in with an echoed refrain.
Once, one of them offered my father quite a price for me.
Two goats I think it was."

"Goats? What for?"

"To marry him, of course. My father politely declined the
offer, and the man went back to his singing."

"You were destined for a better man even then," Miles
teased. "Your father must have seen a different future
written in your eyes."

Lilia gave him a sideways glance. "I don't think *you* were
exactly the sort of man my father had in mind for me, either."

Miles had to laugh. "No, I don't think I was. Remember the night you took me home for dinner to meet your parents? Your mum had cooked American fried chicken, hadn't she? With a crispy crust and all the bones left inside."

"You didn't have a clue how to eat it!" Lilia was chuckling now. "You picked up your knife, tried to stab the chicken with your fork—"

"And it shot straight off my plate into your father's lap."

"Oh, Miles, you were trying so hard to impress them!"

"I botched it."

"Not really. My mom thought you were cute." Lilia let her eyes drift to the window as the bus pulled onto the ferry. Other vehicles quickly filled in the space around the bus, and a horde of foot passengers boarded the upper levels.

"Of course, my dad wasn't too thrilled," she went on. "Well, you *were* my first serious boyfriend. I think he had been hoping I'd go off to college and fall in love with a nice preacher boy."

"Not some strapping Brit with a bad sunburn who intended to cart you off to Zambia?"

"Definitely not."

"He thought I was a heathen, did he? Not good enough for his daughter."

"I don't know many fathers who approve of their daughters' boyfriends. He was protective. But he liked you well enough. That is, until you...until he thought you had..."

"Abandoned you? I can't blame him. Not the act of a loving husband, was it? My mum thought badly of *you* for turning me out, especially when I'd been so ill. Odd that she never knew my father was behind it all along. My mum would enjoy your company now, though. She's a strong woman. Like you."

Lilia dredged up her memory of the lithe, middle-aged woman with graying blond hair and Miles's blue eyes. Lilia had been terrified to meet her, but Miles had insisted. The two women—one very young and uncertain, the other older and content with life—had sat in the shadow of a thatch-roofed umbrella and discussed their favorite artists. Mrs. Kane, as it turned out, sculpted clay statues. Her specialty was figures of Africans—women pounding millet, children rolling hoops, warriors dressed for a hunt. Her works commanded respectable prices in Lusaka galleries, but she was forced to do her sculpting more or less on the sly. Mr. Kane had never approved of his wife's ambitions.

"I used to believe you were just like your father, Miles," Lilia mused. "He was the outspoken one. The bold adventurer, the athlete, the keen-minded businessman. He had a good sense of humor, too. The two of you seemed in perfect harmony."

"Like a pair of bagpipes, eh?" Miles laughed. "No, we weren't out of sorts back then. I always did what he wanted, that's why. But after you...after I lost you...I stopped caring what anyone thought of me. I saw no point in bowing and scraping to my father. I was angry all the time. I fought him."

"Literally?"

"Once." Miles thought it might be time to change the subject. "Care for a fresh mango, Lilia? This chap is peddling them right here on the ferry. Making himself a tidy profit, I should think."

For a moment, she was diverted. The young African held up a pair of heavy yellow-skinned fruit, each shaped like a paisley, each fragrant and ripe. Miles reached across Lilia and rolled down her window. In a moment, he had used some of the currency he had exchanged at the airport to purchase both mangoes.

"Wash them in your room," he said, setting the fruits on Lilia's thighs, "and I'll fetch a knife from the hotel kitchen. Before the day is over, my love, you'll be dining on fresh—"

"So, what did you fight your father over?" she cut in.

He gave a slight frown. She wasn't going to let him off the hook, was she? "We fought over nothing. School, I suppose. After I had recovered from malaria, he wanted to pack me off to Cambridge. I told him I'd lost you, lost my future, and the last thing I intended to do was fly off to England and freeze my—"

"So you *fought* with him?"

"He shoved me about. Told me I'd go whether I liked it or not. Told me to damn well forget about you, forget about chasing around the bush after wildlife and forget about my own frigging dreams. He gave me a whack on the jaw—so I let him have it. Flattened him."

Lilia stared. She couldn't imagine Miles having the temerity to knock down his own father. Mr. Kane had been formidable, a giant of a man with thick brown hair and fists like hams.

"That was the last of it between us," Miles continued. "He let me have my way from that moment on. Of course, he was never happy about it. He had wanted me in the copper business, not the hotel and tourist trade. We don't speak often to this day. In fact, I would say I've grown to be much more like my mum than him. At least I prefer to think so. I may have his size. I may have his stubborn drive and impatience. But I hope I have her open-mindedness, her sense of vision. I hope I'm not cruel. And I know I'm no liar."

"I never thought you were." Lilia realized that his eyes compelled her more strongly than even the sight of her beloved homeland. "Miles, even when I believed you had betrayed me, I never thought you were cruel. Young, maybe. Irresponsible. But never heartless and never a liar."

"I hope you don't think of me as unreliable today."

She shrugged. "I don't know you that well."

"You know me, Lilia. You know I've worked a responsible job every day of my adult life. I've been put in positions of authority. I've never been fired—only promoted. Everything I've done has been successful. It's because I *am* reliable that my company listened to my ideas for this wildlife adventure hotel project. And it's because they can depend on me that the board of shareholders appointed me to carry out the plans."

"I have no doubt you're a good employee," she said. "And I know your supervisors depend on you. But...well, in personal matters—"

"You don't think I can be counted on to make a commitment to a relationship."

"I said I'm not sure. I don't know you that well." She met his eyes. "After all, you're thirty-one, and you've never married again. That doesn't say much for your dedication to making a relationship successful.''

"It doesn't say much for yours, either.''

"I know that,'' she said softly. "I'm not sure I have what it takes. Not after all I went through.''

He stared out the window for a moment, frowning at the passing scenery. Then he cupped Lilia's chin with one hand and turned her face to his. "Look, you want to know why I never married again? I'll tell you why. It's because I never stopped thinking of myself as your husband. Not for ten years. Not with any number of pretty girls making eyes at me. Not even though I'd given up ever seeing you again. Somehow, in spite of it all, Lilia, I thought of myself as a married man. Now if that isn't dedication and reliability, I don't know what is.''

"Welcome to Two Fishes Hotel!'' the minivan driver called. "Please check in at the front desk in the main lobby. And have a wonderful holiday here at Diani Beach!''

They were assigned adjoining rooms. Eager to hurry back outside and explore the beach, Lilia quickly unpacked her bag and rearranged some of the items she had purchased in England. The room was lovely, appointed with a patterned bedspread and matching curtains, a double bed, a chair and table set, and seascapes painted in oil.

She took a moment to examine the bold black signature on each canvas, aware that original paintings could be purchased by the basketful at local markets. With one of these hanging in each Habari Safari hotel guest room, the company would support indigenous artists and accurately portray the African setting.

Lilia had the first pang of uncertainty when she went into the bathroom to change into her bathing suit. She knew she shouldn't care what Miles thought of the alterations in her body after ten years. After all, she hadn't let herself go to pot. But neither was she the rail-thin teenage waif she'd been at eighteen.

She tugged the one-piece maillot suit up her legs and then arranged her bosom in the preformed cups. There was certainly more to arrange than there had been ten years before. Miles probably wouldn't mind that. But there was more elsewhere, too. Lilia smoothed her palms down the curves of her hips. She sucked in her stomach and patted her behind. A little too much here. Not quite enough there.

Of course, she didn't show any effects of childbearing. Not that that made her feel much better. As she aged, her chances of finding the right man seemed dimmer year by year. And bearing a child of her own seemed less and less likely.

Lilia sighed. What wouldn't she give to have little Colin with her at this moment? If only he were in the room, tugging off his britches and pulling at his socks. If only she could slip him into a pair of tiny bathing trunks and run with him down the sand. He would love the beach—all those sandcastles to build. He might be afraid of the water at first, but she would teach him how to splash in the waves and run through the surf.

Fighting unexpected tears when she should have felt gleeful anticipation, Lilia wrapped a towel around her shoulders and started for the door. As she reached for the handle, she heard Miles's voice in the next room.

"Lusaka!" he shouted. "I want Lusaka!"

She knew instantly he was on the telephone. His words had that toneless, clearly enunciated quality people used when they were attempting to be heard over the static of poor connections, faulty wires and sleepy operators who were the standard in Third World countries.

"That's right, Zambia!" His voice was so strong Lilia couldn't help but hear every word. "Industrial Copper Mines, please. I want to speak to William Kane. Executive vice president, William Kane!"

Lilia gripped the corners of her towel. She knew she should leave her room. She shouldn't listen. She ought to just head out to the shore. Stroll on the sand. Wade in the surf. It wasn't right to eavesdrop. But she couldn't move.

"Dad, it's Miles." The voice was controlled now. "Miles Kane, your son. Yes, that's right.... No, I've left America. I'm in Kenya now."

There was a pause. Lilia turned the knob. She really should go.

"Mombasa, Kenya. Dad, I wanted to tell you who's here with me.... It's Lilia Eden. You remember her, don't you? She's the girl I married."

Lilia shut her eyes. *Oh, Miles.*

"Ten years ago," he said. "We were on holiday here in Mombasa, remember? Lilia tells me that while I was in the hospital, you spoke with *her* from Zambia—not with her father.... Well, which of them was it, Dad? Surely you can recall a thing like that. After all, she was my wife at the time."

She should go. This was a private conversation between Miles and his father. But Lilia couldn't make herself open the door. Hearing this confrontation was the final proof to her that Miles had been telling the truth. Their marriage had been torn apart by a man with selfish ambitions for his son. Ambitions that didn't include a young American wife.

"So you *did* speak with Lilia?" Miles confirmed. His voice was hard and angry. "And you told her I wanted to end the marriage? I don't believe you. That's not what Lilia says. She insists you told *her* that *I* wanted to get on with my life. And then you told me that she wanted to forget the whole thing! You lied to both of us, didn't you? I know you wanted great things for me, but you had no right—"

He stopped speaking for almost a minute. Lilia listened breathlessly.

"I *know* you thought I could do better than to get married at age twenty-one!" Miles shouted. "But did you stop to think what *I* wanted? Ten years, Dad! Ten damn years, and I hold you responsible."

Lilia could hear the anguish in his voice. She once believed she had been betrayed by Miles—but he truly had been betrayed by his own father. She couldn't imagine the effect it would have on him.

"No, that doesn't solve everything!" he snapped loudly. "Just because I've found her again doesn't mean we're together. We can't simply take up where we left off ten years ago.... Why not? I'll tell you why the hell not. Because we've both changed. We've both been hurt, and she's not sure she trusts me even now...."

He listened to his father speaking for a moment before he began shouting into the telephone again. "I don't know what she'd want with a worthless tourist-kisser like me, either. But I'll tell you this much. If she does come back to me, I won't let you or anyone else stand in the way. I won't lose her again, Dad. Do you hear me?"

Lilia tore open the door. She stood in the hall for a moment, waiting for the next explosion that would send her down the steps to find solace in the waves.

But Miles was quieter this time. Almost inaudible.

"No, she doesn't know about that," he said. "Because I haven't told her, that's why. I'm not sure I will." Then his voice rose. "I don't give a damn about it! If knowing the truth about me turns her away, then I'll live with it, won't I? At least I'll know she left me for a legitimate reason. It won't be a lie that tears us apart this time.... To hell with you, too, then. Yes, that's what I said, and don't think I won't remember—"

Lilia fled. Her bare feet slapped against the cool tile floor as she ran down the hallway. Clutching her towel tightly around her shoulders, she burst out into the sunshine. Legs churning, she raced down the concrete sidewalk and tore across the swimming pool enclosure where imported Europeans in various stages of sunburn lifted their heads to stare as she flew out onto the sand.

The sea beckoned. Turquoise waters. The distant line of white foam crashing over the reef. The rise and fall of salty waves. The curl and splash of the surf at high tide. Lilia dropped her towel as she ran. Her feet scattered the loose sand beneath the palm trees. Then they sank into the spongy sand near the water. And finally, after ten long years, Lilia ran straight into the Indian Ocean, burst through the surf and dived into the sea.

Her body shot beneath a wave. Saltwater stung her eyes. Sand filtered into her hair. *Miles, oh, Miles!* She thrashed her way to the surface, then streaked up into the bright light. Water streamed down her face, her hair, her skin.

She dived again. Surfacing, she swung into a crawl stroke. Why had she stayed and listened to Miles argue with his father? Why did she care whether Mr. Kane had lied or not?

It had been ten years since she had faced the pain of losing the man she had married. So why was she feeling it all again—and just as strongly?

As Lilia swam, she felt her heart aching not only for herself but also for Miles. How would he react to the phone conversation? His words had clearly revealed how much it hurt him to know he had been betrayed by his own father.

Again, Lilia's thoughts swung to Colin. Parental betrayal seemed to be running rampant. Colin's mother had left him alone in a filthy room for two days when he was no more than an infant. Now he had been returned to that woman. Did Colin remember why he had been taken away from his biological mother in the first place? How would he feel if he ever learned about his past?

The abandonment of a mother... the betrayal of a father...the loss of love...Lilia's loss of both Colin and Miles.

Fighting to make some sense of it, she cut through the water, her arms pumping. And somehow, with the passing of the minutes and the caress of the warm salty water, she felt a familiar release of tension. How many times in her young life had she run to the comfort of the sea with her troubles? The time her mother had been stung by a scorpion... the time her father's life had been threatened for preaching the Gospel of Christianity... the time her little brother had fallen out of a guava tree.

The ocean had been more than her playground. It had been a nurturing bosom in which to cry. It had been a museum of wonders to explore. It had been a magical meeting place where people from all around the world gathered to play.

Lilia kicked over onto her back and drifted on the buoyant water. She let out a deep breath. Here she was. Looking up at the same pale blue sky. Gazing at the same wispy clouds. Floating in the same turquoise ocean.

Why didn't she feel the same? Where had her life taken a turn? When had she begun to separate from this place and all it had meant to her? How could she again belong to it? And did she really want to?

"Caught you!" A pair of strong hands grabbed her around the waist and pulled.

Lilia gasped in a lungful of air before gurgling beneath the waves. Opening her eyes underwater, she saw an unmistakable pair of brown, muscular thighs, a set of baggy swimming trunks and a hard, flat stomach. Propelling herself up, she emerged only inches from Miles's chest.

"You scared me half to death," she admonished him.

He gave a crooked grin. "You didn't wait for me at the room."

"The sea was calling." Searching his blue eyes, she found that she could read nothing in them, as though he had pulled a mask over his face. She ached to lift it and touch him. "I thought I heard you on the phone," she tried.

Again, no sign of emotion. "I had to make a few calls. Thought I'd better check in with the company and let my boss know we made it to Kenya."

"So you called Zambia?" She took another stab, hoping to elicit some sort of response. "Is everything all right...in Lusaka?"

He glanced at the shore, and for a moment she thought she saw a shadow of hurt flicker across his face. Then he gave a shrug. "The usual rot."

She touched his shoulder. "Miles, I—"

"Race you to that coral head, Lilia," he cut in, and shot off in the direction of the outcrop that showed just above the surface of the ocean.

Lilia started after him, instinctively responding to the challenge. As she swam, she acknowledged to herself that Miles was not going to say a word about the phone call. Did his reluctance to talk have something to do with whatever it was he hadn't yet told her...the secret his father had mentioned...something that might turn her away? Or was Miles choosing to keep silent about his conversation with his father in order to minimize and eventually bury his own pain?

Whatever it was, Lilia knew she would have to be patient until Miles felt like talking. If he wanted to deny the phone call and focus on the present moment, then she would, too. With renewed determination to put the past behind her and enjoy the pleasure of her homecoming, Lilia surged forward.

She had lost sight of Miles, but the coral head was almost within reach. Just as she stretched out her hand, she was once again caught from behind and dragged under the water. Through the muffling water, she could hear Miles's laughter. The genuinely happy sound washed away the last of her doubts, and Lilia felt her heart lift.

Okay, Mr. Kane, she told herself. *It's retaliation time.* Smiling to herself, she kicked quickly out of reach beneath the water, darted off into the murky depths, then turned around and homed in for the attack.

Miles was still treading water, obviously searching for his intended prey, when Lilia lunged from behind him. She grabbed his shoulders, gave a swift tug and dunked him.

He might not have been brought up near the ocean, but Miles was no stranger to the water. Instantly, he reached out and caught Lilia's slender ankle. She kicked hard, but his hand only slid up her calf to hold her in place. Both of them burst to the surface as Miles's hand captured her waist.

"You rat!" She laughed, shaking her head to fling water in his eyes. "That was the second time you caught me by surprise."

"Just doing a little deep-sea fishing."

"Well, I'm afraid you caught an octopus." Arms waving, she slithered from his grasp and started swimming on a line parallel to the shore.

Miles matched her stroke for stroke. As they swam, Lilia felt a sense of acceptance wash through her. She wouldn't tell Miles that she had listened in on his confrontation with his father. What had passed between them was intended to be private, and their conversation only confirmed what she already had learned. But Miles's last revelation concerned her. There was something he hadn't confessed. Something that would affect her deeply if she knew.

She swam on. Well, the secret didn't matter. She wasn't interested in reestablishing their relationship, anyway, she reminded herself. The heated emotion in Miles's words to his father only confirmed her position. If she let down her guard with Miles, everything would begin to erupt, to confuse the orderly pattern she needed in her life.

Lilia began to struggle to keep up with Miles. She hadn't realized how out of shape she was. Even at sea level, her breath came in gasps as she paused and let her toes touch the bottom for a moment.

Miles glanced back, then turned and drifted to meet her. He couldn't help smiling as he watched Lilia. She was his waiflike enchantress again, her short hair framing her face with a wet, dark cap, her gray eyes mirroring the sparkle of the water. It was all he could do to keep from touching her. As angry as the telephone conversation with his father had made him, it had also served to confirm everything for him. Lilia *had* once been his—wholly, completely, eternally.

Now, watching her in the water as the purple swimsuit pushed her breasts forward and up in a tantalizing swell of creamy flesh, Miles vowed he would have Lilia again. This was no boyish rebellion against a manipulative father's wishes. The vow arose from Miles's own adult desire. One way or another, no matter what it took, she would be his, and he hers. If not as husband and wife, then as lovers.

"Want to go out to the reef tomorrow at low tide?" she asked, pointing at the long line of pounding breakers in the distance. "We could hire a boat and do some snorkeling."

"Sounds good to me."

"It's not exactly research for the hotel design."

He shrugged. "We'll be meeting with management first thing in the morning. We'll tour the hotel and grounds together, and then you'll be on your own for a few hours while I discuss operations. After that, I'd say we can do as we like."

"How many nights will we stay at Two Fishes?"

"We'll move tomorrow. To Africana Sea Lodge."

"Oh, I love that place!" She sank beneath the waves in sheer bliss at the memory of the round white bungalows set among curving walkways. When she resurfaced, she realized that the mask was gone, and Miles was gazing at her with an expression she was almost afraid to read.

"You're beautiful, Lilia."

"Even without the white bikini?"

"Purple makes your gray eyes turn violet. And, yes..."
He caught her around the waist and drew her against his
body. "I do like the woman you've become."

"Miles!" Lilia caught her breath at the sudden sensation
she felt as her bare legs drifted against his. She put her hands
on his shoulders, intending to push him away. But the electric shimmer of his damp skin paralyzed her. She swallowed. He drifted closer, causing her breasts to brush against
his chest.

His fingers trickled up her back. Where her suit ended,
they found bare flesh and continued upward onto her neck.
She realized she was hardly breathing.

"Miles," she said. "We agreed..."

"We agreed about a lot of things, Lilia. A long time ago."
He toyed with the wet tips of her hair, aware that she hadn't
moved her hands from his shoulders. He ached to kiss her.
Her mouth was parted as if in anticipation. Her breasts rose
and fell as she struggled to breathe.

He pulled her closer against him. Her hips drifted against
his, and he knew she could feel the evidence of his desire.
Still she didn't move. Their toes touched. He felt her thigh
slide up the side of his leg. And he bent his head toward
hers.

Suddenly, she sank out of his arms and shot away. He
pursued, swimming hard. You're not getting away, Lilia.
Not this time, he thought. Not when you want it as badly as
I do.

She was stroking toward shore as if a school of sharks
were after her. When he caught up to her, he slipped his arm
around her waist and swept her up against him.

"Lilia!" Before she could protest, he cupped her head
and kissed her. She blossomed instantly. Their lips slid together, hungry, relentless with urgency. Her hands formed
around his back, her fingers stroking the ridges of his flesh.
He could hear her breathing hard as tiny cries of need rose
from her throat.

He parted her lips, tasted her, and knew her eager response. Her breasts, wet and peaked with tension, slipped
up and down against his chest with the movement of the
waves. As he kissed across her cheek to her ear, he felt her

hands glide into his hair. Their legs moved with the rhythm of the tide, skin stroking upward against skin. His leg floated between her opened thighs, and he heard her catch her breath.

"Oh, Miles," she pleaded. "Miles, please . . ."

"What is it, Lilia?" he said into her ear. "Tell me what you want from me."

She shook her head, swallowing back the words that demanded to be spoken. "No," she said, as if speaking to herself. Then she lifted her eyes. "I'm afraid."

"Afraid of what, Lilia?"

"Of you. Of me." She fought the knot forming in her throat. "I'm afraid it might happen all over again."

"I hope it does."

"The beauty between us lasted a couple of weeks, Miles. But the pain went on for ten years."

"Isn't it time to end that pain, Lilia?"

Fighting the need to be swept into his arms again, she turned toward shore. In the distance, she heard the light, ringing sounds of a bamboo xylophone. "It's time for dinner," she said softly to Miles. "That's what time it is. I'll race you to shore."

And she pushed away from him, cutting through the waves. He gazed at her for a moment, watching her slip away. Then he set his jaw and started after her.

Chapter 8

At dinner that evening, Miles and Lilia were guests of the hotel manager and his wife, a pleasant African couple. The expansive dining room adequately handled the crowd of American, German, Swiss, English, Dutch, Italian and other European tourists. The mixture of languages and clothing ranging from safari suits to bathing suits made no difference as everyone crowded around the long food tables.

"I hung around these hotels all the time when I was a kid," Lilia confided to Miles as they loaded their plates with cheese, crackers, fresh bread, salad and fruit. "But I rarely got to actually eat at them. This is a feast."

"Eat all you want. And the main course is yet to come." He gave her a wink and leaned against her shoulder to whisper, "I'm feeling very hungry myself...aren't you, Lilia?"

Her blush enchanted him. A childlike wonder shone in her eyes as she gazed at the table spread with food, but Lilia was definitely all woman tonight.

Miles could hardly concentrate on dinner and conversation with the hotel manager. Lilia's skin wore a rosy tint from the afternoon sun. Her dress, a drapey, sleeveless bit of enchantment in hot pink, set off the glow of her cheeks. More than that, the neckline came to a point just between her breasts, and Miles found his eyes wandering constantly to the mysterious shadow between them.

Two Fishes Hotel was purely a beach resort rather than a game-viewing outpost, the manager informed his guests as they sat in the lounge area near the pool after dinner. Tourist buses not connected with the hotel *did* take patrons to the nearby Shimba Hills game park. There they observed rare sable antelope in their only major Kenyan stronghold. Other groups of guests participated in organized boating trips for snorkeling, game fishing or scuba diving.

But Miles's primary interest in Two Fishes was its absolute success at catering to its guests' desires. In fact, Lilia could recall when the establishment had been nothing more than a group of small, whitewashed bungalows that rented by the week. Now, the hotel boasted a magnificent swimming pool that wound through the bar and then outside to the open air. The noisy throng in its huge dining room and bustling activity in the kitchens testified to its thriving tourist trade. Miles intended to mirror this establishment's success in Habari Safari's three wildlife adventure hotels planned for the United States.

When a group of African men set up their instruments beside the outdoor pool, Lilia felt a pang of memory. As a girl, she had wandered from hotel to hotel with her friends, listening to bands, watching magic shows, enjoying native singers, and then struggling into bed late at night with her feet worn out from dancing. She could almost trace her girlhood by the dance styles that had been in fashion—from the twist in her early childhood, to the bump, disco and rock and roll.

Though her parents had frowned on their daughter's evening adventures, beachcombing and dancing until midnight had seemed like fairly tame vices compared to what she might have encountered in the States. There was not a chance of keeping Lilia under wraps, anyway, and they soon gave up trying. She was as flighty as a feather, and forever pirouetting around the house. Even now, Lilia was aware that her toes were tapping and her fingers were drumming out the rhythm.

"Care to dance, Lilia?" Miles asked, interrupting her memories. The hotel manager was leading his wife onto the cleared area beside the swimming pool.

Against her own impulses, Lilia shook her head. She didn't think she could handle another close encounter with this man. "No, thanks. I'm pretty tired."

He seemed to accept her excuse. "My head feels a bit mushy, as a matter of fact. Must be jet lag. But—nothing like dancing to clear the fog away. Come on, Lilia."

She let out a breath. "Miles, I told you this afternoon—"

"We used to dance for hours, remember? You in a white dress that flowed around your ankles. I thought I was in heaven. As a matter of fact, I gave up dancing after you. It never had much appeal to me."

"Then you wouldn't be able to keep up with me now," she said, trying to lighten the mood. It bothered her the way Miles kept drifting back to their time together. Of course it was natural, but all the same she wished he wouldn't do it.

"I never stopped dancing," she told him. "I even learned the two-step and the Cotton-Eyed Joe."

"The what?" He was on his feet. "Show me, Lilia."

Before she could stop him, he had pulled her out of her chair and swept her into the crowd on the dance floor. His hand slid around her waist, and he drew her so close she could feel his breath on her neck.

"Who's this Joe chap, anyway?" he asked.

She had to laugh. "The Cotton-Eyed Joe. It's a country-and-western dance. You have to have the right music and a long line of people who all know the steps."

"Damn."

He didn't look at all sorry. Instead, Lilia realized he was practically devouring her with those hot blue eyes. She wished she'd packed something a little more discreet than the low-cut wraparound dress she was wearing. But the knit fabric never wrinkled, and she'd worn it on trips a hundred times.

Now she could feel the heat of Miles's hand through the thin fabric as he led her across the floor in a more traditional waltz. The afternoon sun had only deepened his bronzed features, making his eyes almost shimmer with blue light. He had traded his khaki for a white cotton shirt that looked like something the captain of a ship might wear. Its epaulets and square, pleated breast pockets made him look more formal than she knew he really was.

The music was wonderful—contemporary Western dance songs tinged with the syncopation of African rhythm. Lilia couldn't help but relax against Miles as the warm ocean breeze shifted through her hair.

This is home, she confirmed to herself. The pulse of drumbeats, the scent of frangipani blossoms, the whisper of the surf just beyond the line of palm trees. Yes, this was home....

Or was it Miles who made her feel so comfortable? So at peace. Lilia studied him for a moment. She had the odd sense that they'd never been apart at all. The straight line of his nose was so familiar to her. The way his thick hair shone like gold seemed perfectly normal. She was intimate with the curve of his ear, the angle of his jaw, even the cologne he wore. But how could that be? Jet lag was playing tricks with her mind.

"Like to take a walk on the beach?" he asked, his mouth moving against her ear.

She shivered and felt a curl of anticipation slide into her stomach. She shook her head. "Too many sand crabs."

He chuckled. "Now, that's your weakest excuse yet, Lilia."

"I'm serious. Don't you remember all those pale little crabs sidling back and forth in the moonlight? They scurry down to the water and then scurry back up the shore again. You can't walk anywhere without stepping on them."

"I'll carve us a path through the crustacean jungle, how's that?" Without waiting for an answer, he took her hand and drew her to the path that led down to the sea.

"You'll see what I mean," she warned. As they slipped through the shadows, Lilia was gratified to find that the moonlit beach was indeed alive with tiny transparent crabs.

By the hundreds, they slipped in and out of their holes, bustling to and fro across the white sand with no apparent rhyme or reason.

"We'd better head back to the hotel," she said.

"Take off your shoes," Miles instructed, kicking off his boots. When she hesitated, he pointed at her feet. "Your shoes, Lilia."

She slipped off her heels. "Miles Kane, if you think I'm going to walk *barefoot...*"

But he scooped her up in his arms and strode toward the water. It was low tide, and for a long moment—one that Lilia wished would stop and at the same time hoped would never end—he held her tightly against him as he walked across the teeming sand.

"I don't know how many of the poor things you mashed," she said as he finally set her toes gently into the water.

"Not a one. I assure you, I was very careful." He was smiling at her. "I've been wanting to tell you all evening how beautiful you are, Lilia."

She glanced down at the magenta knit wraparound. "A long time ago, I gave away that white dress you liked so much."

"I don't mind. I realized this afternoon, the past is just that—past. White dress, string bikini, and all. I wouldn't trade the woman you are for that girl-child, no matter how much I loved her."

"Miles, when you think about it, we hardly knew each other when we decided to get married." She started walking into the wind. He took her hand, as he always had. "Back in the States, I decided that it was just the uncertainty of leaving Africa that had drawn me to you. There I was, preenrolled at some college I'd never seen, and already packing my suitcases. I was dreading the moment I would have to set foot on that airplane. Somehow I knew I'd never be back."

"And I promised you a way to stay in Africa?"

"When I met you, everything suddenly looked hopeful to me—instead of hopeless. By marrying you, I knew I would never have to leave. I could almost replicate the way of life I'd known as a child."

"So I was just a convenient escape for you, is that it?"

"I've thought about it that way."

"And do you think that's the truth, Lilia?"

"Well, you might counter that I was just a convenient escape for you, too, Miles. After all, your father was pushing you to go to England. He wanted you studying metallurgy at Cambridge, when you wanted to stay in Zambia and become a game warden. With a wife and children to support, you'd have had a good excuse not to go."

"What a cock-and-bull pack of blarney," Miles snorted.

Lilia couldn't help but laugh at his response. "Okay, maybe not."

"Definitely not. I might have been young and reckless, but I was no fool. Why would I have tied myself down with a wife for the rest of my life merely to escape going to university? No, that wasn't what drew me to you, Lilia, and you know it."

"I know." She sighed and watched the crabs dart into the foam and then dash away. "And it really wasn't the idea of staying in Africa the rest of my life that drew me to you, either."

"I should hope not."

"There was something ... magical ... about you."

"About *me?*" Miles pictured himself sprinkled with fairy dust, twinkling his toes as he flitted from flower to flower. "Magical, did you say?"

"Over the years, I must have met a couple of hundred young men out here on these beaches. In fact, that was half the fun of my baby-sitting job. I loved meeting people of all kinds. And I know I must have danced with every available male who ever vacationed on the coast of Kenya."

"*All* of them?"

"But you were ... I don't know—" she lifted her eyes to the moon "—so different. You were all of Africa rolled up into one person. The sunshine, the fresh air, the wildness—"

"The smell?"

She laughed and swatted him. "You know what I mean."

"Yes, I do. You were that for me, too."

"And you were so...persistent. I couldn't believe the way you kept after me. At first, I thought you were interested in a little fun in the sun. That sort of thing. Just a holiday romance. But you never stopped pursuing me until that night when you..."

"When I asked you to marry me. You were shocked. You laughed and told me to stop teasing. But I wasn't teasing, was I, Lilia? I knew what I wanted even then. I meant to spend the rest of my life with you."

"Maybe you had a touch of the fever."

He caught her hand and swung her around. "I wasn't ill then, Lilia, and you know it."

"You might have been." She wished they hadn't wandered so far from the hotel. She wished she hadn't let this topic of conversation go on and on. "After it was all over, I told myself that you'd been on the verge of malaria. That's why you'd proposed to me. That explained everything."

"I was as clearheaded back then as I am right now."

"*Now* you have jet lag, Miles."

"Lilia, stop pushing me away. Stop denying what happened between us. It was real. It was adult. We both wanted it, and we both intended it to happen."

"All right, I won't deny it," she said. "But will you please stop pushing for it to happen again?"

"Why should I?" He caught her shoulders and pulled her toward him. "You know we were meant for each other then. We still are."

"I don't know that."

"Yes, you do." He shook his head. "Lilia, it won't end badly this time. I swear it."

Her mind flashed to the phone conversation she'd overheard that afternoon. "Miles, what is it you want? A trip down memory lane? A round-trip affair in all the hotels in Kenya? I can't do that, don't you see? I'm not that Lilia Eden who fell in love with you ten years ago." Unexpected tears washed into her eyes. "I'm a grown-up now, Miles! I'm an interior designer. I own a house on Walnut Street in Springfield, Missouri. I sing in the choir at First Baptist Church. I'm trying to adopt a child! I'm expanding my business. I have regular hair and dental appointments set up a year in advance. Things are planned. Things are in order. I don't want—" she sucked in a shaky breath "—I don't want..."

"Lilia," he groaned, catching her against him. He brushed a kiss across her trembling lips.

Her fingers caught his shirtsleeves as his mouth moved over hers. *Yes!* her heartbeat pulsed against her throat. *Yes! Yes! Yes!*

"No, Miles," she whispered. But before she could make herself break away, she ran her hands around his shoulders and leaned upward into his kiss, seeking, urgent with the hunger that raged inside her. He cradled her head, parted her lips, deepened his kiss in an image of the passion they once had shared.

Lilia's hands willfully tangled in his hair, luxuriating in the thick, coarse strands that slid between her fingers. She heard his breath grow shallow, felt his heart thudding against her breasts as their mouths lingered together, playing, exploring, drawing out the sensuality of the moment.

Waves lapped at their ankles. He curved his hands down her back, over the swell of her hips, settling her against him. A rush of heat scattered across her skin at the pressure of his arousal against her pelvis. Not once in ten years had she permitted even this closeness with a man. Now, suddenly, the memory of her intimacies with Miles erupted inside her. She remembered how he had looked as she lay on the sand the night of their wedding, his body rising over her, his eyes soft with desire.

"Miles," she managed to say. What would she tell him? That she was afraid again? Afraid that she wanted him as desperately as she ever had?

"Lilia, I want you so much," he murmured.

She felt his hands slide down the curve of her bottom, over the silky drape of her skirt. He pulled her closer still, and she gasped at the pressure against her thighs. As his mouth worked magic on hers, his hands slipped upward, drawing the hem of her dress over her thighs. His palms molded against her ribs, then lifted slowly, testing the weight of her breasts.

"Beautiful," he murmured.

She thought she might melt into the sea. His hands formed around the swell of her bosom, lifting and then separating the swollen flesh.

"I've been wanting to touch you all night. Tantalized by you. Mesmerized by this one tiny shadow." He slid his finger down the cleavage between her breasts. "I was right...I do love what the years have done to you, Lilia."

A white-hot wave curled down her as his fingers spread apart, pushing aside the fabric of her dress, running streaks of lightning across her silken skin. She kneaded his back, aching for the moment when he would touch her intimately—as she knew he would.

But she had been right, too. The mature Miles Kane knew how to take his time. His fingertips traced patterns over her bare skin as she stood in shivering anticipation. His mouth hovered against her ear, and their ragged, rhythmic breathing came in unison. Slowly his fingers circled her breast, edging ever closer to the tingling peak until finally he stroked across it.

"Miles!" she gasped, but she couldn't break away. His hand played music on her flesh, taunting and caressing until she was sure her knees would collapse. Even if they did, she wouldn't sink into the water—his free hand circled her waist, holding her so close there was no doubt between them of the passion building.

As his fingers spread to cover her breast, the palm of his hand rolling her nipple, she pressed her mouth against his neck. His skin was hot, dry, scented with bay rum, and she kissed him again and again. He toyed with her, and she felt her thighs begin to ache. A deep thrumming began in the pit of her stomach, and it spread downward with a delicious heat. She wanted nothing more than to surrender.

"Lilia, you've asked me not to push you," Miles murmured. "I covet your trust. I won't destroy this magic between us by forcing what you don't want. Tell me, Lilia...tell me what you want."

She trembled as his hands swept up and down her body, molding every curve and hollow, sliding her dress over her bare skin. "Miles," she whispered. "I'm not sure what I want. I only know what I didn't want when I agreed to come on this trip."

"Tell me."

"I didn't want this...this hunger building up between us again."

"Has it?"

She nodded, unable to answer aloud. "Miles, when you touch me, it sweeps me back in time. I feel like I did with you ten years ago."

"Is that wrong?"

"It must be. This isn't ten years ago. This is now. If something happens to us, I want it to be new, different. I don't want a repeat of my past. It hurt too much."

"I won't hurt you, Lilia. I give you my vow."

At the word of solemn promise, she slipped back in time to their wedding night. He had given her a vow then. One never to be broken.

She took his hands in hers and drew them away from her body. "Miles, I used to be a risk-taker. I would try almost anything. Life was a lark for me. Throw an adventure my way, and I'd jump into it feet first. But time has cured my wanderlust."

"Time? Or fear of being hurt?"

"Losing you was the first step. After that, I wasn't so willing to rush into things. I stopped taking the risky path. Losing Colin has sealed me forever, I think. See, I stepped out and exposed myself to pain. I took the risk because I wanted a child of my own so badly. And I lost again."

Miles swallowed, absorbing the double significance of her words. Every time Lilia spoke about Colin, it was like a thorn in his side. He would never meet that need in her. Not as long as he lived. It was the one gift he couldn't give.

"When you hold me," she was saying, "and we dance, or walk hand in hand, or when you kiss me, I feel that old urge start to rise up inside my heart. *Take a chance,* a voice whispers in my ear. *Come on, Lilia, take the risk.* But, Miles, I stopped listening to that voice a long time ago."

"And you're afraid to start listening again?"

She gazed across the sea, beyond the moonlit breakers on the reef. The lights of ships shone in the distance.

"I won't let anything happen to tear us apart, Lilia."
Miles gripped her hands until the blood stopped. "I swear
it."

His blue eyes shone in the silver light, and she wondered
if the moon was playing tricks...or if tears rimmed his lower
lids.

"Let's go back to the hotel," she said. "I'm so tired that
I think . . . I think I'm starting to imagine things."

Miles spotted Lilia's purple bathing suit at the fruit bar
the following morning. She was hovering near a plate of
mangoes, her fork poised over a plump orange oval. The
flesh of each mango had been halved, then cut into small
squares, and the skin had been turned inside out to expose
the juicy fruit. From a distance, Miles watched Lilia spear
a mango and set it on her plate. She wavered a moment,
then jabbed her fork into a second one.

"Look out for the vervet monkeys!" he warned, coming
up behind her.

She jumped and turned her head to the open windows of
the dining room. Instantly, Miles nabbed one of her mangoes and swept it behind his back.

"Oh, those pesky creatures have been trying to steal toast
and fruit off people's plates all morning," Lilia fumed as
she walked beside Miles toward the table she had selected.
"The hotel has had to station waiters near the windows just
to keep the monkeys away."

"That's appalling," Miles commiserated.

"It could be dangerous..." She set her plate on the table
and stared at the single mango. "I thought...I was sure I..."

"What's the problem?" Miles asked, feigning grave concern.

"I would swear I—"

"Take a look at that, would you?" He grabbed her hand
and pointed to the window behind her. Lilia swung around
in her chair. Miles dropped the filched mango back onto her
plate.

She turned around, disappointed. "I guess I missed it,"
she said, then frowned at the two mangoes. Lifting her

head, she fastened Miles with an appraising look. "Did you take one of my mangoes?"

"What?"

"My mangoes. You rat!" She laughed at his guilty shrug.

"Now, Lilia, surely you're not accusing me—"

"I am convicting you. You're a slicker thief than those vervet monkeys."

He chuckled. "I was only trying to protect your delicate stomach. After all, we have a busy day today."

"If I get sick from eating too many mangoes, it'll be the best excuse for a stomachache I've ever had." She popped an orange square into her mouth and shut her eyes as she savored it. "Ohhh, I could eat these all day long."

He studied her, boldly admiring the view of her long neck and half-bare breasts rising above the shelf of her purple suit. When she opened her eyes and saw him, a pink flush crept over her skin.

"Aren't you going to the breakfast bar?" she asked. "The chef makes omelets while you wait."

"As a matter of fact, I am feeling suddenly famished." He gave her bosom one last, lingering gaze. "I've been hungry ever since last night."

She rolled her eyes. "Then go eat—*food!* We have a meeting with Mr. Onyango in twenty minutes. I was afraid you might sleep right through it, lazybones."

"I see you've already been for a swim."

"And arranged for a boat to pick us up at noon. And ordered a box lunch from the kitchen. And packed my bags for Africana Sea Lodge."

"You do have a bad case of jet lag," Miles said sympathetically.

"On the contrary, I'm simply a very efficient person."

"And a very lovely person." He winked and rose to take his plate to the bar.

Lilia watched him walk away, a wash of shivers running down her spine at the backside view of his long, tanned legs, khaki shorts covering tight male buttocks, and a back that swelled into impossibly broad shoulders. If the truth be known, Lilia admitted to herself, it wasn't efficiency or jet lag that had brought her out of bed so early. She'd slept restlessly, wrestling with memories and struggling to put the rush of new emotions into place.

Then, at the first sound of the monkeys playing tag on the roof, Lilia had thrown off her sheet and bounded out of bed. But it wasn't the call of the sea or the joy of her first morning back in Africa that drew her. It was the anticipation of seeing Miles.

She covertly eyed him as he stood chatting with the chef near the small grill at which a fluffy omelet steamed. No doubt about it—the man was majestic. It wasn't only that head of unruly blond hair, or those unearthly blue eyes, or the bronzed glow of his skin. It was the sum of all of him. And the fact that he actually desired her, wanted her and intended to rebuild what they had lost filled her with a sense of wonder.

All night she had struggled with her feelings—tingles running through her at the memory of his hand on her breast, and at the same time fear curling into her stomach at the uncertainty of letting him take such liberties. With each kiss, she had opened to him a little further. With each touch, she knew she might be building a bond so strong that if it broke, it would almost kill her.

"Omelet," he said, setting his plate on the table. "Sausages. Hot, buttered buns. Fresh papaya. And passion fruit juice."

"Don't drink that," Lilia teased, taking his glass of pale yellow-green juice. "Too dangerous."

He caught her wrist and lifted the glass from her hand. Then in one motion, he downed the entire contents. Lilia held her breath. Head tipped back, he tapped out the last drop, then leaned forward across the table.

"Be on your guard tonight, my love," he whispered.

"I always am." She picked up her own glass and drank the last of the liquid. Then she ran her tongue over her lower lip. "But you're the one who had better look out, Miles Kane. Mine was passion fruit, too."

With a coy smile, she rose from the table, tossed her towel over her shoulder and sauntered out of the dining room.

Chapter 9

While Miles met with Mr. Onyango in his private office, Lilia wandered around Two Fishes Hotel taking careful notes on design elements she would like to incorporate in the Habari Safari project. The New Mexico hotel, she was happy to recall, included a wonderful winding swimming pool much like the one at Two Fishes. She had decided that the more she could intertwine fresh air and an outdoor feeling in each hotel, the closer it would approximate the true feeling of Africa.

Of course, a roof of thatched palm leaves would never meet the state building code, and gardens lined with palm trees and bougainvillea vines would not survive even a mild United States winter. There would be no monkeys snatching papaya from tourists' breakfast plates. There would be no open courtyards with African tribal dancers beating their zebra-skin drums.

All the same, Lilia believed she could approximate the ambience. Palm-leaf fans swirling the air around would lend a touch of the tropics. Huge windows would let in the sunshine. Warm red floor tiles would hold the heat.

Exotic plants—split-leaf philodendron, hibiscus and Bird of Paradise—could be grown indoors in the atrium area of each hotel. Outdoor walkways could be lined with aloe, yucca, African lilies and Cape honeysuckle vines for a wash of yellow, orange and green. Lilia decided that wood, wicker, tile, thatch, whitewash and soapstone would become her major design elements. The natural textures and peaceful, earthy colors would set off all the native artifacts in the room.

Her excitement grew as Lilia strolled through the Two Fishes dining room. She drew a rough sketch of the long food bars, each with its own small thatched roof to protect the bowls of fruit and baskets of bread. She had no doubt that even while on a luxury vacation, American visitors would expect their meals to arrive promptly. Fortunately, this fast-food mentality would be satisfied by the food, salad and fruit bars at the Habari Safari hotels. But as Lilia studied the Kenyan dining room, she decided the tableware in the American hotels would clearly set them apart from any drive-through burger joint.

She wanted tables draped in heavy, formal white cotton, set with glasses that shone in the lamplight, and gleaming with silverware that had some heft when a person lifted a knife or a fork. Each dining room ought to feel steeped in time, bathed in formality, wrapped in the genteel tradition the English had endowed upon their former colonies.

From the dining room, Lilia strolled through the Two Fishes lobby. She took notes on the color and cut of the staff uniforms and the design of the check-in desk, and she collected a few of the hotel's brochures. Miles caught up with her in the lounge area, where children swam down corridors of water out to the pool.

"Having any luck with the design?" he asked.

"It's all coming together beautifully." She smiled as he slipped his hand around her waist. "I'm glad I came with you to Kenya, Miles. Seeing the hotel has refreshed my memory, and things are really falling into place."

As they strolled out onto the open patio around the pool, Lilia shared some of her ideas. Miles listened carefully, nodding at each proposal. They found an empty table shaded by a thatched umbrella and ordered some fresh guava juice. Leaning shoulder to shoulder, they read through Lilia's notes. Miles made several suggestions, and she penciled them in.

"Could you design the landscaping for us, Lilia?" he asked. "Are you trained in that area?"

She shook her head. "You'll have to contract that project out to a professional landscaper. But if you agree, I'd like to oversee the design. Especially the plant selection. If you're not careful, you'll have pathways lined with jonquils and tulips instead of red-hot pokers and canna lilies."

"You're hoping to use native African flora?"

"As much as possible." She took a sip of juice as she thought over what she had been pondering. "Miles, if animals indigenous to eastern and southern Africa can survive winter in the southwestern United States, it stands to reason that a lot of the plants can, too. But we'll have to be careful not to introduce anything too foreign or so prolific that it might endanger the native groundcover."

"We wouldn't want to anger our cattlegrowing neighbors."

"Or upset the ecology. You know, the prickly pear cactus was introduced to Kenya from America. It propagates so readily that it's now considered a noxious weed in Kenya—especially in the Rift Valley. We wouldn't want to turn around and introduce an African plant that would become an American pest."

"Absolutely not. It's the same with the animals. I've spent the past two years working in a lot of different areas. But one of my major concerns has been to ensure that the barriers we build will be strong enough to keep all our animals enclosed. And even if they did escape, we're making certain we don't bring in any breed that would threaten local wildlife or domestic animals."

Miles turned his glass around and around in a damp circle on the glass-topped table. "I only have to think about the rabbits that were introduced to Australia," he said, "or the starlings that were brought into the United States, and a shudder of dread runs right through me. If I thought I were responsible for bringing in a permanent pest..."

"You won't be." Lilia covered his hand with hers. "Miles, I really admire the care you're taking with this project."

He looked into her gray eyes and read the understanding that seemed to flow back and forth between himself and this woman. "My future is riding on this, you know," he confessed. "It's a lot of responsibility. You can't imagine the amount of money being invested in this project. If we design and build these buildings, and we import hundreds of animals... and then if nobody shows up to patronize the hotels ... if it fails ..."

He raked a hand through his hair. "Sometimes I lie in bed at night and my stomach ties itself into knots. There are days I would do almost anything to be a game warden again. Tracking down a rogue elephant is nothing compared to this."

Her eyes softened. "But you've always been a risk-taker, Miles. You've always plunged ahead without taking much heed for consequences or hardships. I would have been surprised if you had become a man afraid of his own shadow."

He had to smile at the image. "Not likely, was it? All the same, when I proposed the adventure hotel project, I had no idea I'd be put in charge of it. Nor how much was involved in setting it up. It's not only planning and building the hotels themselves. It's the animals. They're my passion, and if I fail them, I'll feel I've failed altogether."

"You won't fail. Your experience and concern for the wildlife is exactly the reason Habari Safari put you in charge."

"I suppose you're right. Peter Hancock, the general manager in Zambia, called me into his office one day. I'll never forget that." Miles linked his fingers with Lilia's. "I'd been put in charge of arranging the tours for four hotels at the time—in Zambia and Malawi. When Peter summoned me that morning, I imagined that some tourist might have left her handbag on a tour bus, or some such. Lost all her credit cards, that sort of thing. Then Peter said to me, 'Kane, you've really done it this time.' I couldn't think what he meant, though I've never exactly gone by the company's rules. 'Kane,' he said, 'you've been booted upstairs. The London branch has put you in charge of the new project you proposed. Well done, young man.' Then he handed me a set of airline tickets, and off I went. From that moment on, it's been nonstop travel, a hundred meetings a month, new problems at every turn—"

"And then you had to run into a reluctant interior designer."

"Working with you has been the easiest part." He leaned back in his chair and took a deep breath. "In fact, this is the first time since that day in Peter's office that I feel relaxed. It's as if I'm on holiday."

"A busman's holiday. Did your meeting with Mr. Onyango go well?"

"He's had a lot of experience, and he's extremely intelligent. I think his marketing strategies in Europe will pay off for us in the United States. People flock to Kenya from all over the continent. Honeymooners, families, businessmen. I should think we can draw the same type of clientele if we handle the promotion carefully."

"I noticed there were no honeymoon suites planned in the hotels. Don't you want me to design some special luxury rooms?"

"It never occurred to me." Miles mused on that for a moment. He lifted his head, his blue eyes almost depthless. "We didn't have a honeymoon."

Lilia turned her head and studied the sea for a moment. "We never had a marriage, Miles."

"We had a wedding. We both agree on that."

"The marriage was annulled."

"On paper."

"And in my heart." She closed her notebook and slipped it into her bag. "I think that's the part that really counts."

Miles watched as she stood beside her chair. Her tall, slender body called to him now more than ever. Her beautiful smile and caring nature had never faded. Perhaps the evanescent waif now wore a touch of sadness—the sobering depth that life's realities had brought. It only made her seem more whole to him, more womanly. More desirable.

"We're supposed to meet the boat in fifteen minutes," she said, shouldering her bag. "I'm going up to my room to change. See you on the beach."

He couldn't answer as she turned and walked away from him. Perhaps their marriage—their young love—had died in her heart. But as he watched her climb the white stairs, her dark hair sifting in the ocean breeze and her hand lifted in a greeting to one of the hotel staff, Miles knew that nothing inside him had died.

He had married Lilia Eden ten years ago. It was time they had a honeymoon.

She was chatting with the African boatman when Miles walked down the beach fifteen minutes later. A cotton T-shirt topped her purple bathing suit, and a long towel hung from her waist to her ankles.

"Ndiyo," she said. *"Ni sawa sawa tu."*

The boatman nodded. *"Hakuna matata, memsahib."*

Lilia turned and spotted Miles. Her face lit up. "Miles, this is Juma. We've agreed on a price for a three-hour outing to the reef. *Juma, huyu ni Miles Kane. Bwana mkubwa."*

Juma chuckled and held out a hand. *"Jambo, bwana."*

"What's so funny?" Miles asked.

"Oh, I told him you were a very important man. But I don't think such things really matter to a man like Juma." Lilia waded out into the water toward the long, brightly painted outrigger. "He's got his own sense of what's important in life."

Lilia tossed her towel and bag over the thick side of the carved canoe. Countless times she had performed exactly that motion of swinging her things into one of these African outriggers. The slightly spongy feel of the wood, the slick painted sides, the unwieldy framework of the two bamboo rigs that kept the boat balanced all felt so familiar.

The boat ran about twelve feet from stem to stern, and Juma had decorated it with his own special patterns and signs. Supa boat #1, read the yellow lettering along one side. The hull bore bold streaks of red and blue, and thinner wavy lines in gray and yellow. The rudder, with its narrow steering mechanism, had been painted yellow. Near the prow rose a tall mast with a lateen-rigged triangular black sail tied to a bamboo pole.

"I used to be able to scramble into one of these boats," Lilia lamented as Miles helped her over the tall side. Once

seated, she gazed out across the blue water toward the reef.
Colin would have been enchanted by the seascape. Again,
she was stricken with the realization that the little boy was
no longer a part of her life. Even this far away from him, she
continued to turn her thoughts in his direction, wondering
what Colin would think of this or how he would like that.

Swallowing against the ache of memory, Lilia once again
instructed herself to stop denying that she had lost Colin.
She had to get on with life. She had to grow past the anger.
She had to stop tacking "if only" on to every thought. She
had to cease silently trying to barter with God to return
Colin to her arms. It was time to forge hope out of grief and
take pleasure in the new day.

Lilia willed all thoughts of Colin to the back of her mind
and turned her focus on Miles. Ankle-deep in surf, he was
assisting Juma in shoving the canoe over the sand and
through the seaweed. Once it was afloat, they climbed in,
and Juma began to pole his craft through the shallows.

It was a matter of skilled navigating as they slowly floated
toward the reef. The low tide caused the boat to run aground
on sandbars or vegetation-covered coral. Then Juma would
hop down into the waist-high water and pull his boat into a
clear channel.

"We used to pick up shells," Lilia told Miles. "Colin
would have loved to—"

Catching herself, she glanced at Miles. He touched her
hand. "What sort of shells?"

"You could find everything out here. Cowries, huge
clams and the most gorgeous conches. Now I know that we
were contributing to the death of the ecology. In those days,
we didn't understand how fragile it was. All the same, I'm
thankful it hasn't been destroyed... you can still see the
starfish and the shells and the coral."

"And the sea urchins." Miles was studying the spiny little devils as the boat passed through the clear, almost crys-
talline water.

"When you get out of the boat, don't put your feet
down," Lilia warned. "They're tucked into every coral
crevice imaginable. If you step on those black spikes, we'll

be spending the rest of our time here pulling them out of your feet.''

"Great ghosts," he said as the boat passed over a patch of coral darkened with urchins. "There must be millions of them.''

"Fearsome, aren't they? But you should see the shells beneath their spines—perfectly round and pale purple with tiny bumps all over them. They're as thin as eggshells and just as fragile. I used to have a whole collection in my room.''

"Glad I brought rubber-soled shoes.''

Once the boat reached deeper water, Juma unfurled his sail, and they cut through the waves. The reef kept all sharks away—a strong, unbreachable barrier. At low tide, the lagoon within it was a skin diver's paradise.

When Juma tossed his coral anchor overboard, Miles and Lilia donned masks and snorkels and tumbled into the warm salty water. Lilia knew she had come home. Her feet drifted down and her T-shirt floated up, and she began to swim slowly around the outcroppings of coral that rose from the sea floor.

Miles gestured from a distance, and she kicked toward him. He slipped an arm around her shoulders and pointed to a small crevice in the coral head. Within the darkness, a school of tiny fluorescent blue fish darted back and forth. The intruders watched for a while, then swam toward a pair of black-and-white-striped fish. Each was shaped like a triangle, and each wore a beautiful long ribbon that flowed from its back fin.

The spiny black sea urchins were a menace, but it wasn't too hard to avoid them. Lilia showed Miles a poisonous lionfish, its feathery fins each tipped with deadly venom. But the fish merely observed them from its coral cave until they swam away. Sea cucumbers like giant gray slugs lay motionless on the sandy floor. Starfish with bright red or orange points were abundant. And always, there were the schools of brilliantly colored shimmering tropical fish.

As much as Miles enjoyed the tropical ocean paradise, most of his attention stayed on the drifting mermaid who swam just ahead. It was the sight of long, firm legs and a gauzy white T-shirt that motivated him to keep his goggles polished. Lilia's slender waist beckoned him more than any orange-iced starfish, and more than once he swam against her and slipped his hands around the flesh just above her hips.

It was a tantalizing dance. Miles felt like some mesmerized sailor being drawn ever farther out to sea by the lure of the Siren. Lilia swam from one coral head to the next, then paused to wave a beckoning hand. By the time Miles had reached her, had observed whatever magical fish she wanted him to see, had lifted a hand to stroke her bare arm or the long curve of her neck, she was off again with a tempting flash of leg and the delicious swell of rounded bottom.

If Lilia was a mermaid, Miles felt like nothing more seaworthy than a lumbering rhinoceros. He was a strong swimmer, but he knew there wasn't an ounce of grace to his strokes. While Lilia darted this way and that, dived almost to the sea floor and then shot to the surface, Miles doggedly stroked along after her. He knew her dance was nothing more than sheer excitement at being back in the sea again after so many years. But the sight of her always just ahead, her dark hair adrift and her T-shirt floating around her breasts, enchanted him beyond belief.

When the outrigger was just a dark notch in the distance, Miles finally managed to nab Lilia as she was cruising around a chunk of coral. He caught one slender ankle and held her in place until his arms locked firmly around her waist.

Beneath the water, gray eyes the color of the ocean depths stared at him in anticipation. Or was it dismay? With faces covered by goggles and mouths encumbered by snorkels, there could be no underwater kiss. That didn't stop Miles wanting one.

Through the crystal seawater, he could see Lilia searching his face, wariness written in her eyes. Her hands drifted at her sides as he pulled her against his full length. Hard and hungry, he would have liked nothing more than to pleasure his mermaid as only a man could do. He knew she would feel the effect her dance had had on his body. The moment their hips touched, she shook her head and cupped his shoulders.

Using his shoulders for leverage, she pushed upward until her head shot out of the water. "Miles," she spluttered, spitting out her snorkel. "Miles, please don't start this."

He surfaced and tugged off his gear. "Lilia, I can't spend hours in the water with you and not feel anything."

"Then go back to the boat."

"I want to hold you." He took her arm and floated her against him a second time. Their feet drifted downward to anchor on a raised bed of soft sand. "I want you to know what you do to me. You're the most beautiful, most desirable woman I've ever known."

"Miles—"

"I want to make love with you, Lilia."

A rivulet of water ran down the side of her face. She pulled off her goggles and brushed at her cheek. Her hair, plastered to her head, made her look innocent, almost childlike. Miles wondered if he'd crushed her with his bold statement. She swallowed and tucked her bottom lip between her teeth.

"Lilia." He ran his hand down her arms, then under the shoulder-high water to her fingers. "You can't be surprised."

"I'm not... It's just that you told me you'd keep your distance. You said you wanted to earn my trust."

"I'm trying." His hands tightened on hers. "I'm doing my best to be decorous and gentlemanly—everything you say you want from me. But, Lilia, I'm human. I've never been successful at restraining myself from what I want. Especially not with you. If I pretend I don't want you, I'm lying to myself and to you. I want you in my arms... in my bed."

She looked toward the boat. "You know I won't agree to it."

He had to smile. "I didn't expect you to. You didn't the first time I told you what I wanted."

"No, I guess I didn't." She gave him a shy grin, just as she had so many years before.

He couldn't resist drawing her closer, sliding one hand up her back to press her breasts against his chest. Beneath the T-shirt and her bathing suit her nipples had beaded up. The stiff peaks were a pair of brazen interlopers belying her bashful words.

"In those days," he said, tracing a line from droplet to droplet down her neck, "you rejected me on moral and religious grounds. You were saving yourself for your husband, as I recall."

"My beliefs haven't changed, Miles," she returned. "But now there's more reason than ever to deny your blatant intentions."

"Blatant, am I?"

"Always." She laughed, but the touch of his fingertip on her breast made her breath catch. "Miles, it wouldn't be wise for us to make love. You know that."

"I only know how you make me feel."

Lilia's damp, spiky lashes lowered. She shivered as his hand cupped her wet breast. "It's been a long time . . . ten years . . . since I felt this way. I could so easily fall . . ."

"Lilia," he said, capturing her mouth in the kiss he had been denied all morning. Her hands slipped around his chest to his back and her legs moved along his, thigh against thigh. She parted her lips to him eagerly this time. Miles took her, demonstrating with velvet elegance the rhythmic stroke the rest of his body longed to play inside her.

A wave lifted them, pressed their hips together, sank them into a trough that tangled their legs before setting them on the sand again. Miles could feel Lilia's hunger for him blossom as her fingertips worked the muscles of his back. He kissed her lower lip, her eyelids, her cheeks, savoring the salty trace of the sea.

"Lilia," he whispered, "don't hold back. I can feel what you want from me."

She trembled as he gently tugged the bodice of her bathing suit lower and lower. "Miles, we're adults now."

"All the more reason. I want to know you as a woman." The T-shirt floated up and her top rumpled down to expose the full, bare rise of her bosom. He held his breath as he rolled the tight fabric over the crest of one breast. Its rosy tip, taut with the cold, blossomed into his hand.

"Lilia, I . . ." he groaned. "You're more beautiful than I ever dreamed."

Before she could slip away, he bent and nudged the tip of her breast with his lips. Gasping, she caught his head, tangling her fingers through his wet hair. He flicked her nipple with his tongue, then slowly drew a circle around and around it.

"If you keep on . . ." she moaned.

"I will keep on."

He pulled the top of her bathing suit down to expose her other breast. Certain he was in heaven, Miles slipped his hands around her fullness, savoring the ripe, womanly way her breasts rose from her chest. She was heavy and round, made for a man's loving . . . and a baby's suckling.

He tried to shake off the intruding thought—that he could never give her children. "I want you," he said, lifting his head. "But only when you're ready to give me everything, Lilia."

She made as if to back out of his arms, but he held her tightly, savoring the pressure of her bare breasts against his wet skin.

"I'm not ready to give you anything," she said. "Miles, this is all happening too fast. I'll admit I feel the old feelings . . . and a lot of new ones."

"You're a woman now."

"But I'm not sure you're the man I want to let in, Miles."

"Because you're afraid."

"You said it, not me."

The bright sunshine was drying her hair, and the breeze that cut along the tops of the waves lifted the dark brown strands to toss them against her cheek. Miles raised a dripping finger and drew a line along the curve of her jaw. If he won her body again, he knew he would feel victorious . . . a king lion with his prized mate. But would that be enough? Could he go back to his old life knowing he'd bonded with Lilia Eden again, won entrance to her sexuality but failed to win her heart?

"There's Juma on his way over to us," she said softly, tugging her bodice up over her breasts and then pulling her T-shirt hem to her waist. "We ought to eat those lunches I ordered."

Before he could think of a way to end the moment, she had ducked under the water and slipped out of his arms to swim toward the boat. Miles watched her go, her long arms cutting through the turquoise water and her brown hair as sleek and shiny as a shell.

No, he decided. Making love with Lilia wouldn't be enough. He wanted more than just her beautiful body. He needed more than sweet surrender beneath the Southern Cross.

What he wanted, Miles realized, was his wife.

Chapter 10

The Africana Sea Lodge had assigned Miles and Lilia adjoining rooms. Rooms wasn't exactly the right term, for the hotel was actually a cluster of large, round bungalows in the shape of huts. Unlike traditional African huts of mud and wattle, however, these had been built of concrete block. Whitewashed and roofed with thatch, each bungalow had a porch, large windows and a view of the sea. Winding pathways connected the individual huts to lead guests toward the compound that housed the lobby, gift shop, kitchen and dining rooms.

After transporting their luggage from Two Fishes to the Africana Sea Lodge that afternoon, Miles met privately with the manager. Lilia used the time to stroll the grounds and jot down notes. Her notebook bustled with a hundred new ideas and sketches for the Habari Safari wildlife adventure hotels. Kitenge cloth bedspreads...mosquito netting hung from the ceiling over each bed for effect...tables for afternoon tea on the veranda...special rooms, each focused around a specific animal theme—the Rhino Room, the Elephant Suite, Giraffe Lounge, Hippo Bar and Grill... bamboo-slatted shutters on the windows....

"A swim before dinner?"

Lilia glanced up from her portfolio to find Miles leaning against a palm tree near her table by the pool. A wash of adrenaline spilled through her at the sight of him—a figure still unexpected and yet so familiar. His hair glowed with the golden light of the setting sun, and she thought how unreal he seemed to her even now. She knew his eyes and his voice and his clothes—khaki shirt and shorts slightly rumpled. He was the same as ever, only taller, broader, more solid. But how could this man by the palm tree really be Miles?

Lilia swallowed. Could she have lost Colin and found Miles in the space of a few short days? Had she really flown all the way to Kenya? Was she actually sitting at the edge of Diani Beach staring at the man she had once loved in such ecstasy and lost in such pain?

"The water will be warm, you know. Just right for a quick dip." He started toward her. Sunset bronzed his bare thighs, bathing each muscle in light. He was Africa to her—evocative, compelling, sensuous . . . and no longer a part of her life. Or was he?

"Lilia?" His eyebrows raised expectantly.

"No," she said, more in answer to her own question than to his. "I mean . . . I don't think I'll go swimming."

"Too much sun?"

"I'm buried in paperwork right now."

He pulled out a painted wicker chair and sat down beside her. "You look a little pink." His finger traced a line along the tender bridge of her nose. "But I expect you'll go brown."

She looked down at her sketch of a hotel room. It was so much easier to stay detached from him when she was concentrating on her work. But he was a part of the project, inescapable.

"I think my tanning days are over. I'll probably peel," she said, letting her notebook fall onto her lap as she shut it.

"Wait." He slid a hand between the pages. "Let me see what you've done."

Aware of the pressure of his hand—separated from her thigh by only a few thin pages—Lilia opened the book. He bent over, giving her a view of the back of his head. A clean, herbal scent drifted up. He must have showered and shampooed after their swim. She formed a mental image of him standing beneath a stream of hot water, his naked body dripping. Steam rising from his broad shoulders. Rivulets running over his flat brown nipples, down his bare chest. Droplets forming in the coarse growth of the male hair at the base of his stomach. . . .

Stifling the picture, she focused on his head again. She could almost count the different colors in his hair—pale, white-gold mingled with tawny streaks, then sun-ripened wheat blending to soft caramel. Natural curl turned individual locks randomly this way and that. The ends had grown over his collar in a thick ruffle. She closed her fingers around the arm of her chair to keep herself from touching him.

From behind, his shoulders seemed broad, immense. Maybe it was an optical illusion brought on by the seam of his shirt running from sleeve to sleeve. But then Miles placed a finger on her notebook, and his shirt stretched tightly over the muscle. No illusion. Her fingers hadn't lied that morning in the ocean when she'd dug them into solid flesh.

If only she could rest her cheek on that fragrant mane of golden hair. Her eyes blurred at the thought. Unable to resist, she reached out a hand and laid it on his shoulder.

He lifted his head. "This is great, Lilia! What colors do you have in mind?"

She looked blankly at her sketch, then let her hand drop to her portfolio. "Oh . . . natural tones. Terra-cotta. Clay. Cream. Bronze and copper."

"Nothing bright?"

"What would you like?"

"I'm for yellow." He sat up. "The color of sunrise over the Indian Ocean."

She had to smile at the image. "Sounds good to me."

"Remember the morning after our wedding? We lay on the sand near the cliffs and watched the sun come boiling up out of the water."

"Miles . . ."

"You remember it."

She nodded. "I'll find that yellow."

"Give me a whole wall painted in it. I want to remember that morning with you." Leaning back in his chair, he took her hand and laced his fingers between hers.

"I was thinking of Maasai colors," she interjected, hoping to prevent him taking a trip down memory lane. "You know, their tribal shields, their beads and the clothes they wear? Red, gray, black, green."

"And yellow." He winked at her. "Do you know what I was just thinking, Lilia?"

"No." She wasn't sure she wanted to.

"I was thinking that it might have been yesterday that we slipped out of our rooms and got married."

"It wasn't yesterday, Miles."

"It feels that way, though. This is the same beach, the same sunset, the same water. Same tourists, for all we know."

"These aren't the same people."

"How can you be sure of it? Have a look at that hefty chap in the leopard-print thong. Same protruding stomach, same burnt feet, same glass of Pimms in his hand. That's the same bloke who was here yesterday when I asked you to marry me, isn't it?"

"No."

"Quite sure, are you? I reckon we've fallen into one of those sort of time machines. Here we are, Miles and Lilia, on the beach in Africa. Just got married last night." He studied her for a moment, then gave an exaggerated frown. "By George, you've cut your hair since last night, Lilia."

She had to laugh. "Oh, Miles. You know it wasn't yesterday. Everything's changed, not just my hair."

"So...is Africa different for you, Lilia?" His tone was suddenly serious.

"It still holds the same appeal, the same mystery. There's an aura about the people and the countryside that I don't think will ever fade for me. But something's different. Maybe it's not Africa that's different. Maybe it's me."

"Have I changed?"

"A lot."

"For the better, I hope."

"You're more sure of yourself. More settled." She picked at the corner of her notebook. "You have more control of your thoughts and your actions. At least, I think so. Although, judging from your behavior in the ocean this morning—"

"I showed admirable restraint, if you ask my opinion." He grinned at her lack of enthusiasm over his boast. Running a hand through his hair, he gave a stretch. Then he leaned forward, elbows on the table. "What is it you don't like about me, Lilia?"

Taken by surprise, she stared at him for a moment. "What do you mean?"

"What holds you back? Bad memories? Fear of the future? Am I too uncivilized? Not patient enough?"

"All of the above. Except the uncivilized part. I don't mind that."

"Good thing. It's the only part I'm not certain I can change."

She listened to the soft, hollow ring of the bamboo dinner chimes. "You can't change my painful memories, Miles. Not any more than I can change yours. And you can't promise me a future I could be happy with."

"How do you know that?"

"Miles, please let's go to dinner." She stood.

He caught her arm. "Not yet. Tell me why you don't think I can give you a future, Lilia."

"Because the future I wanted...the future I still want...is with a little brown-eyed boy named Colin." Sucking in a breath at the sudden hurt her words unleashed, Lilia pulled her arm out of Miles's grasp and wrapped it around her portfolio. "I'm sorry...I can't stop thinking about him."

"Lilia." His voice was soft, compassionate. "A future with Colin has been taken from you, love. Does that close the door to everything else?"

She swallowed at the aching lump in her throat. "The future I'll be happy with isn't to go backward ten years in a time machine. My future is ahead of me...and...Miles, it doesn't include you."

Before he could argue, she turned and started for her room. "I want to put my notes away," she called over her shoulder. "I'll meet you at our table."

It was the boy, then. Miles gritted his teeth as he watched Lilia walking back toward him from the dessert bar in the dining room. The thick slice of chocolate cake on her plate had put the hint of a smile on her lips, and she looked gorgeous. A sea breeze through the open windows blew her thin cotton dress tightly against her body. He allowed his gaze to trace down her slender length from the pink tinge of her cheeks to her long neck and straight shoulders, from the delectable crests of her breasts to the sway of her hips, the turn of her legs, ankles, feet. He wanted her.

And she wanted Colin.

Miles stuck a fork into his lemon tart. The crust cracked and crumbled onto the white plate. So she was right, after all. He was powerless to provide her with a happy future. Certainly not one that included him. Colin had been snatched away. Nothing Miles could do about that. Except provide her with another child—one of her own flesh and blood. But of course, he couldn't give her that, either.

So, he didn't belong in her life anymore. Any illusions he might have had about reliving the past or building a new life with Lilia were just that—illusions. He was left with a choice. He could ignore her, become merely the business associate she'd said she wanted. Or he could continue trying to break down the distance between them.

With dogged pursuit, he might win her body and claim the prize that was beginning to haunt him every minute with its urgency. And he could force himself to accept that he would never hold her heart again, never earn her trust, never build her a future. She would be merely a warm and willing sexual partner, nothing more. But what was so wrong with that?

He studied Lilia as she sat down across the table from him. Her eyes sparkled in the candlelight. Her mouth promised hours of pleasure. Dropping his gaze, he observed the pair of taut peaks lying in aching readiness for his touch. He imagined her velvet stomach pressed against his, her legs parted, her sweet, womanly pleasures welcoming his penetration.

Another week of constant company, he reasoned, would provide ample opportunity to sample the ecstasy ten years had denied him. But could a week of lovemaking—or a month, for that matter—replace the decade of marital love he had lost? No.

Miles twisted his fork through the lemony custard in his tart. He wanted to sleep with Lilia Eden. No denying that. Could he simply treat her as a brief affair? Why not? She had made it clear there would be nothing else for them. No future. No permanence. No love.

Sex, then. Maybe that would at least soothe the ache.

"How's the cake?" he asked.

Lifting her eyes heavenward, she licked her lips. "Delicious. I suspect there's rum in it." A forkful of crumbly chocolate torte hovered just in front of her mouth. "Aren't you going to try your tart?"

He glanced down at the demolished dessert. "Not hungry, I'm afraid."

"I can't seem to get enough. Maybe it's the swimming. Or the fresh air. I don't know, but I remember feeling this way years ago. Walking all those miles on the beach must have done it. Chasing those kids . . ." Her words faltered, and he saw her eyes soften.

"Lilia—"

"Miles, I shouldn't have been so blunt about Colin. I know he's gone, but I can't stop wanting him." She sucked in a trembling breath. "Needing him. He was an important part of my life. He was everything. It's hard to let go."

"I know." He pushed back his plate. "I have trouble letting go of what was important in my life, too."

Her gray eyes caught his. He watched as she set her fork on the rim of her plate. "Miles, try to understand."

"I do understand. I understand perfectly." He couldn't keep the bitter note from his voice. "You loved me once, married me, lost me, got over me, and that was that. Similarly, you loved Colin, took him into your home, lost him and now you're trying to get over him. Once you've succeeded, you'll be reluctant to admit any child back into your heart. Even Colin—especially if you're not quite sure you'll have him forever. Or have him in exactly the same way you did before. You'd be afraid to risk the hurt again. You wouldn't want it to start all over.''

"No, I wouldn't," she whispered.

When she looked up, Miles was dismayed to see a tear hanging from the end of one of her lower lashes. He'd made her cry with his thoughtless recounting of her most personal pain. Damn!

"Lilia, I'm sorry." He reached for her hand.

She tucked it into her lap. "It's all right."

"No, I—"

"Why don't we dance...I can hear the band by the pool." She rose and brushed her skirt with her napkin. "Let's not talk about anything else tonight, okay?"

She held out a hand. He took it and stood from his chair. Walking behind her, he studied the fragile strength in her shoulders. She was a gazelle, all beauty and skittishness and inner power. He, on the other hand, was a prowling lion, a predator heedless of anything but his own need, his own hunger. He would never earn her trust. Didn't deserve it. Wouldn't know what to do with it if he had it.

But then she turned into his arms and laid her cheek against his shoulder. Her eyes drifted shut. As he slipped his hand around her back and began to sway her to the music, she let out a deep sigh. Her long lashes cast blue shadows on her cheeks. He bent and kissed the soft curve, only to find it damp from the tear he had summoned with his cruel words.

"Lilia," he whispered, "about Colin—"

"Shhh." She spread her fingers across his back. "Kiss me again, Miles. Make me forget everything."

He touched his lips to her cheek, then her ear. Her hair smelled of roses, soft and warm and velvet against his skin. He dipped his nose among the strands and kissed her temple. She purred.

At the sound, the male lion inside him roused to instant alertness. Untamed, it ignored Miles's determination to remain calm, tender, sensitive and gentlemanly with this lovely gazelle. A mating instinct focused his attention on the brush of a pair of firm female breasts against his chest. He felt his breath shorten.

Lilia moved against him, her thighs stroking his with every step. A hunter suddenly onto a scent, he slipped his hand down her back and tucked her pelvis firmly to his. Her eyes shot up in surprise. He smiled. She let out a breath, and he heard its ragged edges.

So... she was aroused, too. Instantly, the lion bolted in a heated course down his chest to settle in his loins. Waiting, lurking. He could feel its heaviness, its rigid tension.

"Smell the frangipani?" she asked, her breath stirring the hair on his neck. "There must be a tree near the pool."

He lifted his nose to the scent. Her lips brushed his bare neck. The lion arched its back, tail twitching. "Lilia," he said. "Do that again."

She rose on tiptoe and her breasts grazed up his shirt. Her mouth parted against the skin on the side of his neck. Wet. Hot. Her tongue darted out to moisten his flesh. The lion poised, muscles swollen and hard, reflexes humming with anticipation.

Miles turned from the poolside dance floor onto the graveled path and began to walk. Lilia slipped both arms around his waist, laid her head on his shoulder, leaned her hip against his. He tipped her chin and bent to kiss her mouth. She stopped, breathing hard.

"The moon has made me crazy," she whispered. He saw it in her eyes, silver and glossy. "I can't think."

"Then kiss me, instead." Before she could reason him away, he slid his hands behind her head and claimed her. Soft, damp, her lips tasted of chocolate and rum. He stroked the seam of her mouth. Tentative and silken, she met his touch.

With a growl that set Miles's loins on fire, the lion demanded satisfaction. He parted her lips, explored, gave promise of a rhythmic dance. She shivered, gently plundered. His hands covered her shoulders, pulled her closer. Her breasts swelled against his chest, and the lion began to roar.

"Miles, I should go to my room," Lilia murmured. "I'm... I'm tired."

He took her hand and drew her down the walkway, then into the shadows of the porch that joined their rooms. Before she could make polite, departing noises, he pulled her into his arms again. This time her hands wound around his neck and her mouth met his in equal ardor. Her fingers slid into his hair, winding and knotting as his kiss deepened.

He spanned her waist with his hands, fitting her against his arousal and then running his palms over the taut, rounded curves of her bottom. She moved one foot, widening her stance to fit him more intimately between her thighs.

With a carnivorous snarl of hunger, the lion lifted its head in a display of male dominance. Miles fought to breathe.

"It's been so long," Lilia groaned. "I'm very...very..."

"Ready." He slid one hand over her breast, wrinkling the loose, gauzy fabric of her dress and confirming that what he had said was true. She was tightly tipped with need. When his palm grazed the crest of her breast, she sucked in a deep, shaking breath.

"Somehow that seemed safer in the ocean," she said.

"Safer than standing just outside your bedroom door?"

"Right." Her voice had gone husky.

"But equally pleasurable, I trust."

"More."

"Now...or in the ocean?" He caressed his thumb across her breast, aware that her hands had slipped down his back to maintain the pressure of his pelvis against hers.

"Now," she affirmed. And when he brushed the shoulder of her dress down her arm, she wriggled her hips in anticipation. "Definitely now."

Miles lowered the strap of her bra to reveal the rise of moondusted skin. The lion began to slink toward its prey in the rhythm of a hundred drums. Nothing could bind the urge to ultimate satisfaction. Miles slid the lacy edge of Lilia's bra downward until her breast pillowed into his bare hand. His fingers tipped her nipple, and his eyes watched it tighten, flame a dark pink and form a hardened bud.

Lilia's breath stumbled. Her hands began to knead his buttocks. He bent his head and took her nipple in his mouth, licking and savoring it. His tongue traced wet circles, then touched its tip again and again. He suckled, nipped, ran his lips up to her neck and searched her earlobe.

She tugged his shirttail from his trousers. Her fingers raked down his back, working the muscle, absorbing him. The sound of laughter floated through the air, and Lilia stiffened. Guests were walking down a path from the dining room.

Miles fumbled for his key, shoved it into the lock and pushed his door open. Drawing Lilia into his moonlit room, he leaned her against a cool wall. Her loose bodice dropped to her waist where it hung, trapped by the ribbon of a belt. He unsnapped her bra and let it fall. Taking her breasts in his hands, he bent to kiss them, first one and then the other.

Head leaning against the wall, she shut her eyes. Miles hovered over her, memorizing the dark peaks that touched his shirt, thinking that he would never need anything or anyone but this woman. Her silver eyes slid open, and her mouth parted.

"Miles, oh, please, don't stop now," she murmured. "If you let me think, I won't be able to do it."

But he wanted her to think. He wanted this passion between them to be more than an act of animal sexuality. He wanted it to be an act of her will.

Restraining the lion, he slowly unbuttoned his shirt. She placed her hands on his heated skin. Her fingertips traced the edges of his nipples. Her palms moved over ridged muscle and down to the flat plane of his stomach. She pulled his shirt away and dropped it to the floor.

"You're unbelievable," she whispered.

The message in her eyes sent the lion roaring again, and Miles caught her firmly against him. Her breasts crushed into his chest. His mouth fell on hers, ravenous. Again she parted her legs to him, and this time he slid one thigh firmly between them. He rumpled the skirt of her dress up her hip, his hand finding sleek, silky leg and then the cushion of round, womanly derriere covered by a scanty wisp of thin cotton.

"Lovely," he murmured. "Too lovely."

His fingers found their way beneath the fragile elastic. She shivered, and her breasts tingled against his chest. He could feel her hands slide down the front of his trousers, and he heard the sharp intake of air as she rubbed one palm down his hardened length.

"Miles, if you don't touch me this minute—" A sharp, shattering ring cut off her words.

"What?" Miles stiffened. "What the hell is ... damned telephone!" He took her shoulders as the strident bell sliced through the air a second time. "Not here ... not in the middle of Africa." Leading her to his bed, he pulled back the spread and seated her gently.

With one hand he stroked her shoulder. With the other he picked up the black receiver. "Kane," he said.

Lilia heard a female voice through the static on the other end. She took a deep breath. Suddenly aware of the open door, she pulled the bodice of her dress up over her shoulders.

"Who?" Miles asked more loudly. "Mum, is that you?"

His *mother!* Lilia flushed with heat. Spotting her lacy bra cup peeking out from under Miles's shirt on the floor, she felt like a naughty kid caught with her hand in the cookie jar.

"Yes, it's Miles," he said. His hand on Lilia's shoulder had gone cold. "Well, you needn't have phoned every hotel in Mombasa looking for me. I told him all I had to say to him."

Miles sank onto the bed beside her. She could see the rigid tension in his thighs. Looking across at her own bare legs, Lilia felt a wash of disbelief pour through her. What on earth was she doing in Miles Kane's bedroom? With her dress half off and her panties askew!

She and Miles weren't married, she reminded herself. She had no right to claim his body as if it belonged to her. Neither the desire to forget about Colin nor the dormant urges Miles had aroused in her gave her permission to simply fall into his bed.

He slammed his fist onto one knee. "No, I don't want to speak to him!"

Lilia shivered. Miles leaned forward, his bare shoulders knotted. She would have made love with him. So easily. So naturally. She would have done it without even thinking. And then what?

What price would she have paid this time? Would Miles walk away from her? He could do that. They were adults, after all. He had his own life. She had hers, as she'd so often reminded him. He could thank her for the lovely Kenyan holiday, and then jet off to Albuquerque or somewhere to build his hotels. And she would be left in Springfield, Missouri, with a battered heart.

On the other hand, what if they made love, and then Miles demanded that they take up where they had left off—as husband and wife? She didn't feel married to him anymore. She had spent ten years erasing that commitment. She couldn't ever again be that naive, that trusting teenager full of dreams. Life had taught her otherwise.

She did want to make love with Miles. No doubt about that. But was she willing to accept the consequences? She glanced at him just as he leaped to his feet and began to pace.

"Put Mum back on the line," he demanded. "No, I do not want to speak with you, Dad. You know why."

Lilia shrank into herself as she watched him stalking back and forth. The consequences of their first attempt at marriage still echoed. This phone call was a perfect reminder of the chaos they had created with their impulsive act.

"Mum, listen," Miles said. "No, you listen to me. Please. I said what I had to say to Dad. I don't want to discuss it anymore.... I *know* it was a long time ago. I realize he was doing what he thought best for me. That doesn't make it right."

He looked down at Lilia. She realized she was chewing on her lower lip. She should go. This wasn't part of her life—this man, these angry Zambian parents of his, this turmoil. She had her own world, her own separate reality. She was an interior designer from Missouri with a Victorian house on Walnut Street and a place in the alto section of the church choir.

"All right, put him on," Miles acquiesced. He lowered his head and rubbed his eyebrows. "What is it, Dad...? Yes, she is here in Mombasa with me. I beg your pardon? *What?*

Oh . . ." He looked up at Lilia, a slightly dazed expression on his face. For a moment he said nothing. When he spoke again, his voice was subdued. "Well, thank you. Yes, I accept it. I'll convey that. I said, I'll pass it along to her. All right . . . you, too."

Lilia tucked a strand of hair behind her ears. She stood and smoothed down the skirt of her dress. As she walked toward the open door, Miles caught her arm.

"Stay," he mouthed.

She shook her head. Leaning against his bare shoulder, she gave his cheek a kiss. "Good night, Miles."

As she slipped out onto the veranda, she heard him speaking into the phone again. "Mum, what's the matter now? No, don't . . . don't cry, Mum. Please, don't do that." She shut the door to his room, but Lilia could still hear his voice as she sat shivering on the veranda.

"No, Lilia doesn't know about it," he said. "Because I haven't chosen to tell her. I realize it's important, but the time . . . the time isn't right. Don't worry about it, Mum. I have to trust that when I do tell her, she won't stop wanting . . . she'll still feel . . . that it won't matter too much." He let out a sigh. "No, I'm not sure. I'm not sure at all."

Chapter 11

Curled into a chair on her private porch, Lilia listened for the expected knock. When she heard it, she shut her eyes and let out a breath. She could let Miles think she'd gone to sleep. Or perhaps that she was taking a walk or sitting on her porch and couldn't hear.

He knocked again, harder this time. "Lilia!" His voice would have woken half the hotel guests.

"Darn that man," she whispered. Lilia unrolled from the chair and wrapped her cotton robe more tightly around her neck. "Just a minute."

She went to the door, unlatched it and peeked through the slit. Miles was standing in a pool of moonlight, his shirt open down the front and his hands shoved into his pockets.

"Am I invited in?" he asked.

She glanced behind her at the still-made bed. "I, uh...I need to...I don't think so, Miles."

He leaned against the post that supported her roof. "Lilia, I think we should speak."

"It's very late. Almost midnight."

He let out a breath. "Come onto the veranda, then. I'll keep my hands in my pockets, how's that?"

She had to smile. "I'll believe that when I see it." Stepping out into the night, she felt the chill of the concrete floor creep up her bare feet. A woven wicker chair beckoned. Ensconced, she tucked her knees up under her chin and buried her toes beneath the robe.

"That was my parents," Miles began, jabbing a thumb in the direction of his room. "On the telephone."

"I gathered that."

"My dad's apologized."

Lilia lifted her head. "Apologized?"

"For lying to both of us. I know—I couldn't believe it, either. I've never heard a contrite word cross the man's lips. But he said he was sorry that he'd engineered our breakup. He's asked you to accept his apology."

A wash of amazement slid down Lilia's spine. Mr. Kane— that formidable fortress of a man—had asked her to forgive him for something he'd done ten years before. "Your mother must have talked him into it," she said.

"I don't think so." Miles studied the distant fringe of palm trees. "I think he realizes it was a mistake—separating us the way he did. He's seen how I chose to make my life. I think he knows I'd have done better with you by my side all along."

Lilia swallowed. "You've done very well without me, Miles. Surely your father sees that."

"In the business world. Oh, yes. He didn't like my jaunt as a game warden, but once I was into the hotel nonsense, I suppose I became almost acceptable to him. At least I was earning good money—always Dad's standard of success or failure. Now that I'm in charge of this wildlife hotel project in America, he seems to have accepted the route I chose."

Miles sat on the edge of a table and propped one foot in a chair. "It's the personal aspect to my life he thinks I botched."

"What do you mean?" Lilia held her breath. Was Miles going to reveal the mysterious *something* his parents were so distraught about? She had decided it must involve another woman. Maybe Miles had had a disastrous love affair after Lilia had gone back to the States. Maybe he had fathered a child. Or maybe he *had* married again—even though he'd told her he hadn't. There could be any number of things. Even . . . even a woman now.

Lilia glanced at Miles. He wasn't answering her question. Her heart began to thud. Maybe Miles was involved with a woman back in Zambia. Someone he lived with. Or . . .

"What do you mean about the personal aspect?" she repeated.

He looked at her. "I've not been much good with relationships since you. Mucked up any number of possibilities—in my father's opinion."

"What kind of relationships are we talking about here?"

"Any sort." He shrugged. "I told you Dad introduced me to a few women he thought suitable. I wasn't interested. Spent my time in the brush with the game. Focused on my work."

"Miles, are you married?" she blurted out.

"What?" He laughed.

"Are you married?" She looked down at the knot she'd made of her bathrobe. "I overheard you talking to your parents after I left your room. There's something you're not telling me. Some secret."

He let out a breath. She saw his Adam's apple run the length of his throat as he swallowed. "I'm not married, Lilia. I told you that straight off. I'm not married now, and never have been since you. Never lived with anyone. Never found anyone I cared about. Not after you."

She felt chastised. "Then . . ."

"In fact, as far as I'm concerned, I'm still married to you." He held up a hand. "I know you don't want to hear it. I know you've gone on with your life and all that. But I've never let go of the marriage we made, Lilia. I can't think what sort of woman could have come along to change that. And I also think that if you would stop and sort through it all, you'd agree that you haven't let go of our marriage, either. We're just as married as we were ten years ago. We want each other just as strongly—"

"No!"

"Yes, Lilia. You can't deny what was going to happen in there." He pointed at his room. "And you can't deny what's happening inside me is the same damn thing that's happening inside you."

"And what's that?"

"I don't know." He stood and walked to the bamboo railing. Leaning his arms on it, he studied the grass poking up through the sand. "I don't have a name for it. Commitment, perhaps. Love..."

"Not love."

"Why not?" He turned on her, his eyes hot. "Why is this so hard for you, when it's so easy for me? Don't you trust me anymore, Lilia?"

"I don't—"

"You would have trusted me with your body tonight. Wouldn't you? We'd have made love. If not for that phone call, we'd be in my bed right at this moment."

"It would have been a mistake."

"Why? For God's sake, why?"

"Because I don't trust...the situation or the future or any of it. I don't."

"Why not? What have I done to earn your doubt?"

"It's not you. Not only you. I've been taught to doubt in a series of lessons, Miles. First, it was losing you, then Colin—"

"I am not Colin, damn it!" He hammered his fist down on the railing. The bamboo splintered, shivered, separated. Both halves swung down to the ground.

"Hell." Miles shoved his hands into his pockets and stared at the broken railing. "I can't force you to trust me, can I?" he said more to the railing than to her. "I only break the things I try to force. I can't seduce you back into trusting me. I can't convince you with words. I don't know what it takes, Lilia."

"Time, I suppose." She placed her feet on the cool concrete again and stood slowly. Taking a porch post in her arms, she leaned her cheek against the smooth wood. "If I allowed myself to trust you, Miles," she whispered, "and gave you myself, body and soul, what then?"

He turned, his eyes soft and his shoulders low.

"You see," she said, "you're not sure, either."

Leaving him on the veranda, she entered her room. As she shut the door behind her, she realized that he still hadn't told her what it was that his parents were so worried about. It was something that might threaten every hope, every dream. And he was keeping it carefully secret.

"Buy whatever you want. We want to go first-class."

Every woman's fantasy, Lilia thought as she stepped out of the hotel van at the edge of Old Town Mombasa the following morning. She hadn't slept well and her eyes were gritty, but she was determined to put the past night's incident behind her.

She had made a natural mistake, she reasoned, swept away by the whisper of the waves and the silver light of the moon. As close as she had come to losing herself to Miles, nothing permanent had happened. The faux pas was erasable, and Lilia had made up her mind to blot it out. And never to let it happen again.

As she felt the heat from the sidewalk begin to warm her ankles, she heard Miles speaking with the van's driver. Earlier, they had stopped off at a bank to convert an enormous sum of dollars into uncountable shillings. His wallet filled with money for their purchases, Miles had acted the perfect business associate.

Shouldering her portfolio, Lilia gazed across the street at the massive structure built on huge pink coral blocks, with high walls, parapets, cannons, battlements and iron-barred gates. The imposing bastion stood on a coral ridge that projected into the Indian Ocean, and it had witnessed treason, murder, assassination, piracy and siege.

"Fort Jesus," she whispered.

Miles took in the landmark. "It's obviously not British."

"Portuguese. It was captured by the Arabs more than once, though. I can't count the hours I spent roaming through the fort, climbing the winding staircases, drifting under the arches, staring at the cannons. I used to imagine that Francisco de Seixas de Cabreira, age twenty-seven, was in pursuit of my hand in marriage."

"Who?"

Lilia took one look at his scowling face and had to laugh. "Francisco de Seixas de Cabreira, of course."

"Somebody you knew from school?"

"Not exactly. He was the captain of Fort Jesus in 1635." She closed her eyes and recited from memory the words inscribed over the outer gate of the fort. "'He subjected to His Majesty the people on this coast who, under their tyrant king, had been in a state of rebellion. He made the kings of Otondo, Mandra, Luziwa and Jaca tributary to His Majesty. He inflicted in person punishment on Pate and Sio, which was unexpected in India, extending to the destruction of their town walls. He punished the Musungulos and chastised Pemba, where in his own responsibility he had the rebel governors and all leading citizens executed.'"

"Friendly chap," Miles snorted.

Lilia grinned. "I didn't think I'd remember all that. I used to whisper the inscription to myself at night in bed as I was falling asleep. 'He made all pay tribute to His Majesty who had neglected to pay it. For these services he was made a Knight of the Royal Household.' A knight at age twenty-seven, Miles. Just think."

"So you had your heart set on a knight, did you?"

"What girl doesn't?" Lilia tucked her purse against her hip, thinking how absolutely sure she'd been that she had found her knight in Miles Kane. He was tall, handsome, brilliant, passionate and determined to rescue her from a fate worse than death—college in the United States.

Lighthearted at the memory, Lilia started across the street to Jubilee Hall. Now a curio shop, it had once been an important and attractive building erected to commemorate Queen Victoria's diamond jubilee in 1897. She had always loved the hall.

Miles followed, his thoughts still on the Portuguese soldier who had captured Lilia's imagination. He hadn't slept much the night before, and had been prepared to convey to Lilia his worst, most sullen mood. But when she failed to appear at breakfast, he had suddenly feared she might have fled back to America. He'd made a fool of himself dashing out of the dining room and pounding on her door until a passing maid had informed him that the *memsahib* had gone down to the beach for a swim.

Of course. Miles had walked down to the water's edge, his heart still pounding, and finally had located Lilia's dark head bobbing among the waves. Eventually, she had spotted him, waved a long arm and emerged from the water.

A white bikini. He had thought for a moment that he was dreaming. But no, she was wearing it—thin straps running over her shoulders, a pair of indecently small cups barely containing her wet breasts, a tiny thong that curved up over her buttocks and underlined her stomach.

Where had she gotten it? Miles still couldn't imagine. And why? Why a white bikini? Surely she knew what it would mean to him seeing her in it. But she had merely smiled and grabbed her towel. Tucking it around her waist, she had flung an arm in the direction of her room and promised to meet him at the van in fifteen minutes.

It was as though the night before had not occurred. As though nothing had happened ten years before. As though nothing were happening now. Was this how Lilia coped?

Miles watched her in the dimly lit interior of the curio shop. She was inspecting a stack of brass trays, clearly Indian in origin. Nibbling on her lower lip, she ran a fingertip over the dusty surface that had been etched and pierced with intricate designs. The dealer spoke in a low voice, obviously adjusting his price as Lilia considered his merchandise.

"What do you think, Miles?" she asked, turning to him.

"About...about the trays?" He could have given her a more succinct opinion on how he thought she looked in her skinny blue tank top and short black skirt. "Intriguing," he said.

"I don't know. He's asking a lot."

"How many trays would you wish to purchase, madam?" the dealer inquired. "Perhaps I can make you a better price."

Lilia winked at Miles before turning back to the trays. "Oh, I suppose we would want...maybe twenty."

"Twenty!" The dealer's mouth dropped open. "My goodness, that will be a very good number. Indeed, for such a special customer, I can lower the price by... three hundred shillings."

"Apiece?"

"Oh, no, madam." His head wagged from side to side. "For all. Please, these are magnificent trays. Finest brass from India. So beautiful. You will not find trays like this in all of Old Town."

"But maybe in Nairobi I'd get a better price."

"Surely not! You see, here in Mombasa we receive these trays directly from ship. We pay no transportation cost, madam. Here we have finest prices. Come now, I will take off five hundred shillings for all the trays."

Miles focused on a pile of brilliantly colored batiks. He sensed it was his turn to put in a doubtful word. "Perhaps we should look around a bit, Lilia. After all, this is the first shop we've been in. Maybe you'll find trays at a more reasonable price down the street."

"Seven hundred shillings." The dealer hoisted a tray in his arms and hurried across the room to Miles. "Best price. Best price in town, I assure you!"

Miles glanced at Lilia. She was scribbling something in her notebook. "You'll have to ask my..." He caught himself. "My associate. She's in charge of purchases."

"Indeed." The dealer swung his tray around and scurried back to Lilia. "Eight hundred shillings, madam. I cannot go any lower."

Lilia frowned at her paper. "I'll buy twenty-five trays and you knock off a thousand shillings total."

"Oh, madam." The man's face fell. "A thousand shillings is very difficult."

Giving him an even stare, Lilia started to put her notebook back in her purse. "Well," she sighed, "thank you, anyway—"

"Thirty trays," the man cut in.

"I only need twenty-five."

"Very well. I give you twenty-five. And nine hundred shillings off the original price."

Lilia smiled. "I'll pay cash."

The dealer's original dismay was quickly snuffed as he waved to his assistant to begin wrapping the trays. Leaping to a row of shelves, he gestured grandly. "And may I show you carvings, madam? I have the best Wakamba carvings in all of Kenya. Finest selection."

Lilia grinned at Miles and began to inspect the row of carvings.

Within fifteen minutes, she had purchased twenty-five trays, a stack of large batiks in jewel tones and ten hanging lamps in pierced copper. Miles gave the dealer the shipping address in the United States, and with a somewhat lighter wallet, he accompanied Lilia out of the shop.

They walked past the Mombasa Club, built in 1897. As when he was a young man, Miles found the buildings of Old Town intriguing and mysterious. A combination of Swahili, Arab, Indian and Portuguese architecture dating back several centuries, they seemed to lean against one another along the narrow, winding streets. Laundry lines stretched overhead from strange, rickety balconies crafted of carved wood or rusty iron. Built of coral and plaster, the houses had tin roofs and shuttered windows. Huge doors of carved wood and brass studs swung open to reveal long, narrow rooms, each opening onto the next, or airy courtyards where half-naked children played.

At the sight of the cavorting brown bodies, Lilia thought of Colin. Some of his ancestors had probably traveled through a town just like Mombasa—as slaves destined for the plantations of Missouri. Though the image cast a shameful light on her own ancestry, Lilia was somehow oddly pleased at the realization that Africa linked her to Colin. In a roundabout way, they were both children of this continent.

For once comforted by the memory of her lost son, Lilia turned her attention again to the city. It was hard to tell one style of architecture from the next, and even more difficult to distinguish shops from houses. Gabled roofs, finials, deep verandas and cunning towers, all mingled together in a state of romantic dilapidation. From open windows and doors spilled an unimaginable array of goods—spices, coffees, teas, fruit, vegetables, sandals, fabric and ready-made clothes. Vendors hawked ears of roasted corn, paper sacks of cashews, ripe mangoes, hot sausages. Arab men on street corners sold thick black coffee from large brass cone-shaped coffee urns.

A babel of languages—Swahili, Arabic, Gujarati, Hindi, English—swirled down the curry-scented streets. Muslim women draped in concealing black *buibui* hurried from shop to shop, their woven baskets filled with tomatoes, eggplant, live chickens, bananas. Indian women swathed in flowery saris or the *khurta* of Punjab minded their children while chatting in the alleys. Bangles, necklaces, earrings, anklets, nose studs and amulets added touches of feminine grace. Men went bare-chested, their loins wrapped in a single length of checkered fabric, or went about their business fully dressed in Western-style shorts, trousers, shirts, even ties.

It was a blend of cultures so diverse, so harmonious, so evocative, that Miles wondered how Lilia had learned to exist without it as part of her life. As they strolled down Mbarak Hinawy Road, he congratulated her on her skillful bargaining. A smile lighting her features, she stepped into the doorway of another shop.

"I'm the best barterer around," she confided jovially. "And once I start speaking Swahili, you'll hear the prices drop doubly fast."

"I knew I had hired an expert interior designer," Miles returned, "but I never guessed you were such an expert shopper."

Lilia chuckled. "You'll save a bundle. Bargaining is the way I grew up. I'll never forget the look on that saleslady's face in Springfield the first time I tried to talk down the price of a skirt at J.C. Penney's!"

By the time Lilia and Miles had traversed Mbarak Hinawy past Anil's Arcade, Arcaf House, Ali's Curio Shop and Mandhry Mosque, Habari Safari Hotels had become the owner of five hundred carved napkin rings, nine large Persian carpets, three sandalwood chests, three hundred lengths of *kikoi* and *kitenge* fabric in shades of red, green, black and bright sunrise yellow, three massive brass-studded Arab doors and a collection of handcrafts that included copper bowls, olive-wood statues, woven sisal Kikuyu baskets and soapstone carvings.

In Government Square, they stopped at what had been the Old Post Office, now a carpet and antiques shop. Lilia found several rare treasures to add to her growing collection. They passed the odorous fish market to indulge Lilia in a stop at the Scent Emporium. Founded in 1850, the shop boasted the largest range of nonalcoholic perfumes in Mombasa.

Miles purchased a flacon of perfume that mingled the heady tropical attar of rose, gardenia and frangipani. When Lilia dabbed the fragrance on her neck, Miles wondered if he'd made a mistake. It was all he could do to keep from taking his exotic enchantress in his arms.

More and more, she reminded him of the girl he had fallen in love with ten years before. She blended easily with the potpourri of cultures as she made her way down the street. She switched comfortably from Swahili to English, delighting the shopkeepers. Using her own money, she lined silver bangles up her bare arms and bought a pair of copper earrings that almost brushed her shoulders. She sipped Arab coffee, munched on roasted corn, laughed and joked with the shopkeepers and completely entranced Miles.

At lunch, they found a small Indian restaurant and dined on curry so hot that Miles's nose turned bright red and Lilia couldn't stop the tears that ran down her cheeks. She showed Miles how to eat with his hands in proper Indian fashion using a flat *chapati* to scoop up the rice and curry.

Glowing with pleasure at the mingled flavors, she insisted on trying a bowl of milky curd and a cup of lentil *dal*. They ate sweet cakes wrapped in thin silver foil for dessert, and then finished off the meal with a handful of licorice-flavored seeds that Lilia insisted were good for the digestion.

As they set off down Ndia Kuu Street for another round of shopping, it occurred to Miles that Lilia had slipped into her own element. She was as comfortable in Old Town Mombasa as he was tracking a cheetah through the Zambian brush. They were born of this third culture and would never be truly English or American, no matter what their language and citizenship might insist. No matter what Lilia herself might insist.

How had she made a life for herself in the middle of America? Was she actually happy there? Miles watched her babbling in Swahili to a carving vendor and wondered what would draw her back to that large old house in Missouri. She was here now, and obviously happy. Would she be willing to give up that American life she was so protective of and reenter this world that was foreign to most but home to her?

Miles sat on a stone bench and studied her from a distance. She was lost in this world now. At home here. Could he use this moment, this happy African holiday, to win her away from the life she had built for herself? Did he want to?

He watched her lift a carving of a gazelle and hold it to the sunlight. Her eyes sparkled and her mouth curved into a smile he hadn't seen since he'd found her again. She was happier in this third world. She belonged to it, as he did. Most importantly, Miles decided, she belonged to him.

And, yes, he would do everything it took to steal her away from her other life. He would woo her, charm her, hypnotize her out of that existence and into this one.

Like the gallant knight she had dreamed of as a girl, he would win her—body and soul.

Chapter 12

Lilia wasn't sure how it had happened. Or when. It crept over her like a mist. It smelled of rose, gardenia, frangipani. It whispered in Swahili, Arabic, Hindi. It danced in shades of red, green, black, gold. It tasted of curry, cinnamon, roasted corn, coffee. It brushed against her skin with the glint of copper and brass, the velvet of Persian carpet, the sleekness of polished olive-wood. It was Africa... home... and it had taken possession of her.

She wanted to blame Miles. He had brought her back, after all. He had slipped gold bangles on her arms and amber beads around her neck. He had bought perfume and curry dinner and the basket purse that hung over her shoulder. He had taken her hand and led her past the Old Harbour where dhows once sailed in on monsoon winds. He had led her up winding stone stairs and across cool walkways that smelled of the Indian Ocean.

It was Miles's fault, Lilia thought as she slipped into a taxi in front of Fort Jesus. This wistful, happy, full feeling that threatened to spill out in a mixture of tears and laughter was all his doing. But it was her fault, too. She had let it happen. Willingly, she had embraced the languages and memories of her childhood. She hadn't hesitated a moment before plunging fully back into her beautiful Africa. It had captured her as easily as a butterfly at a bowl of honey.

And Miles... he was the same man he had always been, after all. As the taxi driver maneuvered through the streets to the edge of Old Town, she let her eyes wander over Miles's face. It was a little older, maybe, but just as handsome, just as honest. She looked at his hands, large and brown. They were the same hands that had loved her so urgently once. Her husband's hands.

Oh, she couldn't think like this! Lilia bit her lip and stared out the window. The taxi driver purchased a place amid the cars and buses on the Likoni Ferry, and the ferry chugged away from shore. As it slipped through the water, Lilia felt the familiar, unreal sensation that she was not moving—and yet the landscape all around her was silently passing by.

Was that what had happened in her own life? Years had slid by, but she and Miles had remained exactly the same. Events, pain, laughter, people had come and gone. But the two young lovers hadn't changed at all. They were just as they had been—mysteriously brought together by fate—by God?—and as essential to each other as were the sea and the sky.

The taxi descended from the ferry, and Lilia heard Miles give the name of a street. It was a name she recognized, a familiar word so common to her that it almost didn't register. But in a moment, she caught her breath.

"Oh, Miles..." Instinctively, she reached for his hand.

The taxi was pulling up in front of her own house—the small, whitewashed, tin-roofed bungalow where she had lived with her family for most of eighteen years.

"I thought you might want to see it."

"I didn't expect... Oh, maybe not... What if everything is..." Her mouth made hesitating sounds, but she was already climbing out of the taxi. Standing, she shaded her eyes to gaze at the graceful columns of the old veranda where her family had spent so many happy afternoons.

"Wait for us," Miles instructed the taxi driver. Coming to stand beside her, he opened the wrought-iron gate. She stepped onto the path and felt the years vanish with the whispered breath of an ocean breeze.

There were her mother's canna lilies and philodendron plants, as bold and green as if she had planted them yesterday. There was the hibiscus shrub, awash in flamboyant crimson blooms. There was the old swing set. The single swing, empty, swayed in the evening breeze.

Miles took Lilia's hand and led her up the walkway. She knew her parents had retired two years ago, but Lilia was gripped with the oddest feeling that her mother might step out onto the veranda at any moment. A dusting of white flour on her cheek, she would be wiping her hands on an apron.

A figure emerged from the house into the half shadows of twilight. "Who's there?"

It wasn't her mother.

"It's me . . . Lilia Eden," she called. Her voice sounded young, uncertain.

"Lilia Eden? Well, heavens to Betsy!" The middle-aged woman waved from the porch. "Lilia Eden, is that you? What do you know about this!"

"Aunt Grace?"

"Sure enough! Come on up here, honey." She pulled open the door and called inside. "Paul, it's Lilia Eden—Madelyn and Bill's daughter! She's right here in Mombasa, coming up our walkway this minute."

As Lilia and Miles approached, a tall man stepped out onto the veranda beside his wife. "Well, I'll be. Come here, girl, and give your old Uncle Paul a hug."

As lighthearted as if she were fifteen years old, Lilia rushed onto the veranda and threw her arms around the missionary couple who had been her personal favorites. Though they were neither of the same missionary organization nor of the same Christian denomination, the Petersons had been her parents' best friends.

"I can't believe you two are living here!" Lilia exclaimed. "Our house full of the Peterson clan. This is amazing."

"Actually, just Paul and I are here now. The kids are all grown up, you know. We sent Stephen off to college last year."

"Little Stevie?" Lilia tried to imagine the freckle-faced child as an adult. "The last time I saw Stevie, he was about eight years old."

"Heavens, he's a head taller than Paul now."

"Oh..." Lilia stared at Grace, still unable to accept the passage of time.

"While the kids were growing up, we lived down the way in the old place you probably remember," Paul said. "Our mission bought this house right after your folks moved out. We had so many good memories of the times we spent with your family here that we were thrilled to get to live here, too." Smiling, he turned to Miles. "And this must be..."

"Miles. Miles Kane. Zambia." Thrusting out a hand, Miles stepped forward. "I believe you might remember me, Reverend Peterson."

Lilia's eyes darted to the missionary. Of course Paul would remember Miles. He was the man who had agreed to perform their hasty marriage that night ten years ago.

Unfazed, Paul took Miles's hand and shook it firmly. "Miles, so glad to see you and Lilia. This is a wonderful surprise."

"Would you like to come inside?" Grace asked.

Suddenly uncomfortable, Lilia had the urge to bolt down the path and climb into the taxi. But Miles slipped his arm around her shoulders. "We'd love a visit," he said, and led her into the house.

It had hardly changed. The same faded blue curtains hung at the windows. The same furniture filled the rooms. The Edens had commissioned the simple pieces from an Indian *fundi*, a skilled carpenter who had built the chairs, couch and coffee table from Lilia's parents' original shipping crates. Grace explained that she and Paul had purchased the old furniture from the Edens, who didn't want to pay the cost of freighting it back to the States. The selling of unneeded furniture was a common missionary practice, but the impact of seeing the house just as she had left it brought Lilia closer to tears than ever.

Even her room was the same—a single bed covered with a simple white cotton coverlet. Shelves were laden with books, some of which Lilia recognized. Her shells had vanished, but she could almost see them as they had been, smooth, mottled, gleaming in neat rows. She looked out her bedroom window at the bougainvillea bushes along the back wall, the patchy grass, the old guava tree. It was this window through which she had escaped to run into Miles's arms. And it was a real window—as solid and undeniable as the fact that she had married the man who now stood at her side.

"I can't tell you how much we miss your folks," Paul said as he led them back onto the front veranda. "Wonderful people, truly godly. And all you kids, too. Every one of you a jewel—especially you, Lilia."

Arriving with a brass tray, Grace passed out glasses of cold tangerine juice. Paul stretched out his long legs and began to tap his toes together. He scrutinized Miles and Lilia for so long that Lilia began to twitch.

"I seem to recall," he began, "an evening some years ago when you caught up with me as I went on my rounds. You wanted to talk to me about some young Zambian fellow who was in Mombasa on holiday."

Lilia tried to smile. "I always trusted your opinion."

"I appreciated that, especially the following day when you brought your mysterious Miles Kane around to my office at the church to meet me."

"I remember that day quite clearly," Miles said. He gave Lilia an affable wink. She wished she could melt into the shadows.

"And the following night," Paul continued, "we all met at the church where I performed a marriage ceremony." He looked from one to the other, seeking confirmation. "But later, Lilia, I believe it was your father who told me that Miles had flown back to Zambia. Malaria, was it? And then you went off to the States for college. When I told your father about the wedding I'd conducted, Bill was floored. Later, he told me the whole thing had been called off. A divorce... or an annulment? I'm almost sure that's what he told me. But maybe I heard wrong, after all. I mean, here you are... together..."

Lilia looked down at her juice. Miles let out a breath. "You heard right, Reverend," he said. "We were separated straight away after you'd married us."

"The marriage was annulled," Lilia confirmed.

"Oh?" Paul frowned. "Annulled. I've never really liked that idea...never really understood how something signed and sealed could be..."

"My father was behind it," Miles explained. He quickly related what had happened. Then he told how he and Lilia had come to find each other again.

At the seemingly happy conclusion, Paul's expression brightened. "Well, that's more like it. So you're back together as you were then."

"Not really." Lilia studied the condensation on the outside of her glass. "A lot has changed. I mean...ten years..."

There was a long silence. Grace eyed her husband. He ran a finger around the inside of his collar.

Miles tapped his fingers on his knee. "It's been a bit awkward."

"Well, I don't know how you *want* the situation to be," Paul said finally. "But in my book...and I believe in His book, too...if neither of you went on to marry again, then nothing has really changed. I'd say that the vows you exchanged in front of me ten years ago still hold true."

"I don't believe a technicality like that...that annulment thing," Grace put in, "can tear apart what's been sealed before the eyes of God."

Paul cleared his throat. "My wife is the more conservative member of the family, you might note. She was appalled that I had agreed to marry the two of you in the first place."

"And maybe you shouldn't have," she added crisply. "They've obviously suffered a lot."

"No, Mrs. Peterson," Miles countered. "Your husband did the right thing ten years ago. Didn't he, Lilia?"

She stared at Miles. What could she say? She felt backed into a corner. Setting her glass on the table, she gave her watch a glance. Then she let out a pointedly casual sigh. "Well, it was all so long ago, after all. Who can think? I'm so tired from shopping all day, I hardly know my own name."

"It's Lilia Kane," Miles said firmly. "And it looks as if I'd better take you back to the hotel before you wilt right here in front of the reverend and his wife."

"We can't have that now," Paul said with a chuckle. He and Grace stood as Lilia shouldered her purse. "Wonderful to see you both again. And Lilia, you're more beautiful than ever."

Grace gave Lilia a hug and then tapped Miles on the chest. "You take care of our girl now, young man," she admonished. "It's high time she had a happy home and children of her own."

Lilia failed to notice the look on Miles's face as he led her down the walkway to the road.

Miles awoke sometime in the middle of the night and lay in his bed, listening to the rustle of the thatch on his roof. Lilia had made certain there would be no repeat of the previous evening's dangerous game. Pleading exhaustion, she had ordered her supper sent to her room, and Miles hadn't caught a glimpse of her since.

He had eaten alone beside the pool. The hotel had served up a sumptuous barbecue on tables piled high with salads, seafood extravaganzas, sweets and fruits. Chefs at open grills had served barbecued fish, beef, pork and chicken. Miles had filled his plate, only to discover that he wasn't really hungry.

He had lingered for a while afterward, watching the Wakamba tribal dancers. Forming two lines, the men and women had performed their pantomime dances to the beat of drums and shrill whistles. The women wore two armbands with an ostrich feather rising upward from each. The men managed to lure several tourists out onto the dance floor.

Miles had witnessed many such performances at the Habari Safari establishments in Zambia and other countries. Restless, he had finally left the enraptured tourists and had returned to his bungalow. Lilia's lights were already off.

As he lay in the darkness, Miles mulled over the conversation of that evening with the Petersons. It was clear that Lilia hadn't wanted to hear her respected friend give any credence to the marriage she had tried to forget. During the ten years, she had convinced herself that annulment was actually a viable concept and not some medieval excuse for divorce. She had talked herself into believing that her marriage to Miles really hadn't taken place at all.

No wonder she had been reluctant to come to Kenya with him. Kenya was home to more than just a handful of happy childhood memories. It was home to the truth—a truth Lilia couldn't accept.

Troubled, Miles slid his legs out of bed and sat up. A mosquito hummed past his ear. He glanced up at the netting that hung in a knot over his bed. Ten years ago he hadn't worried himself about such things as malaria-carrying mosquitoes, never pondered dark possibilities, losses, pain. Now he knew better.

At the sound of footsteps on the veranda outside his door, Miles lifted his head. A thief? Kenya was a relatively safe place, but it wouldn't be wise to take chances. Miles went to his window and pulled back the curtain.

At first he saw nothing but the black shadows of the veranda furniture. The broken bamboo pole had been repaired, he noted with a twinge of guilt. Lilia's door was closed. And then he caught a glimpse of someone moving down the path toward the sea. A soft towel. A white bikini.

Miles frowned. Lilia knew better than to swim at this time of night. Of course there would be night watchmen around the hotel. But out on the beach... A protective urgency sent him across the room to the chair where he had tossed his trousers and shirt. Then he caught himself.

No. Lilia wanted to be alone. How many times did she have to tell him that she could take care of herself? She didn't need him. Didn't want him. She didn't acknowledge their past, and she didn't hope for a future with him. He was nothing to her—not her knight in shining armor, not her happy memory come to life, certainly not her long-lost husband.

Clenching his jaw, Miles turned back to his bed. Probably Lilia's movement in the bungalow next door had awakened him. But what had woken her? Maybe they were so closely tied that what one of them felt, the other sensed as well. Ha! He laughed scornfully to himself. It was all so much romantic malarkey.

Another batch of bunkum was the notion that they'd been brought back together through some sort of heavenly engineering. Miles knew, despite all her church going, Lilia didn't buy that. Pure coincidence had flung them back together. They should do their best to put a good face on it all, so that when this next week was over, they could go on their separate ways with no ill effect.

That was what Lilia wanted. Why couldn't he want it, too? Miles swatted at the mosquito humming near his ear. The insect droned away for a moment, then drifted back in pursuit of its dinner. Thinking he felt a sting on his shoulder, Miles slapped his bare skin. Good thing he'd been taking his antimalarial medicine.

Not that another attack of the disease would make much difference. It hadn't been too long since he'd suffered one of the recurring bouts of malaria that usually sent him to bed for a week. With a high fever and borderline delirium, he endured the malady that had continued to haunt him periodically for ten years. It was a permanent condition, as permanent as the disability the original disease had brought him.

Remembering that he would never be a father, Miles gave a grunt of disgust and took to his feet. Even if everything else between Lilia and himself could work out as he wished, this one fact would destroy everything. Why would she want a man who couldn't give her children? Especially when having a child was the most important thing in her life right now.

Miles lifted his trousers off the chair. Might as well confront Lilia now and seal off the future for good. That would keep him from persisting in these ridiculous daydreams, Miles reasoned. He stepped into his pants and drew them up his bare legs. He could track her down on the pretense of concern for her safety, then broach the subject of the afternoon at the Petersons' house.

With a few terse sentences, he could let her know that he'd been wrong to push a relationship of any sort with her. After a gallant apology for attempting to seduce her the previous evening, he could explain that he'd realized they had nothing in common. He was still a footloose traveler; she was obviously rooted to her own home. He intended to keep Africa as his base; she clearly considered Missouri her permanent residence. She was quite right that they had each made separate, satisfying lives for themselves. In addition, their unhappy memories of the preceding ten years could not be erased by wishful thinking.

Miles pushed open his door and stepped onto the path. Moreover, he would tell Lilia, she wanted what he could never provide. Colin was her dream for the future, and Miles knew he had no hope of bringing the boy back into her life. On top of that, he would inform Lilia, in a matter-of-fact manner, that he could never father a child himself. He was sterile.

Flinching at the bluntness of his own thoughts, Miles forced himself to continue walking. He didn't have to tell her, but she might as well know. She had overheard his conversation with his parents, and this would confirm what he wanted to convey: that it was over between them—and that he would not pursue her again.

The moon cast a rippling blue streak over the face of the ocean as Miles strode out onto the beach. He scanned the water, but the deep indigo shade obscured any distinctive shapes. The translucent sand crabs must have decided party time was over, for the sand was clear and crystal-white. So clear, in fact, that the single set of footprints winding southward near the water's edge was all that marred the sleek surface.

Miles studied the distant strand, but he couldn't make out anyone walking along it. Again he had to force down his protective instinct as he began to track Lilia down the beach. She shouldn't have come out alone. And she shouldn't have wandered this far. Miles passed one luxury hotel and then another without seeing any trace of a slender, dark-haired young woman in a white bikini.

What had brought her out here? What had carried her this far? Anger? She had every right to be furious with him after he'd called her Lilia Kane that afternoon. He had promised to avoid referring to her as his wife, and as before, he had broken the promise.

Or had sadness drawn her onto the moonlit beach? She would be leaving the coast in the morning as they followed an itinerary that would take them to three inland hotels. Miles realized it must be difficult for Lilia to accept that she was leaving Kenya again soon, probably never to return. And of course, she was still mourning the loss of Colin. Her smile could never completely hide the pain always present in her eyes.

He passed a third hotel. In the distance he caught a flash of white. He stopped, straining to see into the darkness. A woman's figure, faintly outlined by moonlight, took shape at the water's edge. He walked toward her. She knelt and touched her lips to a ripple of foam that slid up the sand. In silence, he watched for a moment as she waited for the wavelet to seep back into the ocean.

Then he took a step toward her. "Lilia," he called softly.

Her head darted up. Instantly, she was on her feet. "Miles, what are you doing here?"

"I might ask you the same thing."

"I'm walking. You shouldn't . . . you shouldn't have followed."

"I heard you leave your room. It's not safe to be out alone at night." As he approached, he saw her brush the heel of her hand across her cheek. "I was concerned that you might . . . Lilia? Are you all right?"

"I'm fine," she said. "You can go back to your room. I don't need you."

"I'm aware of that."

"Oh, I didn't mean—"

"Are you crying?" He was close enough now to touch her cheek. The brush of damp skin tugged at his heart. "Lilia, you'll come back to Kenya one day. You'll be a rich designer and you can holiday anywhere you like.... Oh, Lilia, don't—"

"I'm not crying." She sniffled in a deep breath. "Anyway, it's not Kenya. I know I can come back. When I was little, I used to kiss the water every time I had to go home. It was my promise...my vow...that I'd return."

He reflected on the moment she had bent to touch the ocean. The memory of the gesture caught in his throat, crumpling his determination to blurt out a grand, final speech and be done with her.

"You'd kiss it, would you?" he asked. "The sea?"

She nodded. "When I was a little girl."

He dug his hands into his pockets, struggling to recall the oration he'd planned. "Well then, you'll be back to Kenya one day. Perhaps I'll look you up."

She tucked a strand of damp hair behind one ear. "What do you mean?"

He shrugged. "Oh, you know. I'll give you a ring, and we'll have a chat. You can tell me what you've been up to."

"Oh." Nodding, she stuck out one toe and drew a semicircle in the sand. The line clearly divided them, as if it were a boundary not to be crossed.

With some effort, Miles drew his eyes upward from the sight of her long, bare leg. He studied the moon for a moment, fighting to swallow the coarse knot that had somehow formed in his throat. "At any rate," he began, "I thought I should apologize to you, Lilia."

She brushed at her cheek again. "What for?"

"Well, last night, for one. I had promised to keep my distance, and I violated that."

"No, it's all right." She crossed her arms over her stomach where the ends of her white towel came together. "I wasn't trying, either. To keep a distance, I mean. You were right when you said I wanted you as much as you wanted me."

He glanced up in surprise, but Lilia was speaking more to the sand than to him.

"And I've been very unfeeling, too," she said. "It's not like me at all to be so harsh and unsympathetic. But I worked so hard to build layers and layers of protection over that wound...over the memories of what happened ten years ago."

"I know. I've been boorish to try to force you—"

"But this evening at the Petersons', I realized that I couldn't deny our marriage at all. I've been pretending, just totally pretending. I'm so afraid of being hurt again that I couldn't let myself risk getting close to you. You've been trying to prove to me how honest you are, and how trustworthy, and I've just cast all that to the wind as if you're not important to me. But you are important, very important, and I'm...I'm so confused."

This time there was no denying the tear that trickled down Lilia's cheek, and Miles balled up his fists to keep from taking her into his arms. Her words only proved how badly he had twisted her happy life.

"Lilia," he tried again, "I know how important your career is to you, and how very carefully you've built your life..."

"And I don't even care about it anymore!"

"And I recognize how important it is to you to be a single woman with a separate— What?"

"I don't care. That whole life I built is false, don't you see? Miles, I'm not an American, and I never will be. I'm a part of this world, this culture...but I don't even really belong to Kenya, either. I'm somewhere in the middle, like you. I'm a mixture of languages and cultures and people and places, and that's why I've never found anyone I could touch souls with but you, Miles. Oh, I don't belong in Missouri. I've lost Colin, and he was the only thing that tied me there. I don't even want to go back."

"But Jenny and your shop and your house..."

"Walking through Old Town today, I realized that I felt at home for the first time in ten years. Truly at home. And it wasn't just the vendors and the smell of the spices... It was you, Miles."

Miles stared at the top of her bent head. He couldn't trust what he thought he had heard. "Lilia?" he asked. "I'm trying to tell you that I won't pursue...that I'm letting go..."

"I know," she whispered. She lifted her head, and her eyes were dark and shining. "And I'm trying to tell you that I want you to stay."

Chapter 13

"I know how it must sound," Lilia said, again talking to the sand. "A complete reversal of everything I've been saying. I think I'm crazy, too, I really do. This whole thing with Colin has tilted me off balance. But lying in my room a few minutes ago, I kept thinking how ridiculous it was to be alone when my...my husband was next door..."

Her voice trailed off to a whisper. A tear fell off the end of her nose and landed in the sand at her feet. She touched the spot with the tip of her toe. She felt so silly, so mixed up and adolescent. But if Miles was going to be gone from her life in a matter of one week, she thought he at least ought to know how she felt. As crazy as it sounded.

"Anyway, I thought I would walk down the beach and try to figure out how to tell you," she went on when she realized he wasn't going to say anything. "And I don't mind at all if you've done a complete reversal, too, which it sounds like you have, because I think we should be honest with each other. I mean, it's the least we can do to be frank—"

"Lilia, are you going to blather all night, or are you going to come into my arms and let me hold you?"

She looked up to find him smiling at her, a sheepish, uncertain grin that curled the edges of her heart. He held out his hands, and she took a step toward him. The next thing she knew, he was sweeping her up in his arms and holding her so tightly she could hardly breathe as he turned her around and around.

As the moon made dizzy circles overhead, Lilia wove her fingers through Miles's thick hair, and she touched his forehead with her lips. His skin smelled of soap, and as he lowered her against him, she drank in the clean scent of his shoulders and chest.

"This bathing costume," he murmured. "Where did you..."

"It was all they had in the gift shop. It's not even my size." When his eyes roved down to caress her bosom, she felt a flush creep over her neck. "My purple one was wet, and I...I went into the lobby to look for it...something new, and this was the only thing on the rack that even came close to fitting."

"I remember you in a white bikini. You're beautiful, Lilia. Paul was right. You're more beautiful than ever."

"Oh, Miles, at the Petersons' house...my old house...I felt so odd. So off center. I was rude."

"You were confused, and so was I. We've both been confused ever since we spoke on the phone that first time. But, Lilia, I'm not at sea now. I know exactly what to think."

She looked into his eyes and read the message she had been longing for all night. "What do you think, Miles Kane?"

"I think that you fit perfectly in my arms. And I think that our lips would fit perfectly together. And I think that if you would permit me to suspend that set of rules you made in the London airport—"

"Please kiss me, Miles," Lilia cut in.

Before she had time to catch her breath, he brushed his mouth across hers. The touch set a tingle on her skin, and she waited, eyes shut, for his next kiss. When it came, it was feather-light, a whisper of a caress. Tantalized, she hung in anticipation. His lips found hers once again, lingering this time. His fingers formed around the back of her neck, slid up into her hair, cupped her head.

"Miles," she murmured.

He stroked his lips over hers. His ragged breath heated her skin. Pulling her closer, he dampened her lower lip. She molded her hands around his shoulders. The feel of his hot skin and the taste of his mouth took Lilia back in time to a similar night ten years before. The same man, the same moon, the same sea...maybe Miles had been right about the time machine.

"I feel as I did on our wedding night, Lilia," he whispered.

"This isn't our wedding night," she said softly. "It's the first night of our honeymoon."

"Do you mean it? Is this a new beginning for us?"

A curl of uncertainty ran through her at his question. Yes, she wanted to say. A new beginning. The start of our life together. But he hadn't asked for the rest of her life. He hadn't laid out a plan for a future that included her. The dreams...the tiny details they once had pored over so lovingly were absent from this commitment. Where would they live? What would they do? Would Miles want children, a family?

"Lilia," he said softly, tilting her chin to force her eyes on his, "give me your answer."

"All I know is what I told you. I'm finally sure that what Paul Peterson said is true. Our marriage didn't end and... and I'm still your wife."

"That's enough for me."

"But I don't know what it means. I don't know about the future. We haven't talked...planned..."

"Do you want to talk, Lilia?" His blue eyes mirrored the silver moon. "We can find a table and two chairs at one of the hotels along the beach here. We can sit and talk until dawn, if you like."

She could feel his bare stomach pressing against hers. Ten years had passed since she'd known this kind of freedom, this intensity of desire—ten years since she had experienced a man's passion. And now, here, she was free to love again with the man who was her husband.

"Talking is the last thing I want to do," she said.

Miles's mouth lifted into a smile. "Do you remember what you said to me on our wedding night? Just after we'd left Reverend Peterson's church and found our way onto this beach, you threw down your gauntlet. Remember?"

"Of course." Lilia squared her shoulders. "And the challenge stands. Race you to the cliffs, Miles Kane. Last one there's a rotten egg."

"You're on." He set her to one side, leaned his hand on his knee and gave her a wicked grin. "Ready, steady...*go!*"

Lilia burst into a run, her feet pounding over the spongy sand. Her white towel flapped behind her for a moment, then tugged loose from her waist and tumbled onto the beach. Miles was right beside her, step for step, his long legs an easy match for her. But she knew secrets he didn't about the beach.

"You're too close," she huffed. "You're taking up my running space. Move down!"

She waved him closer to the water where she knew the surface was as mushy as quicksand. Her own steps took her away from the water, but not so far up that she was on loose sand. Instead, she chose the strip where the receding tide had formed a concretelike path, solid and as easy on the feet as a running track.

Laughing at her clever move, Lilia burst ahead of Miles. Ahead she could see the familiar, looming coral cliff that had so intrigued her as a child. Its base had been deeply cut away by the tide, leaving the coral riddled with deep caves that had once held pirate treasures. A lone baobab tree grew inexplicably from the top of the cliff, far from the inland terrain where baobab normally thrived.

As Lilia ran, a sense of nostalgia overwhelmed her as she pondered the tree she had once gazed at in childish fascination. Why had the baobab taken root in such a hostile environment? Salty water splashed it at high tide, and the cliff had only a thin layer of soil for the tree to take root in. In spite of adversity, the tree had flourished.

Lilia lifted her head and sucked in a deep breath. She was like the tree. Alone. A survivor. She had withstood everything the years had hurled her way. But now...with the loss of her child . . . her roots had reached coral. She had begun to wither without nourishment, sustenance, dreams.

Glancing over her shoulder, Lilia saw Miles running a few paces behind, his head thrown back and his eyes shut. His gold hair lifted away from his face in the sea breeze. The moonlight picked out silver glints like firefly sparks. A pale platinum light outlined the muscles in his shoulders and traced the lines of his legs.

Miles was her hope, Lilia realized with throat-tightening certainty. He was her sustenance—denied far too long. Her hunger for him flamed through her chest and tingled down her arms. It welled up in fresh tears that she refused to let fall. It settled in the base of her stomach and curled down her thighs to her knees.

Out of breath, she ran beneath the shadowing wall of the cliff to the secret hiding place she had not seen for ten years.

"I won!" she panted. "You're the rotten—"

Miles tackled her around the waist, bringing her crashing to the ground in a puff of soft sand. Rolling together, they tangled legs and arms in a sudden rush of need. Their mouths met, urgently seeking intimacy. Lilia clutched at his shoulders, his back, her fingers digging into the muscle.

"I won," he said, his hands on either side of her face, "the day I saw you for the first time. You're my grand prize, Lilia."

When he kissed her, his hands slipped behind her head. His tongue found hers, the sensual meeting of secrets, the dance of promise. She ran her fingers down his back, marveling at the length and breadth of his frame, then slipped her hands beneath the waistband of his trousers to touch his smooth, rounded flesh.

With a groan of desire, he caught her more closely against him and used his hand to press her pelvis against his. She caught a breath of pleasure mingled with the first shadow of uncertainty as she realized he was ready for her.

Lilia chastised herself for doubting. She had raced Miles down the beach to this hidden place with only one purpose in mind. And as he slipped his hand over the swell of her breast, she felt a flood of eager anticipation. Ten years! She had been so alone for ten years, and now the memory of the ecstasy a man could bring welled through her.

"Hurry," she urged before she could stop herself. "Please, Miles..."

He lifted his head and gazed down into her face. Her features were almost obscured in the deep shadows, but he had no doubt that her lips were parted and her nostrils flared. Her breath was coming in short, ragged gasps, and her hands moved over his body as if they were possessed.

Hurry, she had begged. Oh, he had hurried the first time they'd made love. A randy boy then with the blood of a hot stallion racing through his veins, Miles knew he had made no attempt to stifle his urgency. He had ripped away his bride's white dress, ravaged her breasts with his hands, plundered her body until she was gasping half in fear and half in pleasure, and then he had emptied his life force into her. Had she responded with equal satisfaction? He didn't even know.

Of course he had cared. He had loved her. He had wanted perfection in their loving. But he'd been so young. Inexperienced. Awash in thundering need.

Miles ran his hand over the mound of sweet flesh cupped in white cotton. He was awash in coursing need at this moment, too. And not a great deal more experienced, thanks to ten years spent mostly in the African bush country. But he wouldn't dominate this beautiful woman—no matter how much she begged him to hurry.

"Lilia," he said, leaning against her ear, "do you think this is the same sand we made love on the first time?"

"I... I don't know," she said haltingly, because he had slipped the strap of her bra down her shoulder. "I don't... care, either."

In the darkness, his mouth found the tip of her breast. His tongue began a slow, undulating orbit around the sensitive peak. "We won't know what to do in a real bed," he said, and his breath set a flame on her skin. "We've never had to manage sheets and a mattress."

Lilia caught her breath as he eased her breast fully out of the cup of her bikini and held it in his palm. His thumb stimulated her as his lips roved across her chest. "This suits me fine," she said, desire making her wriggle her bottom into the cool sand. "It's so... natural."

"Does this feel natural, Lilia?" Miles whispered, his mouth on her ear.

She felt his hand slide down her bare stomach. As his fingers trickled over her thighs and behind her knees, she attempted to summon an answer. But her body hummed with need, desire blocking all attempt at reason as her senses overrode her mind. The scent of his naked flesh in her nostrils, the taste of his mouth on her tongue, the solid ripple of his muscles beneath her fingers, and, oh... the delicious play of his hand over the base of her belly.

"I suppose I'll have to find the answer myself," he murmured finally, tracing one finger beneath the tight band of her bikini panties.

Her bra had somehow come apart, and he was nuzzling her nipples, first one and then the other. She moved her hands over his hard, flat chest, molding the swell of sculpted sinews.

Swirling in a sea of lights that danced mysteriously behind her eyes, Lilia finally gave herself to the swaying dance her hips demanded. As Miles pushed her panties down her legs, she unzipped his trousers and pulled them away. He was naked beneath. Did he sleep in the nude? Tantalized by the image, she tried to make out his body. In the darkness she could see almost nothing.

Oh, but she could feel. He was urgent and demanding against her thigh, his body bathed in the soft sheen of male need. As his fingers slipped over and between her thighs, she took him in her hands. Their mouths met again and again as they climbed the heights of rapture.

Her body flooded with silken warmth, Lilia hovered on the brink of release. Miles's mouth stroked across her lips, his tongue playing a wicked game with hers. She fully parted her thighs, giving herself to the pleasure of his touch. Throbbing with barely sustained restraint, she stroked and toyed with him until his voice was a growl of hunger in her ears.

"Lilia," he rasped, "I want to know you... but I won't... I won't hurry you..."

"If you don't hurry, Miles . . . I can't promise . . ."

Released by her words, he slid against her side and eased up on his elbows to hover over her. His hands cupped her head as he gently parted her like an arrow sliding through velvet. Shuddering beneath him, she wrapped her legs around his thighs and met his mesmerizing movements stroke for stroke. Their mouths met, tongues mimicking the rhythm of their passion, naked bodies one flesh against the silvery sand.

"I need . . . need you, Miles, please," Lilia whispered, catching his buttocks in her hands and forcing him hard and deep inside her as he rocked on the verge of explosion.

Finally giving in to his need, Miles thrust deeply, crushing her into the sand and penetrating to the core of her hunger. As her body erupted beneath him, he stroked her once again. This time she dug her fingers into his shoulders as the intensity of her release broke over her in wave after drenching wave.

The deep velvet strokes of Lilia's body drew Miles over the edge of control, and he felt himself rocket into her. The climactic explosion forced him against her, reigniting the pleasure of her own release.

"Lilia," he groaned, "you're everything . . . all I've ever wanted."

Shivering, she ribboned her fingers through his hair, her mouth on the shell of his ear. "Ten years . . . I want to make up for every lost minute of them."

She could feel his contented smile against her neck. "That would involve a great many hours spent in this position, Lilia."

"Exactly." With an instinctive purr of contentment, she ran her hands down his naked body. The anticipation of the pleasures to come sent a sudden, swift flame flickering through her. Surprised, she felt her nipples bead up in tight peaks of eagerness.

"Oh, Miles," she whispered, "when do you think you'll be ready to start making up for lost time?"

Startled, he lifted his head as her hands slipped down his chest to the tangle of crisp curls at the base of his stomach. "Lilia?"

She grinned. Her fingers made soft, stroking motions over his thighs. "I was only wondering."

"Already?" In the pink light of sunrise, he could make out the rose-hued crests of her swollen breasts. Her lips looked full and slightly bruised with passion. Her eyes were violet with desire.

"Already," she confirmed.

And it wasn't long before she convinced his body that he was ready, too.

It was a rather disheveled, sleepy-looking couple who wandered down Diani Beach at midmorning. They took little notice of the sunbathers, fishermen, boaters and snorkelers as they meandered toward the Africana Sea Lodge, their arms wrapped around each other and their mouths hovering close in whispered conversation.

"The Land Rover driver will wonder where we've got to," Miles mentioned after a particularly satisfying interlude spent kissing Lilia. A group of children had paused from their work of building a sand castle to watch. "I think I told him we'd be leaving for Tsavo West National Park at about six this morning."

"Oh, dear," Lilia said, trying to sound chagrined. "I feel so terrible about that."

Miles couldn't help but laugh out loud. "You're a dreadful liar, Lilia."

She brushed a dusting of sugary white sand from her bottom as they turned toward the swimming pool area of the hotel. "Okay, I confess," she replied. "I wouldn't have traded last night and this morning under the cliff with you for anything. Especially not for five hours driving inland on the Mombasa highway."

"We'll have to hurry now, though. Quick showers, pack up our bags and be off."

"Showers, did you say?"

Miles glanced at Lilia to find a secret smile playing around her lips. His heart began to thud heavily. Maybe he'd gotten more in this ten-year-old marriage than he'd bargained for. "Showers," he confirmed.

"Why don't you run up to the lobby and tell the driver we're running a little late?" She gave him a wink over one pink-tinged shoulder. "See you later, Miles."

It took him a good ten minutes to convince the Land Rover driver he'd hired the previous day that all was well. Miles gave the man a generous tip and told him to buy himself something to eat and drink—nonalcoholic, of course—and to wait as long as need be to start the trip. Half running over rough-edged stones in his bare feet, Miles maneuvered the path to his room. As he had hoped, the water in his shower was running.

A good, long nap under the cool shadows of the cliff had rested him adequately, and Miles felt a surge of energy race through his loins as he hurriedly stripped off his trousers. When he stepped into the bathroom, he saw that the curtain had not been drawn. Standing under a stream of steaming water, Lilia smiled at him.

"What took you so long?" she asked.

It didn't take long at all to explore the mysteries of showering with this vixen Miles seemed to have brought out of hiding. Lilia was a nymph under the influence of the warm blast of water. Before Miles could convince himself that this was really Lilia...just a reluctant acquaintance until the wee hours of the previous night...she had pinned him against the shower wall and was licking droplets off his chest. Moments later, she was the one with the wall at her back as they discovered the mysterious and sensual nuances of waterplay.

By the time they wandered up the path with bags slung over their arms and hair neatly combed, Miles felt as though his normally athletic body was on the verge of collapse. Famished, he ordered a huge lunch from the restaurant, loaded the food into paper bags and stowed it all in the Land Rover. He insisted that Lilia take the front seat—she was already chattering in Swahili with the driver—while he sprawled across the back seat in a daze of pleasure-soaked disbelief.

The inland journey began with a ride back across on the Likoni Ferry, a trip through the winding streets of Mombasa town and a beeline across the bridge that linked Mombasa Island with the mainland. Then the Land Rover began climbing upward from the coastal belt to the inland savanna grasslands, site of the wild game parks that made Kenya so popular with European and American tourists.

Before long, acacia and baobab replaced palm trees, round mud huts supplanted whitewashed Arab dwellings and vast golden plains erased the vista of turquoise water. Miles vaguely acknowledged that this familiar terrain made him feel more comfortable than the humid coast had. Still drowsy, he tried to work up enough enthusiasm to acknowledge Lilia's excited exclamations over the wild game that appeared in small herds through the brush.

"Tommies!" she called out, turning to grab his knee and give it a vigorous shake. "Miles, Thomson's gazelles! Right out the window to your left!"

Miles lifted his head and squinted at the group of delicate tawny creatures, their flicking white tails signaling alertness. "Tommies, right you are. We'll have a herd of them at each of our hotels."

"Oh, look—is that an eland? It can't be. It is! It is!" Her fingers dug into his thigh. "An eland. Look how enormous!"

Brushing a hand over his eyes, Miles focused on the great antelope, the largest species in the world. Rarely seen, the eland seemed hardly aware of the stir it was causing in the passing Land Rover. It bent its spike-horned head and returned to grazing as the vehicle flashed past.

Miles sank down into the seat and stared at the bag of fresh rolls, ripe bananas, boiled eggs and chicken sandwiches on the floor. He ought to eat. His stomach loudly informed him it was in need of sustenance. He knew he would need the energy if he intended to sit through an interview with the manager of Ngulia Lodge in Tsavo West National Park. But all Miles wanted to do was stretch out and bask in the luxuriant memory of making love with Lilia.

He knew it wasn't only the lack of sleep that was making him feel off balance. Only a few hours ago, he had set off down the beach, determined to seal off any hope of a future with Lilia. In a matter of minutes, the exact opposite had happened. She had come willingly to him, given him he body, declared herself his wife. Every hostile attitude she had used to keep them apart had vanished.

What had brought on the difference? Miles studied the underside of his eyelids as Lilia shouted from the front seat.

"Zebras! Oh, look, giraffes! Three of them! Oh, Colin would...he'd love the giraffes." Her voice lowered for a moment. "I wish Colin could see this. He'd be all eyes...and bouncing around on the seat...so excited. If only...well..." She fell silent, staring out the window. Miles watched her as she attempted to pull herself together. She swallowed several times and chewed on her lower lip.

Then she took a deep breath and sat forward again. "What do you know? There's a kudu! Hey, a herd of Grant's gazelles. Gosh, Miles, you really should see this pair of Cape buffalo!"

Miles managed a squint, not at the dangerous, ill-tempered buffalo with curling black horns he knew all too well, but at Lilia. Having once again forced her grief into hiding, she was rattling on at the driver, mixing Swahili and English so rapidly that Miles didn't know how the man understood a word. The driver did, however, for his enthusiasm nearly matched hers. By the time an hour had gone by, Lilia was singing songs to him in his native Kikuyu tongue, and he was telling her legends about the wild animals they passed.

Miles groaned and fell back onto the seat. Had their visit to Old Town changed her? Or had she come to terms with her loss of Colin? Had it been the talk with Reverend Peterson? Or had Miles actually said something that made sense to her? He didn't have a clue. All he knew was that once she had been distant, aloof and determined to keep him at arm's length...and now she was eagerly seducing him and embracing every endearment he could lavish on her.

Did she actually think of herself as his wife, as she had said? Did she really intend never to return to her life in Missouri? Miles tried to picture Lilia abandoning the lovely Victorian home she spoke of with such fondness. And what about her shop—all those clients who were counting on her to transform their homes? She clearly loved her work. Did she mean to give it up? Would she simply fail to return, leaving her assistant to tie up the loose ends and sell off Lilia's interests?

Miles couldn't imagine that. More importantly, he wasn't sure he wanted it. Lilia needed a creative outlet. She needed more than Miles could give her as a husband. She was full of life, energy and imagination that demanded to be channeled into something. Or someone...a child, perhaps? Once again, the reality of his situation settled over Miles like a lead weight.

Could Lilia have placed her hopes for the future on the illusion of becoming a mother? With a sinking feeling, Miles stared at the back of her dark brown hair. Shining, it bobbed and bounced as she chattered with the driver. Could that be the one thing that had brought such vitality back into Lilia's life—the dream of having a child of her own?

Miles shut his eyes and clenched his jaw. Finally, he understood what had brought about the change in Lilia. It was nothing the reverend had said. It wasn't a shopping trip in Old Town. It wasn't Miles or his commitment to her. It was the promise of a baby...the baby Lilia expected would come as the fruit of her lovemaking with Miles ... the baby Miles could never give her.

Chapter 14

Tsavo West National Park epitomized Africa in its essence. As Lilia slipped up through the square hatch of the Land Rover and leaned her elbows on the warm metal roof, she had to blink back tears. They threatened to blur the sight of lush golden grass, sky as blue and depthless as a mountain lake, thorny acacia that lifted their branches too high for all but the lithe giraffe to feed on tender leaves, and animals... so many animals.

She knew these savanna plains with the intimacy born of hours spent basking in the sun that burned down to parch the tall elephant grass and brighten the stripes of grazing zebras. In her early childhood, when Kenya had still permitted hunting, Lilia had accompanied her father on trips in search of wild game to feed the family. They had spent long days stalking through the brush, then gathered around a campfire that shot sparks into the ink-black night. Those expeditions had provided zebra hamburgers, eland steaks and antelope pot roast for the Eden family.

Lilia's father had explained that hunting was a means to survival in Africa. She had certainly witnessed the continent's ecological balance at work, observing plant-eating gazelles and antelopes as they fell prey to cheetahs and li-

ons. All the same, Lilia had not been sorry when Kenya
banned hunting. She had despised the sharp crack of rifle
fire that brought the end to an animal's sunny days on the
plains. She hated holding a still-warm leg while her father
began the butchering. And she had wept over the glaze of
lifeless eyes.

Lilia's memory of the sweep of trackless brush could be
traced back to those earliest moments of her existence in
Africa. After hunting was outlawed, the Eden family had
continued to travel the savanna. In their efforts to start new
churches among the African people, they journeyed down
dry, sandy riverbeds that served as crude roads. They drove
upland to Nairobi to shop for supplies and to fellowship
with other missionaries. They wandered through these same
game preserves on family holidays, keeping the children in
touch with the raw, elemental aspects of creation.

Like the turquoise waters of the Indian Ocean, the golden
savanna intertwined with Lilia's heart to form the essence of
her core. Seeing this beloved homeland again, she could
hardly speak. The excitement of traveling down the highway ended the moment the Land Rover drove through the
gates of Tsavo West. She fell silent, absorbing like a thirsty
nomad the sight of round gray elephants who lifted their
trunks to sniff the air, shaggy hyenas sunning on the dirt
road and mingled herds of zebras, Grant's gazelles, harte-
beest.

Jostled from his nap by the bumpy road, Miles stood to
join Lilia in the open roof hatch. He looked sleepy and
rumpled, and she ached to feel his arms around her at this
moment. Instead, he stared at her with a look of mingled
confusion and uncertainty in his blue eyes.

When he turned away to observe a tree bearing hundreds
of the teardrop-shaped nests of weaverbirds, she took a deep
breath. "What's the matter, Miles?"

He faced her again, swallowing with difficulty. "Lilia, I
need to talk to you."

His voice held an uncharacteristic note of solemnity that
sent a stab of uncertainty into her stomach. She lifted her
chin. "What do you want to talk about?"

"Us." He raked a hand through his hair. "Me, I mean. Or really... the future."

She glanced at the driver, who was pretending not to listen. "Oh... the future."

"Not what you're thinking." He let out a breath. "There's nothing I want more than... well, than you. Everything that happened... everything between us is wonderful. Or, not exactly wonderful because...." He pounded his fist on the roof. "Hell, I can't say what I'm—"

"You wanted to see the baboons, *bwana?*" the driver called, slowing the Land Rover.

Miles groaned inwardly. He'd forgotten that a knock on the roof was the signal in Africa to stop a vehicle. A family of baboons sat by the side of the dirt road, their canine faces uptilted at the Land Rover. Doglike snouts and golden eyes acknowledged the foreign presence. Several stopped their grooming to wander across the road. Completely unafraid, they stared placidly as if wondering whether one of the onlookers might toss out a forbidden banana or bit of candy.

Miles didn't give a damn about the baboons, he wanted to inform the driver. How many thousand of these gray-furred creatures had he seen in his lifetime? He had little interest in the zebras or the elephants or even the family of cheetahs he had noticed in the distance. In fact, this whole journey inland seemed to be slipping past him like so much mist on a river. The vast plains of Africa were as familiar to him as the back of his hand, so well known as to border on the routine.

Miles loved Africa and its animals, but on this day they seemed insignificant next to the knots in his stomach over telling Lilia he could never father children. He gripped the edge of the roof hatch, impatient for the Land Rover to start forward again. Conscious of the driver, Miles counted on the growl of the engine to drown out his words so he could talk freely. His need to tell Lilia everything had become a bitter taste in his mouth, and now it demanded spitting out—no matter how much Miles dreaded the moment when her soft gray eyes would register the truth.

Lilia had continued to stare at him for a moment after the Land Rover had stopped. He could already see the hurt forming on her face. When he said nothing, she turned to the baboons.

"Twelve," she counted. "They're not apes, you know."

"Right. The Cercopithecidae family."

"Oh." Of course Miles knew about baboons, Lilia admonished herself. An expert on African wildlife, he had studied every species and its characteristics and habits. He had examined these animals, lived and worked with them, researched their prospects for survival in the United States.

Lilia glanced at Miles. Disinterested in the baboons, he was studying a patch of the roof where the green paint had flaked off. A curl of dismay slid through her stomach. What had happened to bring on his dark mood? As the baboons went back to their grooming, she tried to remember the sequence of events that might have led to this moment.

Miles had come out to the beach the previous night with every intention of severing their relationship. She had sensed it in his stride and in the tone of his voice. But instead of letting him end things between them, she had blathered on and on about having found her home and about wanting him. Then they had made love.

Of course they had. What man in his right mind would refuse a moonlit beach and an eager woman in a white bikini? Especially if only hours before he had declared that she was his wife. Though Miles may have loved her with his body, Lilia realized with sickening swiftness, he had already divorced her from his heart. He had come onto the beach to tell her that—and had been prevented by her sexual advances.

She flushed at the memory of the way she had flung herself at him that morning in the shower. Vague memories of sermonic denouncements of the demon lust drifted through her thoughts. Well, she did hunger after Miles. Even now, the image of his naked body kept intruding on her mind and sending trickles of desire down her spine. She wanted Miles—his mouth, his hands, his rock-hard thighs. If they were husband and wife, as they had agreed, there was nothing wrong with such brazen passion. It belonged in a marriage.

But could Lilia really claim a spiritual union with Miles? She glanced at him again and saw the muscle flickering in his clenched jaw. He had failed last night to tell her that he wanted out of the relationship—and now he was trying again to make his feelings clear.

The dismay in Lilia's stomach knotted into certainty as she stared at the baboons. Whatever it was Miles had to say, she didn't want to hear it now—not in the presence of the driver. Not in the midafternoon when all of Africa seemed to be listening.

She focused on the baboons, hoping for a way to steer the conversation away from dangerous ground.

"A baby," she announced.

Miles lifted his head, his blue eyes more tumultuous than ever. "I know, Lilia . . . that's what I'm trying to . . ."

"A baby baboon in its mother's arms." She pointed. "See its little pink face? Must be a young one."

"A baby baboon." Miles brushed his hand over his forehead. What was he thinking? For a moment, he had imagined Lilia could read his mind and knew what he had to tell her. He had to regain control of this. But the thought that she would reject him again—after all they had shared the past night—gave him an almost physical pain.

"Its fur is so dark. I'd forgotten that about the babies." Lilia was gazing at the tiny baboon, who was peering out from the cradle of its mother's lap. "It looks more like a chimpanzee than a baboon."

"At this age," Miles managed to say. "But it won't be long before its nose grows into a snout and its fur turns gray."

"Well, enough baboons for the day. I guess I'll take my turn at resting." Lilia slid down into her seat so that Miles couldn't resume his train of conversation. She had no wish to allow the man she had given herself to body and soul to sever that bond while jolting along in a Land Rover. For that matter, she didn't particularly relish the thought of hearing his grand finale speech that evening at the hotel. In fact, she didn't want to hear it at all.

But if she had to, Lilia decided, she would choose the time and place. And she would give herself time to prepare for it, so that her own response would be mild, mature, unemotional.

She nodded at the driver, who put the Land Rover in gear and left the baboon troop behind him in a cloud of dust.

The words of an Andrew Lloyd Webber song played through her mind as Lilia wandered around collecting notes at both the Ngulia and Kilaguni lodges in Tsavo West National Park. Miles's meetings with the managers of each hotel gave Lilia the time she needed to investigate the decor and to sort out her thoughts.

As the song asserted, she wanted to be let down easy, no big song and dance. No long speeches, no long looks, no deep conversations should prolong the moment when Miles announced that he had made up his mind that, after all, they didn't belong together.

Maybe she couldn't specify that he tell her only on a Sunday, but she knew she didn't want it to happen here—not at this beautiful game preserve where her heart had been so full. She took note of stone veranda, banana bark baskets, soapstone salt-and-pepper shakers, but her mind felt detached from the portfolio she was building. Would there really be a Habari Safari hotel in America? Could it ever capture the wildness, the majesty of Africa? Did she want to be a part of trying to recreate that elusive grandeur—especially if Miles had severed himself from her?

Lilia sat down beside a particularly impressive arrangement of Kenyan arts and crafts. She pulled a pad from her attaché case and began to sketch the display. Again her thoughts roamed back to the night she had spent with Miles beneath the cliffs. As her hand drew a draped tablecloth and a collection of beaded gourds, her mind wandered to the moment when Miles had pulled down the strap of her bathing suit. The power of the memory sent a swift, tugging sensation deep in the pit of her stomach, and she crossed her legs to try to distract the surge of desire.

Studying the gourds, she saw not rounded, golden flasks but the curve of a male buttock, hard and smooth beneath her hand. Maybe it was simply the fact that she had been a single woman for ten years and was entering her sexual prime that had made her feel so eager for Miles's touch. Perhaps it was merely a physical aspect he had awakened in her, and without him in her life, she'd eventually get over it.

Lilia tucked her hair behind her ears and returned to her sketching. But she had relished the way his hands molded over her breasts, his thumbs tipping their peaks. At the thought, her nipples began to tingle. Well, this was completely ridiculous. Miles was preparing to tell her to forget everything, and here she was salivating over the mere thought of his fingertips on her body.

Lilia recrossed her legs, but the throbbing between her thighs seemed to have settled in permanently. Looking down at her drawing, she realized what a mess she'd made of it. The beaded necklaces looked like a jumble of peas, and the philodendrons in artistic clay pots resembled very old elephants more than tropical plants.

Annoyed, Lilia tossed her pencil and sketch pad into her case, leaned back in her chair and shut her eyes. Instantly, the image of Miles hovering over her, his mouth a whisper away, flooded her mind. Her lips felt hot, so she ran her tongue over them. At the memory of his thighs sliding between hers, her back began to ache with a sweet, pulsing need that slid deeply inside her body.

Sometime during her stay at the beach, she had abandoned her sensible white bra with narrow elastic straps and wire underpinnings. Now she regretted it. Beneath her soft pink cotton shirt her breasts swelled, their tips contracting into embarrassing tight nubbins that demanded Miles's touch.

Knowing she should get up and walk around the pool to distract herself, all Lilia could do was luxuriate in the pool of desire into which she had inadvertently slid. She remembered Miles's lips heating the side of her neck. She dwelled on the picture of his mouth forming a perfect, damp circle around her nipple, and his tongue tipping the sensitive peak until she cried out. As she remembered the way his fingers had danced against her moist, silk skin, her breath went shallow. Her breasts tipped even tighter, speaking of their need for his caress.

What would it be like never to know Miles's touch again? Even as her mind formed the thought, she rejected it as impossible. She still had nearly a week with him. So what if he didn't want to spend the rest of his life with her? Did that mean she should deny herself the remaining nights to engage in pure carnal pleasure with the man who she now thought of as her husband?

Would the consequences be more than she could bear? She would have to live with a heart full of memories, perhaps, but she had learned to suppress those. An emptiness that would defy description would settle over her, but she had survived that, too. What else?

The memory of Miles's body driving into hers sent Lilia to the brink of need even as she sat alone on a chair in a hotel lobby. But as her mind continued down that course, recalling the way he had loved her, she remembered the ultimate moment of that union...the spilling of his life force into hers. The realization of its significance sent a wash of ice down her heated veins.

A baby.

She might be pregnant even now. With Miles's child.

Lilia's eyes flew open. How could she have failed even to consider such a thing? Of course, last night had been impulsive, a torrent of emotional and physical release. But not to have even thought of the possibility that she might have conceived?

Sitting upright, Lilia felt a mixture of disbelief, fear and utter joy. She looked down at herself, her long legs, her full breasts. She placed a tentative hand on her stomach. At this very moment, a tiny life might be flickering inside her—infinitesimal cells dividing, multiplying, eventually forming into brain and spine, head, heart, eyes, ears, miniature feet and fingers. The fingers of a baby...her baby!

Panic gripped her the next moment. She would never take another sip of alcohol on this entire trip, just in case. She would be careful to eat right. Get plenty of rest. She would veer away from cigarette-smoking tourists. She would refrain from drinking sodas full of caffeine. How soon would she know for sure?

Leaning forward, she tried to recall the crucial dates the obstetrician would ask. Yes, this was almost exactly the right time of her monthly cycle for conception. Then she ticked off the ensuing months, all nine of them. A March baby! A springtime birth! Could she do it? Could she actually endure the reputedly excruciating pain of labor and delivery? Of course she could. And then she would hold her own tiny, wriggling bundle in her arms.

There was no question that she would nurse her baby, filling the helpless infant with the warmth and nourishment of mother's milk. She would be there to observe each new movement from the moment the little one rolled over, through the stages of sitting and crawling and walking.

All the things she had done with Colin and had ached to do with him in the years that had been stolen, she would do with this child of her own flesh—repeating favorite nursery rhymes, taking walks through fall leaves and spring flowers, singing songs learned in Sunday school, building sand castles at the beach.

There would be bridges to cross—the first day of kindergarten, the first loose tooth, the first trembling kiss. And Lilia would be there... a mother.

Seized with elation, she curled over and hugged herself.

"Prefer to eat dinner here at the lodge?" Miles asked behind her.

Lilia straightened, reality intruding with a disconcerting suddenness. There was Miles to consider in all of this... Miles with his tender touch, his deep concern for all life— and his determination to topple what they had just begun to build.

"Lilia?" he asked, coming around toward the display of native crafts. "You look a bit pale. Feeling all right?"

Pale! she wanted to exult. Of course I'm pale—I'm pregnant!

"Umm...oh, I'm fine." She read the seriousness in his eyes. She didn't know for certain that she had conceived. Actually, it was probably not as likely as she wished. And maybe...maybe this very possibility was what had upset Miles. Maybe he had been trying to tell her that he didn't intend to build a permanent, stable future with her—at least not one that included a family, babies, children.

What had he said in the Land Rover? He had wanted to talk to her about the future. *There's nothing I want more than you,* he had plainly told her. *Everything that happened between us is wonderful. Or, not exactly wonderful because...* Because what? Because of the future. Miles wanted a life with her perhaps, but he didn't want a relationship that included a child.

While she had been elated to think about a pregnancy, maybe Miles had been dismayed. Lilia studied him as she stood to gather her belongings. Miles was everything she had ever wanted in a husband. Everything she still wanted. She had no doubt he would provide for her, protect her, delight her. She knew—probably much better than he did—what a wonderful father he would make. Warm, compassionate, understanding, he was also fun and playful—exactly the sort of stable yet interactive father a child would need.

"Dinner?" he repeated for the second time. "We could eat here at Ngulia Lodge before we head out."

Lilia tried to concentrate. "Aren't we staying here tonight?"

"Actually, I booked a couple of self-help bandas." He shrugged. "I've thought of incorporating private guest cottages with kitchenettes at some of the hotels I'm working on. It seemed the thing to do to stay at one for the night."

"Well, let's eat there then." Lilia glanced at the white-clothed tables laden with crystal and silverware. "To tell you the truth, I'm sort of tired of the luxury hotel atmosphere."

"We don't have any food... but I suppose I could arrange with the kitchen to collect a few things."

"That sounds all right." He gave her a look she couldn't read before turning to walk away. As his broad shoulders disappeared around a corner, Lilia wondered what the hours to come would bring.

As Lilia stood over a small gas stove and ground pepper onto a pair of thick steaks, she decided the Ngulia Self-Help Bandas were the right choice for this evening. Secluded, the row of small whitewashed bungalows were perched on a hill, overlooking a water hole. Lilia and Miles had been assigned the two largest cottages, as the others were unoccupied. Their driver had stayed behind with other tour-bus drivers and the hotel staff in quarters provided at one of the lodges.

While Miles opened cans of peas and spread butter on bread still warm from the oven, Lilia grilled the meat. A cool breeze drifted in through open windows. The sun slanted across the horizon, casting bars of orange light into the little kitchen.

"That shade of tangerine always brings back memories," she told Miles over her shoulder. "It's watering time for the elephants."

As he poured the peas into a saucepan, Miles couldn't help but smile. "Shall I have a look?"

"I wouldn't want to miss a moment of it."

He slid a pair of binoculars from their case and left the kitchen for the front veranda. Lilia used a pair of tongs to flip the sizzling steaks. So far, neither she nor Miles had said a word about the subject brewing between them. She had managed to fill in every silence on the journey to the bandas with her observations on hotel decor and her plans for the sites in the States. Miles had responded politely, his focus directed on maneuvering the dirt road without driving into any ant bear holes, and then on unloading the Land Rover.

All the same, Lilia knew what was coming. And she knew she had a choice. She could sit down with Miles and hear him out, as any considerate human being ought to do. He would tell her how he felt about their future and about families and so forth, and then she would nod and reply that she understood completely. They would acknowledge that their actions the previous night had been spontaneous and merely a result of unfinished business from ten years ago. Then they would agree to keep at an emotional distance for the rest of the trip.

Or Lilia could take the upper hand and play out the cards she chose. If she really wanted a baby of her own...and she definitely did...she could sidetrack the conversation. As she had this morning in the shower, she could tease and flirt and lure Miles back into bed. That he would make love with her, she had almost no doubt.

His brain might tell him to back off, to prevent any chance of complications such as pregnancy. But in spite of his keen intelligence, Miles had always been a man whose body spoke loudly, demanding its way. He was physical. He was male. And most importantly, he wanted her. She knew that, and she knew she could use his desires to accomplish her own ends.

Giving the peas a stir, she pondered her situation. Would it be right to use Miles? Could she in good conscience manipulate him into her bed and employ his body as nothing more than a fertilizing device? Part of her argued vehemently against the idea. She had never used or coerced people. To do so would be demeaning to both parties. And she wouldn't find it easy to put Miles in the role of breeding stud, rather than lover and husband as she had come to think of him.

No, she couldn't do it.

Lilia opened the oven door and checked on the bread she was keeping warm there. When she straightened, her hand brushed against her stomach. Instantly, her thoughts fell on the tiny life she hoped was growing inside her. *Oh, please,* she whispered in unconscious prayer.

She looked out the window and saw Miles scanning the horizon for elephants. The set of his shoulders told her there was no doubt he fully intended to separate from her. He would leave her high and dry with nothing to show for all this turmoil but a heart full of painful memories. Why shouldn't she claim something meaningful out of it— something she wanted and something that Miles could give her? Why shouldn't she bear a child?

Of course, if she resumed life in Springfield among all her friends and clients and suddenly began to swell with pregnancy, she would receive more than her share of raised eyebrows. Missouri was definitely conservative, middle-class America, with its biblical values firmly in place. That was part of the reason she felt so comfortable there.

How could she reasonably explain an impulsive teenage wedding, a surprise reunion, a sudden trip to Africa, a whirlwind fling and a second abandonment by her husband? *Oh, sure,* people would think. *Lilia Eden flew off to Africa and had herself a romance. And now she's paying the piper.*

But she wanted those consequences. What did she care what people thought of her? If she wanted a baby, why shouldn't she have one—no matter what it took?

Outside on the veranda, Miles lowered his binoculars and slipped his hands into his pockets. Lilia's eyes traced over the breadth of his shoulders, the tapering of his waist and hips, the fine, golden sheen of hair on his legs. She thought of his blue eyes, and pictured how that color would look in a small, pink face. A blond little boy, perhaps, with Miles's inner strength, Miles's stubborn persistence, Miles's deep compassion.

As she turned back to the kitchen, it occurred to Lilia that she ought to look for the pair of silk panties she had packed. She would need them after dinner.

Chapter 15

"Seventeen of them," Miles told Lilia when she joined him on the veranda. "Mothers and babies."

Standing so close that her shoulder brushed against Miles, Lilia took the binoculars and swept them across the dusky plains. As she adjusted the focus, a long line of elephants came into view. A huge female with flapping ears and an enormous pair of white tusks led the way, followed by her matriarchal clan. Aunties, sisters, cousins and babies drifted toward the water hole that reflected the deep pink of sunset in the valley below the bungalows.

"So few," Lilia commented. "Hundreds and hundreds used to come when I was a girl."

"Poachers." A note of bitterness edged Miles's voice. "That grand mama in the front had better look to her own hide if she means to stay alive. No doubt someone would love to turn her tusks into piano keys or a pair of earrings."

Lilia lowered the binoculars. The elephants were now so close she could see them clearly. "The last time I was in Tsavo, only four rhinos were left."

"It's a damned shame. You can't save elephants and rhinos without a good cash flow to provide game wardens with weapons and ammunition against the poachers. And you

can bet most of the cash flow will have to come from outside the country—from private donations and foreign aid."

The elephants had slowly formed a ring around the water
hole. While the matriarch kept watch, the others dipped
their trunks into the cool pond, then drained the water into
their mouths. Two calves went in knee deep. In a moment,
several of the larger elephants followed suit.

This was not a merry band like those Lilia had seen in the
past. There were no wobbly babies cavorting on the bank,
no impulsive teenage bulls spraying one another, no flop-
eared young cows wading through the shallows. In fact, the
elephants were somber, as if they sensed the cloud of doom
that hung over them.

While the sun sank beneath the horizon, they went about
their task of drinking. There was a heavy, stoic air about the
herd. As the last of the pink light hung in the acacia
branches, they began to amble away, one after the other.

With a sigh, Lilia turned back to the kitchen. Miles had
set napkins and silver on a small table on the veranda. Lilia
filled white crockery plates with the steaks and vegetables,
and she and Miles settled into wicker chairs. As they ate the
delicious dinner, another line of elephants came from the
opposite direction to form around the water hole.

"The elephants are the reason I proposed the hotel project," Miles said as he poured himself a glass of wine. Remembering her hoped-for condition, Lilia opted for orange
soda. "Not only elephants, but rhino, leopards, cheetahs.
All the endangered species. We won't be able to keep them
in our enclosures. Not at first, anyway. But I hope to raise
awareness. I hope to collect donations eventually. I've
dreamed..." He let out a breath. "Well, it's a bit far-
fetched."

"What, Miles? Tell me your dream."

He gazed at the elephants for a long time before speaking. "They've given me so much, these animals. Pleasure.
Excitement. Good fun. I've dreamed that I could give
something back. In some small way, I'd like to do my part
to save these animals. To ensure that they go on—here in
Africa, where they belong."

Lilia's eyes misted. She couldn't do it. She couldn't use Miles. He was a man—sensitive and deeply concerned about his world. Why wouldn't he want a child of his own? Maybe she should ask him. If she tried hard enough, perhaps she could convince him how right they were together and how a child would only add to the beauty of their union.

"These elephants have a keen intelligence," he was saying, wrapped in his own thoughts. "They're not like a cow or even a dog. They mourn their slain family. They minister tenderly to their ill. They remember everything—not only sources of water and vegetation, but events. They know when things happened, and how. I feel a responsibility to preserve them. No matter what it takes."

Lilia mused for a moment. "We could incorporate the endangered species as themes in the hotels. Focus an area in the lobby on each of them. Put up displays that show their plight. Call for action in a subtle but definitive way."

"I like that." His eyes showed the first spark of the evening. "If you constructed them right, the displays could blend with the rest of the decor."

"I know I can do it."

Lilia considered going for her notebook, but Miles was rising from the table and carrying his empty plate into the kitchen. He seemed to consider the conversation at an end. Lilia took a last bite of her steak. The sun had gone. A chill that made her wish for a sweater had settled across the land. Stars began to glimmer in the deep purple night sky. Acacias stretched black thorny limbs above the horizon.

Standing, Lilia went to the rock wall that edged the veranda. It was somehow both comforting and frightening to realize there was no artificial light as far as her eyes could see. No headlights, no lanterns, no campfires. Certainly no electric bulbs burning behind glass windows. Nothing but utter blackness . . . and somewhere within it, the faint grunt of a lion.

"No moon tonight," Miles commented as he joined her. She realized he had already carried her plate into the kitchen and cleared the table. "Lions are out."

"On the ridge behind us?"

"A bit to the south, I should think." He listened for a moment. "Hyena. On the plain. Must be guarding a kill."

Lilia strained to hear the eerie yapping that confirmed Miles's observation. "At least we won't be bothered by too many mosquitoes this far up."

"I wouldn't be too sure about that. Once we light a lantern, we'll draw all sorts of nasties."

Smiling at the image, Lilia leaned on the rock wall and shut her eyes. The cool breeze bathed her face and bare arms. The air was marvelous—fresh, raw, earthy. Completely untainted by man. She took a deep breath.

Miles moved beside her, his elbow coming to rest next to hers on the wall. Her heart flopped against her ribs and began to thud at twice its normal pace. She braced herself. This was it, she realized, the moment when he made his statement of closure. She could almost feel the tension emanating from him. She would accept it gracefully. She *would*. He cleared his throat.

"Lilia," he began.

"Oh, Miles…" Without further thought, she slipped her arms around his shoulders and began to kiss his neck. "I've been wanting to do this all day."

Well, it was true! But she hadn't meant to actually do it. She'd meant to let him have his say and deliver the message that had been troubling him for hours. Now instead of speaking, he was turning in her arms, responding just as she had predicted. His hands slid around her waist and up beneath her arms, his palms grazing the sides of her breasts.

"Lilia," he said thickly against her ear, "I must talk with you."

"Tomorrow," she heard herself say.

"Tonight."

"Miles, I need you tonight." And that was true, too. Her body was betraying her just as deeply as she felt she was betraying Miles. Instead of the cold, calculated seduction she had contemplated, she found herself the one seduced.

Miles's mouth had discovered hers, his lips heating her skin and his tongue making silken promises. His hands curved over her breasts, warming the flesh beneath her pink shirt. She moved into his embrace, allowing their stomachs to touch, their thighs to press together.

Part of her mind demanded rationally that she back away this very minute and allow Miles the grace to have his say. The other part of her brain argued fiercely that she deserved to carry this man's baby, and she deserved a future of happiness with or without him.

But it was her body that prevailed. Miles kissed her deeply, and she felt her knees turn to soup. His hands slipped under her shirt, and she sensed the electric waves that zipped through her skin to tighten the tips of her breasts. Her fingertips grazed the sides of his neck, brushed over his ear, slid through his hair. She heard his breath grow shallow.

This was all Miles's fault, she reasoned with faulty logic as he kissed the throbbing pulse point at the base of her throat. His unabashed desire had eroded her convictions. When he touched her, she couldn't think straight.

Of course she couldn't. He wore the scent of Africa—the raw air, the sunburned grass, the windswept plains. His skin was firm and hot beneath her hands. As he pulled her hard against him, she felt the male animal emanating from his body. Like the lion in the distance, he called to her, beckoning, luring, demanding.

"Miles," she whispered, the sensible part of her mind trying for one last stand. *Miles,* she wanted to say, *go ahead and tell me that you're not interested in making a future out of this. You don't want that kind of permanence. You don't want a home, a family... a baby.*

"Miles, please hold me tighter," was all she could manage to say.

"Lilia," he said, his mouth against her neck, "Lilia, I can't promise you... I can't give you..."

"It's all right, Miles." And it seemed to be. No promises, no dreams... but why not a child? Some tangible evidence that once they had truly loved.

"You don't understand," he tried again.

"I do."

"No, it's complicated. It's just that I can't—"

"I understand one thing right now, Miles Kane, I want your hands on my breasts and your body lying next to mine. I want your lips on my bare skin. Can you give me that? If you can't give me your heart, can you give me your touch?"

He shuddered as her hand slid down the front of his trousers. Struggling to clear his head of the fog her caresses evoked, he lifted his eyes to the path of shimmering stars sprinkled across the black sky. "I need to explain," he said hoarsely, his body alive to the stroke of her fingers. "I must talk with you, Lilia."

"Tomorrow," she whispered. "Love me tonight, Miles, the way you did under the cliffs."

Unleashed, he let out a groan of desire and swept her up in his arms. The thud of the bungalow door swinging open silenced the rising chorus of night music across the African plain. In a moment, it swelled again, a mingled melody sharpened by the chirp of crickets, the huff of a lion, the sorry weeping of a bush baby, the shrill laughter of a hyena, the croak of a frog in the water hole.

Barely lit by the stars, the single narrow bed formed a cushion for Lilia's body. She stretched out on the cool sheets, her legs tingling with anticipation. Miles loomed over her, a massive shadow stripping away his shirt and trousers.

"Lilia," he said as he took her in his arms on the bed. "You must understand...I don't want to hurt you. Ever."

She had discarded her clothes, so that it was bare skin that moved against him in the darkness. In the soft light, he could barely make out her eyes, luminous and hungry. Her pale shoulder and curved hip wore a thin veil of silver.

She sighed. "When we're like this, nothing can hurt me. It feels so right. So perfect."

But it's not, he wanted to cry out. *You're not permitted to dream of the things other women dream when their husbands hold them and love them. With me, you have no promise of family, of children. With me, you lose...just as you lost Colin.*

Determined to tell her, he pressed his lips against her cheek. But as he took a deep breath, her fingertips slid down the length of his chest and came to rest on his thighs. Her sweet breasts lifted against him, their pebbled crests grazing his nipples. Her mouth covered his, and her tongue flicked across his lips. And he forgot what it was he had meant to say.

He smoothed his hand down her length, like a blind man memorizing every plane and hollow. Her skin was velvet, her hair a whisper of satin. She smelled of lilacs and tasted of oranges. If he could have prolonged the ecstasy of holding her, he would have.

But her hands found him, set him afire, taunted him into a raging flame. He bent over her, kissing and suckling her nipples until he felt her hips begin to sway on the bed. Her mouth tormented his neck, her fingers played a primordial song on his back, her palms urged him to meld into her dance.

"You're my heaven," he murmured, as he felt her legs slip apart beneath him.

She moaned. "Oh . . . Miles. Please."

"Everything. All I've ever wanted."

He poised above her, savoring the moment to come. Her tongue traced a line down his neck and she formed her hands around his arms.

"All I'll ever want," he said. "For the rest of my life."

As he moved toward her, he heard her breath catch. She stiffened slightly. "What?" she whispered. "Wait...what? What did you say? What am I doing?"

Her thighs fell together and she rolled out from under him. Before he could react, she was sitting on the edge of the bed, her face buried in her hands.

"I can't do this!" she said, sobbing. "I can't believe what I was about to... Oh, Miles."

He stared at the silvery curve of her back. What had he said? He couldn't remember. Whatever he'd said, this couldn't go on without honesty between them. He would insist on the truth, at all cost. But what was she feeling? He could hardly think beyond the roar of his body. He needed her! He had to have her... had to ease himself.

"Lilia," he said thickly, touching her shoulder.

"Miles, it's all about children, isn't it? It's about babies."

A sudden chill surged through his veins, instantly cooling his ardor. He ran a hand through his hair. Mouth suddenly dry, he swallowed. It felt as if he had an old bone stuck in his throat.

"Well...I suppose it is," he managed to say. "Children."

How had she known? Had she overheard something during his telephone conversation with his parents? Or did she simply want to tell him herself how important it was to her to have a baby?

He looked up. Dragging a sheet, she had walked across the room to the window. He could see the dark curve of her hair, the long silhouette of her neck. What had upset her so deeply? He rubbed the back of his neck. Maybe she didn't want to have a baby, after all. Maybe she was cutting off their lovemaking out of fear of pregnancy.

He could certainly reassure her on that count.

"I know how you feel about children," she was saying, her voice so tremulous he felt his heart quake. "That you never were the family-man type."

"I wasn't?"

She looked at him. "Were you?"

"Under the circumstances, I didn't give it a great deal of thought."

She turned back to the starlit window. Before she could speak again, he dragged on his trousers. The urge to bolt was so great that he decided the least he could do was be clothed. He now knew—without a doubt—that the moment he told Lilia what he had to say, she would reject him. And her rejection would be more unbearable than any pain he'd ever known. He would have no choice but to leave.

He wanted to leave now.

"Anyway," she said, letting out a shaky breath. "You wanted to tell me something today. I wouldn't let you. And...now I think you'd better."

He stood and shoved his hands into his pockets. Lifting his chin, he took a deep breath. "It is about children," he said. "About the future."

"You know, you would make a wonderful father." She was clutching the sheet tightly against her throat. "You're very understanding, very kind. You're just exactly the sort of father a little boy or girl would adore.''

Miles clenched his fists inside his pockets. "Possibly."

"It's true. I knew it the moment I saw you and Colin together, the moment you lifted him onto your shoulders. Did you know he spoke, Miles? For the very first time, Colin spoke. It was the day you and I met at the zoo. You had just walked away, and he said bye. 'Bye, Mice.' That's what he said. 'Bye, Mice.'"

She was crying now, pressing the corner of the sheet against one eye, her shoulders shaking ever so slightly. Miles swallowed at the dry bone in his throat. His eyelids felt like sandpaper. He could feel the muscle in his jaw twitching.

"Lilia," he said. The word came out as a croak. "I can't... can't be a father."

She lifted her tear-streaked face, and he saw the look in her eyes. Dismay. Confusion. Rejection. In the next moment, he was out the door, striding down the long veranda, headed for the Land Rover.

Lilia stood immobile. Miles couldn't be a father. What did that mean? Why not? She heard the Land Rover's engine cough and roar to life. Where was he going? He couldn't leave now, in the middle of this.

"Miles!" She ran out of the bungalow. The Land Rover was pulling onto the road. Sheet fluttering, Lilia tore across the gravel in her bare feet. "Miles, wait! Wait!"

The Land Rover stopped abruptly, and she grabbed the door handle. Flinging it open, she saw Miles slumped forward over the steering wheel.

"Miles, please talk to me." She climbed onto the seat beside him. His hands were knotted around the wheel. In the starlight, his lowered head wore a silver-white mane.

"I need to go out there, Lilia," he said, his voice clotted with pain. "I find comfort on the plains."

"Find comfort with me, Miles. Let me be your place of peace."

She reached out and laid her fingers on his shoulder. With the flick of a hand, he pushed her away. "Don't. I might want you too much."

"Miles..." Fear like an icy hand twisted around Lilia's throat. "Miles, you have to talk to me."

"Why did you pull away in bed?" he demanded, lifting his head. His eyes were red-rimmed, their blue irises glowing with anguish. "Because you were afraid you might get pregnant?"

Lilia looked down at her hands. "I want to have your child, Miles. Very much. I want it so badly that... I would have done anything. I pulled away because I had considered using you to father a baby, even though I knew you didn't want to have children. When we were making love tonight, you said something about the future—that I'm all you'll ever want. I suddenly realized I couldn't make love with you, even though my feelings had gone way past the stage of using you. I hadn't given you the chance to say what you had to say to me. To...to tell me how you felt about the future. About us. About having a permanent relationship...and children."

Miles was silent for a long time. Lilia felt the chill of the cold metal floor creep around her ankles and up her legs.

"Was that all you wanted from me under the cliffs the other night, then?" he asked finally. "And in the shower? A baby?"

"No! I wasn't even thinking about that. It hadn't occurred to me until today at the lodge. And then having your baby was all I could think of. Especially since I know how you feel—"

"You don't know a damn thing about how I feel!" Miles exploded. He flung open the Land Rover door. The night air cut through his lungs as he waded through the thigh-high grass. He hadn't cried in ten years—not since he'd lost Lilia. Now he was choking back the lump in his throat, cursing the sting in his eyes, fighting to place anger where sorrow demanded expression.

"You haven't told me how you feel!" Lilia called behind him.

"How could I?" He whirled on her. "You cut me off. You wouldn't let me talk."

"I didn't want to hear it."

"Why not?"

"Because I don't want to end what we've just begun, that's why!" Her anger sought to match his own. "That's what you've been trying to tell me, isn't it? That you don't want a future. You don't want permanence. You don't want children."

"Is that what I said in the bungalow a few minutes ago?"

"No," she whispered.

"No." He looked up at the sky. Like a fireworks display frozen by time, the stars emblazoned the blackness. A swath of sparks cut through the center of the night, a diamond path across ebony velvet. Miles brushed a fingertip under one eye.

"I would offer you a future," he said softly, "but it wouldn't be the one you wanted. It wouldn't be the one we dreamed of ten years ago. What I have to offer is myself. That's it. No cozy little family sitting round the fire. No children. No grandchildren. Just me."

He could see Lilia shivering under the draped sheet that left her arms and shoulders bare. Shoeless, she stood in the prickly grass. She didn't understand, and he knew he would have to say it out loud. Exactly as it had been said to him.

"I will never father children," he stated, claiming the doctor's speech as his own. "I no longer have that option. The malaria I contracted ten years ago was accompanied by a high fever. The prolonged, elevated temperature in my body destroyed all my reproductive capabilities."

He squared his shoulders. "So you see, Lilia. I will never be a father. And if you stay with me, you'll never be a mother. It's as simple as that." He took a deep breath. "I'm sterile."

Chapter 16

Lilia stared at Miles. A waterfall of images poured through her. Her marriage to Miles. Their first lovemaking. His sickness. Her college. Her design studio. Colin...

It was Colin all over again. There would be no Colin. There would be no child for her. Not through adoption. Not with Miles.

Feeling as barren as the biblical Hannah who had begged God for a child, Lilia placed a hand over her empty womb. Seeing the gesture, Miles straightened.

"I know how much it means to you," he said. His voice was stiff with suppressed emotion, the English accent stilting his words. "Nothing to be done about it, of course. Permanent situation."

She read the hurt etched in his face. Her mind formed words of sympathy, understanding, acceptance. But the messages wouldn't filter down to her mouth. All she could think of was Colin. Small, fluffy-haired Colin with his little cloth elephant and his big brown eyes.

It's Colin, she wanted to say. *My arms ache for my son! My heart grieves day and night for him!*

But instead of explaining, all she could do was cry. Tears started in the corners of her eyes, filtered through her lashes, rolled down her cheeks. Her breath came in shallow gasps. She had to explain. She could see Miles's face changing, his expression altering from pain to resignation.

"Oh, Miles—"

"I'll send a Land Rover for you in the morning," he cut in. "You can do as you like after that."

"Now wait—"

"You don't need to explain, Lilia. I've gone over it all in my mind a thousand times—starting ten years ago." He took the keys from his pocket. "I should have told you from the beginning."

He swung around and started for the Land Rover.

"Miles, stop!" Lilia ran after him, but he was already climbing in, shutting the door. The engine sputtered to life. "Miles, will you please wait?"

The Land Rover started down the rutted track. Lilia followed as it gained speed. She hammered on the metal side with her fist and called his name, but Miles drove on. In a moment, the vehicle had outpaced her, and she was left alone on the road, her sheet tangled around her legs and dust swirling into her hair.

"Fine!" she shouted after him. "Don't give me a chance to say anything. Don't hear me tell you that I love you, Miles Kane!"

The vehicle's lights moved away toward the lodge. Lilia sniffled. A cricket chirped somewhere near her foot.

"I love you, Miles," she whispered. "That's what I want to tell you. I love you."

The headlights disappeared behind a ridge, and Lilia let out her breath. Well, this was the perfect end to a confusing mess. Miles had confessed his deepest pain, and then like a rogue elephant with the raw stump of a broken tusk to torment him, he had stormed off to nurse his agony alone. And here she was alone in the bush, unable to console or comfort him in any way. She couldn't even contact him. She had neither protection nor transportation, and wild animals were all around.

Picking up a fallen tree limb as a small pretense at defense, she started back to the bungalow. Her bare feet ached. Her eyelids felt like a pair of thick lemon peels. She rubbed her finger under her nose, then dabbed her cheek with a corner of the sheet.

Miles was a rogue elephant exactly, she decided as she climbed onto the veranda and slumped into a wicker chair. For ten years, he had lived with the throbbing, open wound of knowledge that he would never father children. No doubt that knowledge had contributed to his agreement to annul his marriage to Lilia, an action that had only added to his pain. He had felt sure, even as a young man, that she would turn him away.

When he finally had bared his soul to her, he was so sure of rejection that he had chosen to read it in her eyes. But Lilia wasn't rejecting Miles. Was she?

Gazing out at the utter blackness of the night, Lilia pulled the folds of the white sheet over her shoulders. Would she ever accept a childless life? Could she be happy with Miles, knowing he couldn't give her a baby? And when would she ever be able to admit that she had lost Colin forever?

Feeling the tears start to well up again, Lilia clenched her jaw. It was time to take a good, hard look at this situation. Time to put her head in gear instead of her heart. First of all, she had to face her loss of Colin. As much as she loved him, as often as his little face played in and out of her dreams, Colin was no longer a part of her life. She had to find some way to accept that.

Like Miles, who had escaped rather than face the pain of loss, Lilia knew this trip to Africa was an attempt to flee the knowledge that Colin was gone. It was so much easier living without her son in Kenya than it would be when she returned to Missouri and the home they shared. But she couldn't run forever.

Second, Lilia knew she had to face the fact that she was committed to the hotel project, and in good faith she should finish at least the preliminary stages. After all, Habari Safari had spent an enormous amount of money sending her to Kenya to build a portfolio. She had no ethical choice but to complete it.

Third, she had to talk to Miles. Perhaps there was too much water under the bridge to ever build a successful future out of the rubble of the past. Maybe she would find that, indeed, she couldn't accept a husband who couldn't promise her a family. Whatever happened, she didn't intend to end this holiday with Miles Kane the way she had ended the last one—with an aching heart, broken vows and words left unspoken.

Lilia knew now that she did love Miles, and she had to tell him that much, no matter what. If only she could find him.

The African driver appeared early the following morning. He said nothing to Lilia about the disappearance of the *bwana mkubwa*. Instead, he helped her load her bags—and Miles's—into the Land Rover, and then drove her to the lodge.

Lilia inquired at the front desk, only to learn that Miles had not spent the night there. Instead, he had driven to the airstrip, where he had taken a plane out at dawn. Checking their itinerary, Lilia realized he must have flown to the slopes of Mount Kenya, where he was to interview the managers of two luxury hotels. Aware that Miles had scheduled a night at Naro Moru, Lilia decided she had no choice but to fly there herself and try to track him down.

"When will the next plane leave for Nairobi?" she asked the African woman behind the reception desk. "I need to book a seat."

"The last flight of the day has just gone. There won't be another until tomorrow morning, I'm afraid. We'll have two more groups of tourists flying in this afternoon, but nothing going out again today."

"But I need to..." Lilia squelched her frustration. "What would you suggest I do to get to Naro Moru as quickly as possible? This is urgent."

"A medical emergency?"

If you consider a broken heart a medical emergency, Lilia thought. "No," she replied, "this is personal."

The clerk checked her notebooks and schedules. "Your driver could take you to Nairobi today. Late this afternoon, an Air-Tours flight leaves for Mount Kenya. It is possible you could stay at the Safari Club and then be driven to Naro Moru early in the morning tomorrow."

"But I have to get to Naro Moru tonight, or I might miss..." Lilia tucked a strand of hair behind her ear. "Did Mr. Kane leave any messages for me? I'm Lilia Eden. Or Lilia Kane. Whatever."

"Permit me to check." Giving her a curious glance, the woman went into a back room. Lilia chewed on her lower lip. If she couldn't make it to Naro Moru by nightfall, she might as well forget it. Miles had scheduled only one night there. She studied her itinerary.

Common sense told her to skip Naro Moru, and try to catch up with Miles at Maasai Mara National Park. She had never felt comfortable in the chilly rainforest that cloaked the foothills of Mount Kenya. Leopards and shy bongos lurked beneath the canopy of leaves and tangled vines. Mists crept through the lush undergrowth. It was a mysterious, drippy, frigid place, and only the tent camp at Naro Moru had ever been able to lure Lilia from the sunny climate she seemed to need for survival.

But she had to talk to Miles. She didn't want to spend one more day without settling things between them. Why had he left her? She knew why. All the same, she felt abandoned by him. It was the same creeping, desolate, empty feeling she had first known when his parents whisked him away to the hospital in Lusaka.

Resisting the grip of dismay, Lilia reaffirmed her decision to find Miles at Naro Moru and talk things through—even if it meant renting a Land Rover and driving from the Safari Club to the camp alone at night. She was placing her itinerary in her bag when the clerk returned with a slip of folded paper.

"Here's a message for you, Ms. Eden." She slid the paper across the desk. "It came by telephone."

Lilia tried to swallow her eagerness as she flipped open the note. She knew it might be nothing more than a curt message from him. The note read:

Lilia, please phone me. Family services was trying to locate you. I don't know why.

Jenny Larsen

It took two readings before Lilia finally accepted that the message was not from Miles, but from Missouri. Lilia pictured her blond assistant, and then she focused on the words "Family services."

Colin! It must be something about Colin. Lilia's heart fluttered with a mixture of excitement and fear. Colin. Or maybe not. Maybe there was a new child ready for adoption. On the other hand, it could be nothing more than a new form to fill out or a report to make. But Jenny had phoned all the way from the States to let her know.

"I need to make a long-distance call," Lilia told the clerk. "Overseas. Do you have a telephone I can use? I have a calling card."

"Of course, madam. But I should warn you that our telephone has not been responding well for two days."

Lilia's spirits sank. This was the flip side to the natural beauty and wonder of the Third World—difficulties with transportation and communication. At this moment, the sight of a hundred healthy elephants wouldn't take the place of her need for a clear connection to Missouri and, following that, a quick flight to Naro Moru.

She thanked the clerk and asked her to wait a moment while she spoke with the driver. "We'll go to Nairobi after I've made a telephone call," she told him.

"In Nairobi, you will find a better telephone, *memsahib*."

Lilia pondered that for a moment. It was true. In Nairobi she would find the conveniences of the modern world. She would taste reality again, and she could think logically. But Nairobi would have to wait.

"I'll try here, first."

She followed the clerk into a back office and spent the next two hours shouting at various overseas operators. Static crackled across the line. She was cut off twice. Over and over she heard the recorded message that all the international circuits were busy. There were so many numerical codes to dial, she lost track. Finally she heard a faint but familiar voice at the other end of the line.

"Huh? What?" Jenny mumbled.

Lilia glanced at her watch, realizing she'd forgotten to calculate the time in Springfield. "Jenny, it's me, Lilia!" she said loudly into the receiver.

"I can't hear.... Who is this? Hey, it's two in the morning! What do you mean by calling me at this..."

"Jenny! It's Lilia in Africa!"

"Decent people are asleep at this hour of the..." There was a brief pause. "Who?"

"Lilia! I'm calling from Kenya."

"Gosh, Lilia! It's great to hear your voice. I've missed you so much. Oh, wow—is this really Africa? I can't hear you very well. Are you there?"

"I'm at the lodge where you left the message. Jenny, what's going on? Why did you call?"

"That lady was here today. Well, not *here*. I'm at home in bed right now. Did you know it's two in the morning? What time is it over there in Africa?"

"What lady?" Lilia shouted.

"Huh? Oh, the lady from family services. Your caseworker."

"Jean Banes. What did she want? Is Colin all right?"

"She wouldn't tell me a thing, but I'm thinking they might have another baby for you. She said she was trying to get a message through to you, but she couldn't. She missed you at Mombasa, and then the phones weren't working right. She wanted to find out if I had talked to you."

Lilia couldn't think what to say. Of course the caseworker wouldn't tell Jenny anything. But Lilia didn't have Jean's home phone number, and it would be hours before the family services office opened in Springfield.

"I really wish you had called sooner, Lilia," Jenny was saying. "I've had so much trouble with Mrs. Kaufmann. I showed her all your plans, but she doesn't want to work with me. She says you're the decorator, and she won't work with anyone else. And then Mr. Bilton's silk plants came in and they're the worst I've ever seen. So fake-looking, you wouldn't believe it. Nothing like the ones we ordered at market. I've just been going crazy. The wallpaper place shorted me two rolls on the Exeter house project, so we re-ordered, and then the new rolls didn't match. They were practically green instead of blue. There was a big nubby flaw running right down the middle of all that fabric that came in for the new restaurant and then—''

"Jenny, first thing in the morning I want you to tell family services I called. I'm going to drive to Nairobi right now—''

"In the middle of the night? Is that safe?''

"It's ten o'clock in the morning here.''

"Golly! That's wild, isn't it? It's two over here. Two in the morning—like the middle of the night, you know?''

"I'm going to drive to Nairobi and call family services from a hotel there. I'll stay at..." She racked her brain trying to think of a place. "The Norfolk Hotel. That's where I'll be. If I can't get them, tell them to try me. Please, Jenny, can you remember the Norfolk?''

"Okay, I wrote it down. Are you coming home soon? I could really use some help. Where's Miles? How's everything going between—''

"I'll be back as soon as I can. Just hold the fort for me, will you?''

"Sure, Lilia. Don't worry.''

But as Lilia hung up the phone, worry was all she could do. The driver had wandered off during her long telephone saga, and it took another half hour to round him up. Then he insisted on loading the Land Rover with jugs of fresh water and boxes of food.

While he was occupied, Lilia decided to send a message to Miles in care of the Safari Club at the foot of Mount Kenya. But the phones were down completely by this time, and Lilia had no choice but to leave a short message with the clerk at Ngulia Lodge there in Tsavo West. After scribbling out the address of the Norfolk Hotel and writing a message telling Miles she wanted to speak with him, she asked the clerk to relay the information if Miles Kane happened to telephone.

There was hardly any chance that he would call, Lilia knew. She had seen the look on his face—the total shutdown of emotion. He had faced his pain by locking it away, by severing himself from every reminder. She knew he would avoid contact with her at all cost. From the moment he had revealed his secret, the ball had been in her court. Of course, she had done nothing but cry—which had only seemed to confirm Miles's certainty that she would reject him.

If they were ever to work through this, it would be up to her to initiate a meeting and start the conversation. Now she would have to be the one to break down walls. But could she find him? And was there time before she would have to fly back to the States?

With a sigh of frustration, Lilia climbed into the Land Rover and set off down the infamous Mombasa highway. She quickly realized she had been selective in her memories of the long trip, focusing on the majestic panorama of distant purple hills, golden plains, scrubby acacia and groups of gazelles or giraffes. Now as the Land Rover traveled the narrow road, she was vividly reminded of every deep pothole and every bathroom stop that had served to make the trip seem endless when she was a child.

The pit stops required the fortitude of a Greek stoic, Lilia decided. Roll of toilet paper in hand, she trekked through thigh-high elephant grass in search of a tall red anthill to hide behind. It required luck and some skill to avoid the mamba snakes, stinging safari ants and curious passing tourists that took the place of clean, pine-scented service station bathrooms in the United States.

Nearly six hours of driving finally brought the first view of Nairobi, Kenya's modern capital. Lilia hardly noticed the bougainvillea that grew along the medians in shades of deep magenta, crimson, soft pink and gold. The high-rise offices that mingled with stone colonial buildings failed to bring the rush of excitement she had always felt on arriving in the historic city. Nose buried in her itinerary, she ignored the throngs of Africans who mingled easily with Asians from India, Britons who could trace their heritage in Kenya to the turn of the century and tourists from every corner of the world.

"The Norfolk?" the driver asked as he maneuvered the Land Rover through the dense traffic circling a roundabout. "It is not far."

They pulled into the parking lot of the old hotel as the sun set over the eucalyptus trees. Lilia breathed a sigh of relief and climbed out of the vehicle. She learned at the front desk that there would be a room for her, and that the telephones were working for overseas calls, and that there were flights each morning to Mount Kenya.

Breathing a prayer of thanks, she followed the porter to her room. The faithful driver had given her his address and had asked her to write to him and his family when she got back to America. As she walked into the lamplit room, Lilia slipped the address into her portfolio. She had the feeling it might be her last connection with Kenya.

A quick dial brought the crackle of the overseas operator. Lilia checked her watch and then gave the number of her credit card and the number for the family services office. A distant voice answered.

"Hello—hello?"

Oh, no, an echo. There was nothing worse than the echo caused by a faulty satellite relay. Even static and sleepy operators were better than this.

"I'm calling long distance to speak with Jean Banes—speak with Jean Banes," Lilia said, hearing herself repeated in a hollow voice.

"What—what?"

"Jean Banes—Banes! I'm calling from Africa—from Africa."

"Do you hear a funny echo—funny echo?"

"It's the phone system. Where is Ms. Banes—Ms. Banes?"

"Jean Banes is out of the office. She's working on an emergency case—emergency case."

Lilia shut her eyes. "This is Lilia Eden. Let me speak with someone in charge—someone in charge."

"I'm familiar with all the cases—all the cases."

"Listen, Jean Banes sent a message to Africa telling me to call her—to call her. I need to know why—know why."

There was a pause. "Did you say Africa—Africa?"

"Yes, now please tell me if there's any new information on the Colin Jefferson case. I was his adoptive mother—adoptive mother."

"Oh, you're *that* Lilia Eden—Lilia Eden."

"Yes, why? What's happened—happened?"

"I'm sorry. I can't release any information by telephone—by telephone." The woman hesitated a moment. "Jean should be out the rest of the day, but you can call back tomorrow—call back tomorrow."

"I can't wait until tomorrow. Find Jean and tell her to phone me immediately—immediately."

Lilia gave the number of the hotel twice before hanging up. Her nerves felt like the frayed ends of a live electric wire. She ran her fingers through her hair and stared at the floor. What if something terrible had happened to Colin? Jean would call her about that, of course. Lilia couldn't stop the images of disaster that flooded her mind—he had darted into the street and been hit by a car, he was deathly ill with pneumonia, his birth mother had gone off and . . .

Miles! If only she could talk to him. He would understand how she felt. He would be there to listen, to console. His strong arms would wrap around her and barricade the confusion while she sorted through her emotions.

But Miles wasn't with her. And she had to find him. Another round of dialing and shouting into the receiver brought the manager of the Mount Kenya Safari Club on the line. He told Lilia he had spoken with Miles that afternoon, and didn't expect to see him again. Miles was staying at the tent camp at Naro Moru, and of course there were no telephones there.

The manager offered to send a message down in the morning, but he couldn't guarantee it would reach Miles. Mr. Kane, the man informed Lilia, had planned to fly out at dawn to Maasai Mara National Park. She might leave a message for him there, if she liked.

Lilia spent the next half hour trying to call the Serena Lodge at Maasai Mara. She finally reached someone who told her there was no Miles Kane registered, but that the clerk would leave a message for him to telephone her at the Norfolk Hotel if he showed up.

As Lilia hung up, she realized her hand was trembling. For so many years now, she had lived a solitary life—self-sufficient, competent, generally content. But she had chosen to open the door to her heart and let love back in. Love's joy brought with it pain, risk and the unbearable desire to be reunited with the loved one.

As she clenched her shaking hands into fists, Lilia sensed she was engaged in a battle. She felt desperate to keep her two loves alive and determined to bring them both back into her life, no matter what the cost. As firmly as reason spoke, her heart called out louder.

Chapter 17

Miles dipped his bare feet in the icy stream that ran just a few yards beyond the canopy of his tent. The chill crept up through his ankles right into his teeth. He shivered and gave his shoulders a muscle-relaxing shake as he began walking through the shallow water.

This was exactly what he had needed. A river of melted snow from the peaks of Mount Kenya. A tent with the evening sunlight filtering through the olive green canvas. A crackling fire and the scent of wood smoke clinging to his sweater. The bright flash of a jewel-blue Malachite kingfisher as it dived into the stream to snap up a silver fish.

He needed Africa. This continent was his solitude, his comfort. Africa was his mistress, Miles thought as he meandered downstream, in much the same way the sea was wife and lover to a sailor. The roar of lions and the prancing of zebras on the plains had healed him once before. He trusted they would again.

Africa was reliable. A man could trust this confidant to be changeless day after day. He couldn't say the same about a woman—a bundle of confusing contradictions. If a man needed to be alone, Africa was large enough to escape in. And it was bold and seductive enough to keep him happily occupied and content for years. The cycles of rain and drought, plenty and famine, life and death comforted Miles even in their intensity. He knew them, could count on them, understood how to go on living as they unfolded.

But a woman with a sad gray eyes...a woman whose words rejected him one minute and lured him the next...a woman whose body welcomed him and then pulled away...

Miles pushed back a branch covered with creeping vines. A man couldn't depend on a woman's love in the same way he could rely on a comfortable mistress who demanded nothing but his presence. Lilia needed things he didn't have. She needed not only a child—though God knew that was his ultimate inadequacy—but she needed communication, too, tenderness, sympathy and understanding.

As much as Miles loved her...and he knew without a doubt that he did love Lilia more than he had ever loved her before or would ever love anyone...he had to admit that he didn't possess the refinements a man needed to make a good husband. More than once he had compared himself to a rugged Cape Buffalo—single-minded, stubborn, unemotional.

He really didn't know how to talk to Lilia, either. One didn't learn such things from a father who dominated his wife at every turn, or from a life spent in solitary communion with speechless animals. Lilia needed a man who could say the right things at the right times. Someone who understood those fears and joys and sorrows that flitted across her face like the shadows on Mount Kenya. All Miles knew to do was hold her in his arms and listen—and that wasn't much good.

As much as Lilia needed someone she could talk to, she needed a man with a tender streak to his personality. She was resilient and strong, of course, but she was a person who required a measure of gentleness. She needed patience. She wanted softness, at times, from her man. Miles didn't think he had an ounce of any of those qualities.

He had always been hard, dogged, domineering. Just like his father, in a disheartening way. Not at all the kind of man who would make a good husband for a woman like Lilia.

And that was why, Miles decided as he turned around and spotted the lantern light of his tent camp, he should put this mess with Lilia behind him and return to his mistress—to Africa.

Lilia managed to reserve a seat on the Air-Tours plane headed for Maasai Mara National Park the next morning. It wouldn't leave until nearly noon, so she spent the hours after breakfast wandering through the courtyard of the hotel.

Lilia was sketching the leather-hooded vehicle when a messenger with a chalkboard found her. "Miss Lilia Eden?" he asked. "You have received a telephone call. Please follow me."

As she hurried down the paved stone walkway, Lilia's thoughts swung back and forth between Miles and Colin. If Miles had phoned, what would she say to him? *I love you, and I want to be your wife again forever, and it doesn't matter if we never have children?* Or, *Miles, I'm flying to the Mara in a few minutes, so stay put and don't ever leave me again.* Or, *You rat, how could you just drive away without giving me a chance to talk?*

But what if Jean Banes was on the phone? What if something had happened to Colin? Or what if family services had another child for her to adopt? Did she really want a new baby? Lilia swallowed, her palms clammy as she followed the messenger into the hotel's main office. She picked up the receiver that was lying on the receptionist's desk.

"This is Lilia Eden."

"Lilia, Jean Banes here." The caseworker's clipped voice carried clearly and almost static-free across the line.

"Oh, Jean—how is Colin? Is he all right?"

"I need to know when you expect to be back in the States, Lilia."

"Well my ticket is for..." Lilia fumbled through her cluttered purse with one hand while she held the receiver with the other. "Wednesday. That's three days, isn't it? But I won't arrive in the States until Thursday. I'll land at the Springfield airport that night." She gripped the ticket. "Why? What's happened?"

"Would there be a way for you to come back any sooner than Thursday, Lilia?"

"Well, I...I might be able to get an earlier flight. I don't know exactly. I'd have to check with the airline. Jean, what's going on?"

"I'm really not at liberty to talk about this over the telephone, Lilia."

"Does it involve Colin?"

"Yes."

Lilia shut her eyes. "Is he all right?"

There was a pause. "Yes."

"I'll leave on the first flight out."

"Give me a call after you arrive in Springfield. I don't normally do this, but here's my home telephone number."

Lilia scribbled the information on a scrap of paper. The pen slid through her damp fingers. She heard Jean Banes give a crisp farewell and Lilia offered some vague response in return.

Straightening, she stared out the window. It was Colin. Something had happened, and suddenly she needed Miles more than ever.

Miles stepped through the low door of the airplane onto the top platform of the rolling metal stairs. He lifted his head and drew in a deep breath of musky air scented with dry grass and fresh, sunlit breeze. He definitely felt better than he had the night before.

The midnight hours had been the worst. He hadn't slept a minute, tossing and turning on his low cot, thinking about Lilia and what he might have said differently to her. No matter how much he had ordered himself to blot her memory out of his mind, she filtered back in, her gray eyes soft with tears, her body warm and loving.

As he made his way to the waiting Land Rover, Miles pushed a hand through his hair to roughly organize the thick rumples around his collar. He'd left his comb and the rest of his baggage at the Ngulia bandas with Lilia. But even though he had been wearing the same clothes for three days he definitely felt like a new man.

He had decided he would interview the manager at the Serena Lodge, and then he'd take a ride out into the park to have a look at the game. No doubt a few hours with the elephants and wildebeests would ease this twisted pain in his stomach.

"Mr. Kane?" The African tour guide held out a hand to greet him. "Welcome to Maasai Mara. Mr. Njoroge, the manager of the Serena Lodge is expecting you. I understand this is your final stop before you return to Zambia."

"That's right." Miles winced at the memory of his plan to ask Lilia to accompany him to Lusaka. "Off to Zambia to meet with the *bwana mkubwa* of my hotel project."

Chuckling the man handed him an envelope. "You speak Swahili very well. A message for you, sir."

Miles flipped open the envelope.

To: Miles Kane
From: Lilia Eden
I need to talk things over with you. I'm staying at the Norfolk Hotel. Please call me.

He read the message twice before folding it and stuffing it into his pocket. *Talk.* He wouldn't have a clue what else to say to her. He'd said it all already, hadn't he? Told her the whole situation in clear, concise terms. What more was there to talk about?

No, he didn't want to talk—at least he didn't want to hear Lilia's gentle farewell speech, the sort of soft, consoling words she would want to say under the circumstances. If she didn't want to end things between them—if she wanted him badly enough—she could damn well come out to the Mara. She had the schedule. She knew where he was.

The last thing he wanted was a long, stilted "Dear John" conversation over Kenya's telephone system.

Miles settled into the front seat of the Land Rover and stretched out his legs. Through the window he could see the stretch of wide, grassy plains dotted with groups of antelope and acacia trees. He loved Lilia, and he wanted her. But his mistress was beckoning.

* * *

The first international flight with an empty seat didn't leave Nairobi until midafternoon. It was scheduled to depart the Nairobi airport for Amsterdam at three p.m., and Lilia could catch a connecting flight to Chicago shortly after midnight. She would be in Springfield by the following afternoon.

Lilia debated flying to Maasai Mara and trying to talk to Miles before boarding her three o'clock flight. But if any of the local planes were delayed, the international connection would be impossible.

Once again, she attempted the telephone. By the time she got through to Serena Lodge, the manager told her that Miles Kane had visited him earlier that morning and had already gone off on a tour of the park. He would be spending the night at Cottar's Camp. Yes, Mr. Kane had been given her message.

Lilia let out a breath and hung up the receiver. If Miles didn't want to talk to her, what could she do? Let him go just like that? She felt forced into a corner by his actions, and anger and sadness jockeyed for position in her stomach.

Swallowing at the thick lump that was forming in her throat, Lilia stood and shouldered her bag. She wanted Miles more than she had ever wanted anything or anyone in her life.

But Colin needed her. Jean Banes had made that much clear.

If Lilia failed to return to the States, there was no way of knowing what might become of the child. It was essential that she go, even though her heart pulled her to stay here in Africa and try to straighten things out with Miles.

If she didn't get in touch with him now, she knew he would be gone forever. He would return to Zambia and bury himself in his work as he had done before. Even if she was able to track him down through Habari Safari's offices, she doubted that Miles would ever agree to speak with her. If they were this close now—both physically and emotionally—and he wouldn't talk, time would only weaken the bond. They had both learned to heal from the pain of lost love, and they would learn again.

Her heart aching, Lilia spent the next few hours trying to make good on her commitment to the design project. She toured the shops of Nairobi, selecting furnishings for the hotels. Unable to summon fresh inspiration for the task, she used the list of ideas from her portfolio to select sandalwood chests, bolts of native fabrics, beaded jewelry and gourds, sisal mats, batiks by the dozen and scores of carvings.

Worry about Colin ate at her like termites, and she felt as though she were wandering around in a fog. She couldn't keep her worst fears at bay, no matter how she tried. As she worked through her worries over her little boy, she tried to sort out her feelings about Miles. Could she really just fly away to the States without even talking to him again?

Her portfolio was a painful record of every hotel where they had stayed, every moment they had shared. Like a film in slow motion, the memories flitted across her eyes. Arguing in the London airport, feasting at the Two Fishes food bar, snorkeling around the reef, dancing beside the pool, kissing under the moonlight. She could see Miles hammering his fist on the bamboo pole so hard it splintered. And in the next instant, she saw his blue eyes aflame with desire.

In a blur, she managed to find the church she had attended while her family was on holiday in Nairobi. She sat through the Sunday service, her eyes blurred with tears. If she had ever needed divine help, it was now. Somewhere in the haze she heard herself praying for Colin and his safety. And then she prayed for Miles, begging God to bring him to her and asking for peace to accept it if he didn't come.

She wandered out of the church and stopped for lunch at the Thorn Tree, a sidewalk café on one of Nairobi's busiest streets. As she sat sipping a soft drink, she thought about how deeply she had loved this very spot as a girl. The Thorn Tree Café had been exotic and mysterious, with its towering acacia that grew several stories high to shade the clutter of small, round tables beneath.

Here Lilia had watched in fascination as groups of American tourists garbed in fashionable khaki "safari suits" paraded into their vans for outings in the game parks. She had stared at the elderly British couples who took tea promptly at four. She had gaped at the astonishing younger set of African, British and Asian teens in their various stages of rebellion. Through the years, the miniskirts, Beatle haircuts and bell-bottom trousers had given way to orange-dyed punk mohawk hairdos, chains, zippers and leather vests. Under the same thorny umbrella, all the languages of Europe mingled, business associates schemed, lovers cooed and tourists gawked.

The Thorn Tree Café had been part of Lilia's Africa. But as she chewed a spicy samosa, she felt a strange sense of alienation creep through her. She was more like one of the tourists than a citizen. All her feelings in Mombasa to the contrary, she had to admit that she didn't really belong to Africa anymore. And as much as she loved it, Africa didn't belong to her, either.

She had gradually lost all connections to this continent over the years. Her parents had retired. Their house had been sold. Though the beaches and the ocean and the Thorn Tree Café were a part of her heritage, they would go on without her when she left. They didn't need her . . . and she really didn't need them, either.

Now, it seemed, she had lost the final, slender strand that had linked her to Africa's heart. Miles.

He had been her dream, her hope. He had been her escape. He had been her fantasy lover, as illusive as a mirage. Lilia took a pen from her purse and began to scribble on the napkin beside her plate.

Dear Miles,
I loved you when I was eighteen. I love you now that I am twenty-eight. I couldn't wish or pray you back into my life then, and I can't seem to do so now, either. As I released you before to your own separate future, I release you now. God go with you, my love.

                                                                  Lilia

She folded the napkin and wrote Miles's name on the front. As she was leaving the outdoor café, she pinned the napkin to the message board that circled the trunk of the huge thorn tree. Thousands before her had left such notes. Cryptic scribblings on tattered scraps of paper had clung to the board for all the years of her childhood, and it was covered even now with messages in every language imaginable.

Lilia had always believed these wonderful notes led to happy reunions and dreams-come-true for people from Egypt to South Africa and from Germany to India. In her imagination, the message board was like a central mystic jewel in a web of invisible filaments that encompassed the globe.

But as she walked away from her own fluttering scrap, Lilia again had to tip her head to reality. The truth was more insistent than her fantasy: Miles would probably not stop at the Thorn Tree Café on his brief layover in Nairobi before flying back to Zambia. And even if he did, a man as focused and practical as Miles would never think to look on a message board for a nostalgic, romantic note that would lead him to a happily-ever-after ending with a lost love.

As she had predicted, Miles was not at the Norfolk when she returned, nor had he left a message. She gathered his belongings and checked them into storage at the front desk. Although she considered leaving him yet another note, Lilia decided she had spread her heart thin enough. He wasn't in love with her so deeply that he would fight to make their reunion permanent. There was nothing she could do to change that fact, and she had to accept it.

Lilia packed her own bags, storing away the frangipani perfume Miles had given her, and turning instead to practical matters. She took a taxi to the airport and exchanged her ticket. As she sat in the terminal, she watched every gate in a last hope that Miles would walk suddenly into the room, his eyes as blue as the African sky and his smile as warm and welcoming as its sunshine.

Miles didn't come, and Lilia tired to focus on Colin. Even as she imagined his soft brown arms tight around her neck and his round bottom heavy on her lap, she knew that the future could hold any number of possibilities—and only the slimmest was the return of her son. For the hundredth time she wished for Miles, aware that his presence would comfort her during the long hours to come.

But her flight was called, and Lilia boarded the blue-and-white jumbo jet alone. As she settled into her seat, and as the airplane swooped into the sky, she realized that she had finally and completely left Miles Kane in Africa. And that she would never see him again.

"Miss Eden has gone," the receptionist told Miles as he stood in the cool lobby of the Norfolk Hotel. Evening was sending long blue shadows over the courtyard outside, and the sweet tropical perfume of frangipani hung heavily in the air. Miles hardly noticed. His nerves still simmered from the headlong dash he had made that afternoon.

While staring blankly at a family of elephants, he had suddenly ordered the driver back to the airstrip. Asked why, Miles hadn't been able to respond. He still wasn't sure what had taken hold of him. At the landing strip, he had bulled his way onto a flight for which he hadn't been booked, and he had sat like a broiling volcano on the verge of eruption while the small plane flew to Nairobi. From the airport he had taken a taxi to the Norfolk Hotel, where he now stood trying to accept the words the receptionist had just told him.

"What do you mean, *gone?*" he asked.

"She is not here. She has vacated her room."

"Look, that's ridiculous. Miss Eden sent a message to me at the Serena Lodge in Maasai Mara National Park. She said she was staying here at the Norfolk Hotel, and she wanted to talk to me."

The woman shook her head. "I'm sorry, sir, but she checked out shortly after noon today. She called for a taxi to take her to the Nairobi airport."

"The airport!" Miles exploded. "What the hell for?"

"I assumed she was to return to the United States. Are you a relative?"

"Damn right. I'm her husband."

"My goodness." The woman glanced at a co-worker next to her. "Mr. Otieno, do you know of Miss Eden's plans?"

"She was using the telephone a great many times yesterday and this morning," the man reported, "giving and receiving messages."

"What sort of messages?" Miles demanded.

"I do not know, sir. I believe she was phoning you, phoning the airport, phoning the United States. She went out this morning for several hours. When she returned, she checked your bags here with us at the desk, and then she took a taxi to the airport."

Miles looked at his watch. It was nearly six. If Lilia had left the hotel at noon, she would have had a midafternoon flight. She'd be somewhere over the Sahara Desert by now. Unless her plane had been delayed.

"May I have my bags, please?" he asked. Maybe she had left a message. He could find out which flight she had taken and perhaps call the airport in time to stop her from boarding. But what guarantee did he have that she'd wait? If she had been in such a hurry to leave, maybe he ought to just let her go. Obviously she had wanted to get away as quickly as possible.

"Your baggage, Mr. Kane." Mr. Otieno set the pair of battered leather bags on the floor at Miles's feet. There was no message.

Miles rubbed the back of his neck. So she was gone. Flown away, back to her former life. Her comfortable American world that didn't demand any towering commitment, any risk, much possibility of either passion or heartbreak. She had escaped to where it was safe and secure, as far as she could get from Miles and the storm he had made of her life.

"Any rooms available here?" he asked.

"Of course, Mr. Kane. And would you like a reservation for dinner in the Ibis Grill Room?"

"No, thanks. I'll eat out." He motioned in the direction of his bags. "Place these in my room, will you please?"

As he walked out of the lobby onto the raised veranda, Miles saw the cars and taxis pulling up to unload guests for the evening. He stepped down onto the sidewalk and wandered beneath the tall jacaranda trees in the direction of the city's center.

As he wandered along, Miles tried to piece back together the shattered fragments of the past two weeks. By some unfathomable chance, he had found Lilia. From the moment he had heard her voice on the telephone, he had known he loved her. Seeing her laughing at the zoo and then later wrapped in the distress of losing her little Colin, Miles had known she was still the deep and compelling woman she had always been to him.

The passing days has only drawn him closer and closer to her, until finally he had admitted to himself that he wanted her on far more than a physical level. He had longed for her commitment to him; had taken steps to win it; had lived in trepidation of the moment she found out he could never give her a family. When his confession had spilled out and he had seen her gray eyes fill with tears, Miles thought he had never been cut so deeply.

Now as he walked blindly down the streets of downtown Nairobi, he tried again to think what he could have done to prevent her leaving. Could he have lied to her? Could he simply have failed to tell her he couldn't father children until they were living together as husband and wife? Miles flinched at the thought of deceiving Lilia any longer than he had. Two weeks had been more than enough.

But the news that Miles could not give her children—coming on top of her loss of Colin—had been too much for Lilia to bear. Should he at least have stayed with her there at the bandas the night he had told her the truth about himself?

Miles jammed his hands into his pockets as he walked. He couldn't have stayed. He didn't want to hear her words of rejection. Sure, she had rejected him before on this misguided reunion of theirs. More than once. But he had been well aware that those brief protests were mingled with desire. She had been afraid of her own passion, but she had wanted him—and he knew it.

This was different. This rejection was over something he couldn't change about himself. It was a fundamental part of him. It was who he was—a sterile man, incapable of giving life.

As he sat down at a table in a sidewalk café, Miles realized he had spent years feeling as sealed off and lifeless in his heart as he was in his body. Only Lilia Eden had been able to bring out the warmth in him, the potential for dreams, the utter joy he so rarely felt.

When a waiter appeared at his table, Miles stared blankly at the menu for a moment, then ordered the first thing his eyes fell upon. He watched the man walk away through a hodgepodge of tables cluttered with what appeared to be an international assortment of people. A group of teens were chattering in Italian behind him. Three African men were discussing business at the next table. A collection of German tourists were poring over a tattered map. A Japanese man had posed his large family for a portrait beside the trunk of an enormous thorn tree that dominated the middle of the café area.

Miles lifted his head and studied the spreading branches of the tree overhead for a moment. Its slender limbs caught the starlight, while at its base the world crowded close. He was as out of place as that thorn tree, Miles thought. A Zambian trying to live in Kenya, or America, or some other equally foreign place. A white man dwelling in a black man's country. An English speaker in a land of Bantu tongues. Lilia had told him she felt as alien as he did. But she had slipped away, back to the cradle of her secure middle-American life.

Miles ate his sandwich quickly and decided his ears needed a rest from the babble. He would go back to the hotel and get a good night's rest. In the morning he would call the airport and arrange for a seat on a flight to Zambia.

Rising, Miles, flipped a few shillings on the table as a tip. He stuffed his hands into his pockets and walked out onto the sidewalk from beneath the branches of the thorn tree. Behind him, the breeze tugged a white napkin from its pin on the tree trunk message board. The scrap of paper fluttered to the floor beneath a table, where it would lie until the early hours of morning when a tired waiter with a broom arrived and the message was swept away.

Chapter 18

Lilia rubbed her eyes as she stood on the porch of her house on Walnut Street. For the third time, she tried to fit her key into the keyhole of the front door. Her body told her it was the middle of the night, but Missouri's clocks insisted it was four in the afternoon. It was hot—much hotter than it had been in Nairobi—and so humid that Lilia's shirt was stuck to her back.

She finally managed the lock, and the door swung open into her cool foyer. Stifling the urge to collapse onto the couch, she set her bags by the door and went into her office. Her desk was just as she had left it, stacks of sample floor vinyls here and piles of memos there. Thanks to Jenny, her answering machine's red light wasn't blinking. She picked up her telephone and punched in a set of numbers.

Thank you, Lord, for American telephones, Lilia was praying silently when the family services secretary answered.

"How can I help you?" the woman asked.

"I need to speak with Jean Banes. She's a caseworker."

In a moment, Jean's reassuring voice was on the line. "I'll be right over, Lilia. Don't go anywhere."

As if she would. Lilia left her office and lugged her bags into the downstairs bathroom. They seemed twice as heavy as they had when she'd started out. She washed her face and brushed her teeth, then dabbed on a little foundation and mascara. As she combed her hair, she decided she resembled a zombie more than anything else. She hoped she wouldn't have to see anyone but Jean before she could get a night's rest.

The trip had been a nightmare. Not only was there the expected turbulence over the Sahara, but a sudden headwind had rocked her plane all the way across the Atlantic. Lilia had hardly slept. As she walked across the wooden floor of her living room, it seemed to sway and dip beneath her feet. Sixteen hours of flying with only a short break in Amsterdam had frazzled her nerves.

She had tried reading magazines, watching the in-flight movie, talking with her seatmates, anything to take her mind off Miles. Or Colin. Her thoughts had bounced like a rubber ball between the two.

Just when she had convinced herself that Colin was all right, certainly in the secure hands of Jean Banes, she thought of Miles. The image of him standing on the beach, holding out his arms to her brought a wave of fresh tears every time. When she managed to dam up the emotion of losing Miles, her mind pictured little Colin with his big brown eyes as he had waved goodbye to her from the back of Jean Banes's van.

She had sobbed halfway around the world.

Now she sat on the edge of the couch, her fingers in knots as she waited for the sound of the van in her driveway. When the doorbell rang, she nearly jumped out of her skin. She smoothed down her skirt as she hurried across the foyer to the door.

"Jean, come in." Lilia grabbed the older woman's arm and practically dragged her inside. "Tell me what's going on."

In the living room Jean seated herself, then opened her briefcase and dug around for a file. "I'm so glad you could come home early. I really hated to interrupt your vacation, because I'm not sure—"

"Tell me about Colin!" Lilia dropped into a chair.

Jean took a breath. "Well, his birth mother has been arrested."

"Oh, no! Where's Colin? Who's taking care of him?"

"I'm not able to tell you that."

"Let me take care of him! I'm cleared for fostering. I'm cleared as a preadoptive home. What did his mother do to get arrested? What's going to happen to—"

"Colin will be fine."

"That judge should never have given him back to her!" Lilia jumped up from the chair. The floor dipped under her feet. "Oh, I just... I can't believe this. Was Colin with his birth mother when she... Well, what did she do?"

"Why don't you sit down again and let me explain."

Lilia sank into a chair by her fireplace. "I can't believe he's had to go through all this again. All this...confusion...and now he's living with strangers again. Does he have his elephant?"

Jean smiled. "He has his elephant."

"Has he been talking? Has he said anything?"

"No. Not since he left you." She opened her file. "Here's the situation, Lilia. Colin's mother was caught selling an illegal substance—"

"Drugs. Oh, I knew it!"

"She sold the drugs to an undercover agent. Colin was not with her. He had been left alone in the house."

"Alone!"

The police found him there when they went to search the house. The most incriminating part of the situation for the birth mother is that she was selling drugs on a street that adjoins public school property.

"What does that mean?"

"It means she's in big trouble."

"What's going to happen to Colin?"

"That all depends on her."

"On *her?* What rights does she have now that she's committed this crime?"

"She's still Colin's birth mother, Lilia. She retains parental rights even though family services has taken Colin back into protective custody. His mother hasn't been convicted of anything. Her case certainly hasn't had time to go to trial.''

Lilia knotted and reknotted her fingers. "Will you put Colin back in my home until his mother's situation is resolved?''

Jean sighed. "We've talked that around and around. We would like to, of course, but we're very concerned about the emotional bond between you and Colin. You made your feelings about him clear during the weeks after we had to take him away. And I have to admit that even though Colin doesn't talk, it's quite obvious he has been grieving deeply for you.''

"Oh, no.''

"He has been extremely upset, displaying not only emotional but also physical symptoms.''

"You mean he's sick?''

"Stomach problems. Inability to sleep. Constant crying.''

"Dear Lord.'' Lilia buried her face in her hands.

"We feel that if we placed Colin here in your home again, the bond between the two of you would be restored immediately. If that happened and his mother somehow managed to work her way out of this, she might ask for Colin again. I don't think it would be healthy for you to have to give him up a second time. And I'm sure it would be downright damaging for him to leave you again.''

"So you're going to leave him in foster care? Indefinitely?''

"His birth mother has a hearing in three days. Things will be a lot clearer after that.'' Jean studied Lilia for a moment. "The reason I asked you to come back from your vacation early is to clarify one point with you. This is very important, and I want you to think it through carefully before you give me an answer.''

Lilia swallowed. "Okay.''

"If by some chance Colin's mother agrees to give him up, do you want to petition immediately for termination of parental rights and custody? Before you say anything, think for a minute. You've had several weeks of life as a nonparent again. You've been through a lot.''

"An emotional roller coaster."

"Letting Colin back into your life isn't going to make things easier, Lilia. Children are difficult under the best of circumstances. A little boy like Colin, with his background and the recent trauma he's been through, is going to require an extra measure of love and patience from you. The years to come could hold a lot of unexpected surprises— many of them unpleasant."

"I know."

"What Colin has been experiencing may erupt in any number of ways. He's already speech-delayed. He may continue to have emotional problems—bed-wetting, tantrums, withdrawal—there's no telling what. He could have social problems and be unable to make friends, or he might display unacceptable behavior in public places. He could have academic problems. Our testing has shown that Colin is intelligent, but he might easily become an underachiever. His lack of speech may introduce reading problems or difficulty with other essential skills. He might have a very hard time separating from you, Lilia, out of fear of losing you again."

"Yes," she whispered.

"I want you to be aware that we have another preadoptive home where we could place Colin. This is a loving couple with several children. A strong family unit." Jean shut her file. "Lilia, here's what I'm asking. Would you want to take Colin again if he became available? You've been through an extraordinarily difficult experience with this adoptive procedure. No one at family services would blame you if you didn't want to put yourself in for a lifetime of possible problems. I certainly wouldn't."

Lilia stared at the empty grate in her fireplace. She knew she wasn't thinking clearly. It wasn't only the jet lag. Her heart ached for Miles. It was as if their physical union had bonded them emotionally again. She felt married . . . or perhaps widowed would better describe it.

All the same, there was not a shred of doubt in her mind as Lilia looked up at Jean Banes. "Colin is my son. He always will be, whether he's living only in my heart, or in my home, too. Once you love someone that deeply, you never let go.''

Jean let out a breath. "Thank God." As she stood, she couldn't help but laugh. "I told my supervisors you'd want Colin back. They couldn't believe it after all you've gone through. But then . . . they don't know you."

Lilia walked the caseworker to the door. "You're my only link to him," she said softly. "Please make sure he's all right."

Jean Banes took Lilia's hand and squeezed it lightly. "I'll call you Thursday afternoon to let you know how everything's going."

Lilia shut the door and walked across the foyer to the bathroom. As she picked up her bags to carry them upstairs, the unmistakable scent of frangipani perfume drifted through the evening air.

For three days, Lilia went through the motions of life. She shook the white sand of Diani Beach from her sandals. She rinsed salt from the Indian Ocean out of her two bathing suits. When she hung the white bikini on the line to dry, she couldn't believe she had actually worn the minuscule thing.

Once her bags were unpacked and her clothes had been washed, she slept for about twelve hours straight. She woke up certain that her world would feel right and normal. It didn't. Her breakfast was tasteless. She told herself she was just missing the mangoes. Her car was hot and stuffy. She told herself she was just used to driving on the left-hand side of the road. The streets seemed cluttered with neon signs and run-down buildings. The people on the sidewalks looked bland and colorless.

Jenny, of course, was beside herself to have Lilia back in the studio. Actually, she had managed things very well. Lilia found files neatly stacked, curtains ready to be hung, wallpaper books on the right shelves, a clientele list that was bulging with requests.

Lilia set aside Wednesday afternoon to put her Habari Safari portfolio in order. She typed up a long letter and a list of recommendations. She noted every decorative item she had purchased in Kenya, along with its expected shipping arrival date in approximately three months. After organizing and coloring several of her sketches, she placed the file in a heavy envelope.

Then she typed a second letter to the Habari Safari head office. She thanked the management for the opportunity to work on the project, and she informed them that her local clientele required so much of her time that she would have to be excused from completing the hotel design. Before signing off, she listed the names and addresses of several studios around the country that had worked with exotic decor and that probably would be delighted to take on the wildlife adventure hotel project.

She sealed and stamped the envelope and dropped it in the mail on her way home that evening. Without the portfolio to remind her of her trip to Africa, Lilia felt sure her aching loneliness for Miles would begin to fade.

A heat wave had begun to waft across Missouri by Thursday morning. The sun burned down through the layer of white film that always seemed to hang over the sky. Steam drifted up from sidewalks and streets. Air conditioners churned at full power. Flowers wilted. Birds fell silent. Trees drooped.

Lilia had a headache all day. She and Jenny spent the morning attempting to hang a long-swagged valance around the top of a huge bay window. The mauve fabric shifted and slumped and slithered out from their hands. They finally got one side up and the other fell down. By noon, Lilia was ready to scream.

"I don't know what happened to you in Africa," Jenny said as they ate take-out egg rolls in the studio late that afternoon. "But I sure wish you could go back there and undo it."

"What's that supposed to mean?"

"Golly, I feel like I'm working for Grumpy from the Seven Dwarfs."

Lilia stared at her plastic bowl of hot mustard sauce. "I'm sorry," she said softly. "I'll try to perk up."

"What's the matter, Lilia? Did something bad happen over there? Or was it something to do with that phone call from the caseworker? You came rushing back early, and you're just not the same person you were when you left."

Lilia had to smile. "No, I'm not."

"Is it Miles Kane?"

The name rocked through her with the force of a dynamite explosion. She forced down the bite of egg roll, but she couldn't speak.

"You're in love with him, aren't you?" Jenny said. "I can see it written all over your face. That's why you're not really with it here at the studio. You're with him, wherever he is. Where is he, anyway?"

"I don't know," Lilia managed to say.

"You mean you flew off and left him in Africa?"

Lilia nodded.

"Why'd you do that?" Jenny tossed her egg roll on the table. "Good grief, Lilia, you're not the type to love a man and leave him. You've never been casual about anything in your life. Whatever you do, you do it with all your heart— your design projects, renovating your house on Walnut Street, taking me on and teaching me the business, adopting Colin—"

"It was Colin," Lilia cut in. "That's why I came back."

"What's happened with Colin?"

"His mother's been arrested. He's back in foster care."

"Heavenly days! What next?" Jenny shook her head. "Are they going to give him back to you?"

"I don't know."

"It's no wonder you're a wreck. You're being jerked around all over the place. They give him to you, then they take him away, now they might give him back, or they might not. What does Miles think about all this?"

"I don't know."

"You mean you didn't tell him? Lilia, did you fly back to the States without telling all this to the man you love?"

"It's not like you think with Miles, Jenny," Lilia said. "Not romantic and dreamy. It's all been very difficult. It's not really *love* in that sense of the word."

"Oh, sure, like love is supposed to be easy and perfect all the time. Give me a break, Lilia. I know you better than that. You're practical enough to have started this business.

You've got a reasonable head on your shoulders. You know when love is real and when it isn't."

"Maybe so."

"So why did you leave him in Africa?"

Lilia stood and walked to the window. "I don't think it would have worked out between us." Then she shook her head. "That's not true. It would have worked. It would have been beautiful. But he didn't have faith in me. He didn't believe my love was strong enough to overcome the obstacles. Or maybe he didn't love me enough. I don't know, Jenny. But Colin needed me, and I had to come back."

"Miles needs you."

Lilia turned. "He doesn't need anyone. He's lived perfectly well for thirty-one years. He spent the last ten years without me—and I spent the last ten without him. We can go on, Jenny. We'll survive."

"Of course you will. You don't need him like some simpering, dependent wimp. But you want him. You love him. Your life would be a lot brighter with him in it."

"Yellow. The color of sunrise over the Indian Ocean."

"What?"

"That's how bright my life would be with Miles Kane in it. Sunrise yellow."

Jenny shook her head. "You're in love, Lilia Eden. Like it or not. Now would you get over here and finish writing up this order form so we can lock up and go home? My Sunday school class is having a barbecue tonight, and I'm so hot I've got to have a shower before I can face anybody. I swear, that valance was nearly the death of me."

As Lilia drove home, she decided she would finish mowing the rest of her backyard. In spite of the heat, she had managed to do about half of it with her push-mower in the past few evenings. She could open the window of her office and set the telephone on the sill in case Jean Banes called.

All day her thoughts had drifted uncomfortably over the last time Colin's fate had been in the hands of a court. She had lost him then. Her mental tape recorder told her she would again. But Lilia was determined to replace negative thoughts with action. A good hour or two pushing a lawn mower back and forth would take care of that.

As she drove around the corner and started up her street, Lilia noticed an unfamiliar blue car parked in her driveway. Jean Banes always traveled in the family services van. She checked her watch. It was well after five. Maybe Jean had come to visit in her own car.

Trying to calm herself, Lilia pulled up in the driveway and set her brake. The front porch was empty. The swing drifted in the slight hot breeze. She shut her car door and walked to the side of the house.

"Jean?"

She could hear something whirring in her backyard. Her spine prickling, Lilia walked down the narrow side yard. It was her lawn mower, she realized. That was the whirring sound.

Sure enough, over by the far fence a man was bent over her mower. He had crouched down, as if inspecting the blades. His broad, bare back gleamed a golden brown in the sun.

Lilia's heart lunged into her rib cage. She knew that back.

"Ruddy thing needs oil," Miles said, straightening. "Hello, Lilia."

"Miles." The word was nothing but a breath.

He slipped his hands into his pockets and stared at her. "You're looking very...very beautiful."

"Miles, you're here." Lilia caught her breath. He must have found her note at the Thorn Tree Café. "You're here!"

Dropping her purse, she ran toward him. He held out his arms and swept her up. At the feel of his warm skin beneath her fingers and the pressure of the solid wall of his chest against hers, everything inside Lilia broke loose. She pressed her lips into the curve of his neck as his hands stroked up and down her back.

"I had to come," he said. "Lilia, I love you. I want you in my life, no matter what."

"Oh, Miles, I thought I'd never see you again."

"I took the risk and came here, hoping we could work our way past the barriers between us. I had to let you know what you mean to me. That night at the banda, Lilia, I saw...I saw your face when I told you I can never be a father. I knew how devastated you were." He swallowed. "Telling you I couldn't give you a child was the hardest thing I've ever done. I thought I was prepared for your reaction. But when I looked into your eyes and read . . ."

"No, Miles, I wasn't—"

"Lilia, having you stolen from me a second time by a situation beyond my control was more than I could stand. I couldn't think clearly. I couldn't see beyond my own pain."

"But you stormed off into the night. You didn't give me a chance to tell you how I felt."

"I didn't want to face the moment when you would slip through my fingers again. During the next few days, I fought with myself, but I couldn't bring myself to call you and hear those final words. Nor did I want you to come after me. Just to see your face again would have destroyed me. I tried to convince myself what had happened between us didn't matter—neither the good nor the bad of it. I told myself I didn't need your love. Africa would fill the empty space in my heart. But it was a lie, and I knew it."

Reading the open pain on his face, Lilia felt her eyes fill with tears. The thought that Miles had spent days in torment—just as she had—gave her no sense of satisfaction. She ached for him.

"And then I realized I couldn't go back to Zambia," he was saying. "I couldn't do anything but come for you. I went to the Norfolk in Nairobi—but you had gone."

"And that's when you found my message?"

"What message?"

"On the board at the Thorn Tree. I told you I loved you." He shook his head. "I never saw your note."

The realization that he had come all this way—again risking her rejection—flooded through Lilia in a wave of tenderness and love. "Miles, I had no choice but to leave Africa," she told him. "There was a telegram from the adoption agency. Some kind of trouble, but it wasn't clear what. I was terrified something had happened to Colin. I called the States, and my caseworker asked me to return to Springfield immediately. Before I left, I searched for you

Miles. I sent messages everywhere I knew you'd planned to go. I spent hours on the phone."

"Lilia, I didn't know."

"I wanted you to understand that my leaving Africa had nothing to do with us, Miles. I'll admit that when you told me we could never have children together, I was surprised. But I wasn't devastated. I've lived for years with the reality of never becoming a mother. Living a childless life wouldn't be the worst thing in the world. The worst thing would be living without you."

"Oh, Lilia, we're meant to be together. We can make our love work. I intend to see to that." He kissed her damp cheek. Then he held her away from him a little and looked into her eyes. "Lilia, will you live as my wife again?"

She held her breath for a moment, absorbing his words. And then her heart lifted. "Yes, I will, Miles Kane. Anywhere you want. I'll be your wife until you're as old and gray and wrinkled as an elephant."

Laughing, he caught her up and turned her around and around. "We'll make it legal as soon as possible. I love you, Lilia."

She smiled for the first time in days. His shoulders felt so real, so permanent. The blue sky shone in his eyes as he gazed at her.

"I love you, too, Miles," she whispered.

He let her slide slowly down his length until her feet touched the ground. "If my job is a problem," he told her, "I'll find a new one. Here in Springfield, if this is where you want to live."

"Miles, I'm so proud of your work. Please don't stop what you're doing. I want to be a part of it. And it doesn't matter where we live as long as we're together. You're my home—that's what I realized. It's not Africa or Missouri or even this house. It's us. Our love gives me shelter and nourishment."

"Lilia, I want you to know something else." He let out a breath. "If you still want to adopt, I'll be the best father I can be. I'll love our child as if his birth were a result of our own lovemaking. Colin taught me that about myself. Please tell me about him. Is he all right?"

"I think so. I have to trust—" She couldn't continue for a moment. The joy of knowing this man loved her and wanted to spend the rest of his life with her mingled with the awful uncertainty of Colin's future. As she struggled to bring her emotions under control, Miles slipped his arms around her and held her.

"I have to trust that he's being taken care of," she finally whispered. "His mother committed a crime, and his future is up in the air again. I'm expecting to hear something from the caseworker soon."

"We'll fight for him, Lilia. We won't give up no matter—"

"Mice!" A tiny voice cut through his words. "Hi, Mice!"

Swinging around, Lilia saw Colin racing across the yard. The stuffed elephant dangled by its trunk from one of Colin's hands. His tiny legs churned as his feet ate up the space between them.

"Colin!" Coming to life, Lilia bolted toward him. He jumped into her arms and grabbed her tightly around the neck.

"Hi, Mama," he whispered into her ear.

"Oh, Colin, honey, I missed you so much. I love you, sweetheart. I love you, my precious little boy."

"Wuv-oo, Mama."

Lilia choked back a sob as she felt Miles's arm slip around her back. Colin peered over her shoulder and grinned shyly.

"Good to see you again, little lad," Miles said, giving Colin's tummy a poke.

Jean Banes was right behind Colin. "Lilia, may I speak with you alone for a moment?"

Reluctant to let Colin go, Lilia buried her nose in the soft fluff of his hair. For a dizzy moment she drank in the sweet, boyish scent of her son. Then she turned to Miles.

"Can Miles hold you, Colin?" she asked.

Miles held out his hands, and Colin immediately climbed into his strong embrace. For a moment they studied each other. Then Colin's face broke into a radiant smile. Miles's eyes swam.

"Hey, let's have a look at that mower of your mum's," he said. "It's as rusty as an old gate. We'll have to put some oil on it, if we're to keep this yard in shape all summer."

Miles swung Colin onto his shoulders. The little boy dug his fingers into Miles's hair and gave a giggle of delight.

"Someone you know well, I take it?" Jean Banes asked, nodding in the direction of Miles.

"My husband. Or was. Or will be. Whatever."

Jeans' eyebrows lifted. "Sounds interesting. But I won't ask." She flipped open her file.

Taking a deep breath to try to calm herself, Lilia looked over the caseworker's shoulder.

"Spent all afternoon in court," Jean said. "Colin's birth mother decided to use Colin as a bargaining tool. It's not uncommon."

"What do you mean? How did she use him?"

"Well, she knew she could be spending the rest of her life in prison. You sell drugs near school property, you might as well write your own sentence. So she offered to relinquish her parental rights to Colin if the court would reduce her sentence to fifteen years."

Lilia held her breath. "And?"

"The court agreed to the plea bargain. Family services had already reviewed your case. We had a very good relationship with you, and we knew Colin was grieving for you. Your petitions for the termination of parental rights and for custody were put before the court. The court granted your petitions. And so, Lilia . . . Colin is now your son."

Speechless, Lilia glanced at the back of the yard. Colin was bending over the lawn mower, his eyes studiously investigating the mysteries of the machine. Miles was talking away to him, pointing out this and that.

Lilia turned back to the caseworker. "No one can take him away?"

"Never. The adoption is legal. He's yours."

"I just . . . well, *both* of them . . . all at once. . . ."

Jean smiled. "I wish you all the greatest happiness."

"Thank you . . . for everything."

"I'll leave Colin's things on the front porch."

But Lilia didn't hear her. Turning, she walked across the lawn. Miles looked up, his blue eyes glowing. He scooped Colin into his arms and met Lilia halfway.

"It's final!" she said. "Unchangeable. No one can take him away again."

For a moment Miles couldn't speak. Tears shone in Lilia's beautiful gray eyes. He swallowed, fighting for control. Then he kissed Colin's warm brown forehead.

"Hey, laddie," he said softly, "you've got your mum back now. You won't ever lose her again. Nor will I."

"You have a daddy, too, Colin," Lilia said. "Miles is going to be your father. How does that sound?"

Colin looked from one to the other, studying them solemnly. Then he grabbed them both in his strangling grip and squeezed their necks.

"Us," he said.

"Forever," Miles whispered, and he kissed Lilia to seal the promise.

*   *   *   *   *

And now for
something completely different
from Silhouette....

Unique and innovative stories that take you into the world of paranormal happenings. Look for our special "Spellbound" flash—and get ready for a truly exciting reading experiênce!

In February, look for
One Unbelievable Man (SR #993)
by Pat Montana.

Was he man or myth? Cass Kohlmann's mysterious traveling companion, Michael O'Shea, had her all confused. He'd suddenly appeared, claiming she was his destiny—determined to win her heart. But could levelheaded Cass learn to believe in fairy tales...before her fantasy man disappeared forever?

Don't miss the charming, sexy and utterly mysterious
Michael O'Shea in
ONE UNBELIEVABLE MAN.
Watch for him in February—only from

Silhouette
R O M A N C E™

Take 4 bestselling love stories FREE

Plus get a FREE surprise gift!

Special Limited-time Offer

Mail to Silhouette Reader Service™

**3010 Walden Avenue
P.O. Box 1867
Buffalo, N.Y. 14269-1867**

YES! Please send me 4 free Silhouette Intimate Moments® novels and my free surprise gift. Then send me 6 brand-new novels every month, which I will receive months before they appear in bookstores. Bill me at the low price of $2.89 each plus 25¢ delivery and applicable sales tax, if any.* That's the complete price and—compared to the cover prices of $3.50 each—quite a bargain! I understand that accepting the books and gift places me under no obligation ever to buy any books. I can always return a shipment and cancel at any time. Even if I never buy another book from Silhouette, the 4 free books and the surprise gift are mine to keep forever.

245 BPA ANRR

Name _____ (PLEASE PRINT)

Address _____ Apt. No. _____

City _____ State _____ Zip _____

This offer is limited to one order per household and not valid to present Silhouette Intimate Moments® subscribers. *Terms and prices are subject to change without notice. Sales tax applicable in N.Y.

UMOM-94R   ©1990 Harlequin Enterprises Limited

HE'S AN

AMERICAN HERO

January 1994 rings in the New Year—and a new lineup of sensational American Heroes. You can't seem to get enough of these men, and we're proud to feature one each month, created by some of your favorite authors.

January: CUTS BOTH WAYS by Dee Holmes: Erin Kenyon hired old acquaintance Ashe Seager to investigate the crash that claimed her husband's life, only to learn old memories never die.

February: A WANTED MAN by Kathleen Creighton: Mike Lanagan's exposé on corruption earned him accolades...and the threat of death. Running for his life, he found sanctuary in the arms of Lucy Brown—but for how long?

March: COOPER by Linda Turner: Cooper Rawlings wanted nothing to do with the daughter of the man who'd shot his brother. But when someone threatened Susannah Patterson's life, he found himself riding to the rescue....

AMERICAN HEROES: Men who give all they've got for their country, their work—the women they love.

Only from

INTIMATE MOMENTS®

™ Silhouette®

IMHERO7

SILHOUETTE... Where Passion Lives

Don't miss these Silhouette favorites by some of our most
distinguished authors! And now you can receive a discount by
ordering two or more titles!

SD	#05772	FOUND FATHER by Justine Davis	$2.89 ☐
SD	#05783	DEVIL OR ANGEL by Audra Adams	$2.89 ☐
SD	#05786	QUICKSAND by Jennifer Greene	$2.89 ☐
SD	#05796	CAMERON by Beverly Barton	$2.99 ☐
IM	#07481	FIREBRAND by Paula Detmer Riggs	$3.39 ☐
IM	#07502	CLOUD MAN by Barbara Faith	$3.50 ☐
IM	#07505	HELL ON WHEELS by Naomi Horton	$3.50 ☐
IM	#07512	SWEET ANNIE'S PASS by Marilyn Pappano	$3.50 ☐
SE	#09791	THE CAT THAT LIVED ON PARK AVENUE by Tracy Sinclair	$3.39 ☐
SE	#09793	FULL OF GRACE by Ginna Ferris	$3.39 ☐
SE	#09822	WHEN SOMEBODY WANTS by Trisha Alexander	$3.50 ☐
SE	#09841	ON HER OWN by Pat Warren	$3.50 ☐
SR	#08866	PALACE CITY PRINCE by Arlene James	$2.69 ☐
SR	#08916	UNCLE DADDY by Kasey Michaels	$2.69 ☐
SR	#08948	MORE THAN YOU KNOW by Phyllis Halldorson	$2.75 ☐
SR	#08954	HERO IN DISGUISE by Stella Bagwell	$2.75 ☐
SS	#27006	NIGHT MIST by Helen R. Myers	$3.50 ☐
SS	#27010	IMMINENT THUNDER by Rachel Lee	$3.50 ☐
SS	#27015	FOOTSTEPS IN THE NIGHT by Lee Karr	$3.50 ☐
SS	#27020	DREAM A DEADLY DREAM by Allie Harrison	$3.50 ☐

(limited quantities available on certain titles)

AMOUNT	$	
DEDUCT: **10% DISCOUNT FOR 2+ BOOKS**	$	
POSTAGE & HANDLING	$———	
($1.00 for one book, 50¢ for each additional)		
APPLICABLE TAXES*	$	
TOTAL PAYABLE	$	
(check or money order—please do not send cash)		

To order, complete this form and send it, along with a check or money order
for the total above, payable to Silhouette Books, to: **In the U.S.:** 3010 Walden
Avenue, P.O. Box 9077, Buffalo, NY 14269-9077; **In Canada:** P.O. Box 636,
Fort Erie, Ontario, L2A 5X3.

Name: _____

Address: _____ City: _____

State/Prov.: _____ Zip/Postal Code: _____

*New York residents remit applicable sales taxes.
 Canadian residents remit applicable GST and provincial taxes.   SBACK-JM

Ⓥ *Silhouette*®
™

It's our 1000th
Silhouette Romance
and we're celebrating!

Join us for a special collection of love stories by the authors you've loved for years, and new favorites you've just discovered.

**It's a celebration just for you,
with wonderful books by
Diana Palmer, Suzanne Carey,
Tracy Sinclair, Marie Ferrarella,
Debbie Macomber, Laurie Paige,
Annette Broadrick, Elizabeth August
and MORE!**

Silhouette Romance...vibrant, fun and emotionally rich! Take another look at us!

As part of the celebration, readers can receive a FREE gift AND enter our exciting sweepstakes to win a grand prize of $1000! Look for more details in all March Silhouette series titles.

**You'll fall in love all over again
with Silhouette Romance!**

As seen on TV!
Free Gift Offer

With a Free Gift proof-of-purchase from any Silhouette® book,
you can receive a beautiful cubic zirconia pendant.

This gorgeous marquise-shaped stone is a genuine cubic
zirconia—accented by an 18" gold tone necklace.

(Approximate retail value $19.95)

Send for yours today...
compliments of ▼ *Silhouette*®
™

To receive your free gift, a cubic zirconia pendant, send us one original proof-of-
purchase, photocopies not accepted, from the back of any Silhouette Romance™,
Silhouette Desire®, Silhouette Special Edition®, Silhouette Intimate Moments® or
Silhouette Shadows™ title for January, February or March 1994 at your favorite retail
outlet, together with the Free Gift Certificate, plus a check or money order for $2.50
(do not send cash) to cover postage and handling, payable to Silhouette Free Gift Offer.
We will send you the specified gift. Allow 6 to 8 weeks for delivery. Offer good until
March 31st, 1994 or while quantities last. Offer valid in the U.S. and Canada only.

Free Gift Certificate

Name: _____

Address: _____

City: _____ State/Province: _____ Zip/Postal Code: _____

Mail this certificate, one proof-of-purchase and a check or money order for postage
and handling to: SILHOUETTE FREE GIFT OFFER 1994. In the U.S.: 3010 Walden
Avenue, P.O. Box 9057, Buffalo NY 14269-9057. In Canada: P.O. Box 622, Fort Erie,
Ontario L2Z 5X3

FREE GIFT OFFER   079-KBZ
ONE PROOF-OF-PURCHASE
To collect your fabulous FREE GIFT, a cubic zirconia pendant, you must include this
original proof-of-purchase for each gift with the properly completed Free Gift Certificate.

079-KBZ